To David Hus,

THE DENOUEMENT

by BARRIE JAIMESON

Copyright: © BARRIE JAIMESON 2017

AUTHOR'S NOTE

Most of the names and places in this novel have been changed. Anyone who knows Maldon, where I live, will recognise many of the locations but in no way does the narrative intend to imply anything good or bad about those places. The same applies to Bourrouillan, in which I have spent many happy hours and Potsdam and Berlin, neither of which I have set foot in yet.

I have to extend my thanks to all those who have helped me in my endeavours, especially: The Queen's Head, Maldon (for letting me use the bar as my office!); Rosy Perry (for proof-reading); my long-suffering family (for everything else) and mostly you for buying this book.

THE DENOUEMENT

PROLOGUE – LONDON 2005

'OK. That's a wrap!' The floor manager came onto the set. 'Well done everyone! Have a good weekend.'

Greg Driscoll was heading for the bar at the studios where he was filming the latest episode of the comedy drama 'Gone for a Song', a story of a young female busker trying to make it in the world of pop music. Greg played a rather sleazy promoter who convinces the busker he can help her break into the big time.

'Oh, Greg,' hailed the floor manager. 'Can you phone your agent? He said he needed to talk to you quite urgently. And get out of your costume before you go to the bar, please!'

Greg sighed. His costume was just a suit, which he had to admit was not the sort of thing he would normally wear to go to a bar – or anywhere else really – but he was thirsty. It had been a long day in the studio. He turned round, however, and went to his dressing-room. It was nine o'clock on a Friday evening and his agent, Denis Young, would not be in his office at this time. He changed from his suit into his Levis and a t-shirt, took his phone from his pocket and checked the screen. Three missed calls from

Denis, two from the agency number and one from Denis' private phone. What was it that was so important? Denis, of all people, would know his recording schedule. He must have known he wasn't available on a Friday. He hadn't left any message on his voicemail, which presumably meant he had something personal to tell him. He hoped it was nothing serious. He touched the screen to call Denis back but there appeared to be no signal in the studio. This happened a lot. Maybe they had some way of blocking the signal so it didn't interrupt the recording. Greg locked his dressing-room door and went to the bar.

'Gone for a Song' had proved to be a popular programme and was in its second series. Greg had been an actor for over thirty years. He'd had some success early on - well a major role in a rather short-running soap opera which he went straight into from Drama School. A few small parts in repertory theatre as well as on TV had followed and he'd appeared in a number of commercials – one of which had resulted in him unwittingly smuggling drugs and the death of a girlfriend in terrible circumstances; something which still haunted him. He'd moved to a small town on the Essex coast called Maldon and work had become rather intermittent, so when Denis had come up with the interview for a pilot programme of a new drama about the music industry he'd leapt at the chance. The producer snapped him up and told him he was exactly what they'd been searching for, signed him up before the scripts had even been finalised, and involved Greg in the development of story. He was instrumental in turning what could have been a rather bleak storyline into the successful comedy drama they were now filming.

Greg travelled into the studio in London for rehearsals and recording days. Denis had negotiated a very good fee for him and arranged for the studio to pick him up from home to take him there. The film company also paid for a taxi to take him back. It was a luxury that Greg enjoyed and was happily getting used to.

In his days in the soap opera world, Greg had regularly been photographed by the Paparazzi falling out of various night clubs but he avoided those places now and tried to only drink in the studio bar when he was not in Maldon. He was safe in Maldon; the local paper did not employ any Paparazzi!

There were just a couple of cast members in the bar when he arrived. They were both older actors, who'd been in the business quite a while – young actors didn't seem to drink any more – and he bought a round and sat down with them. At ten-thirty, Greg's phone managed to pick up a signal and a call came through. It was Denis.

'Where have you been?' Denis sounded stressed.

'You know where I've been, Denis. It's Friday. It's the day I record.'

'I know but I left a message with the studio. Didn't you get it?'

'Yes I did, Denis, but there's no signal here.'

'How come you're talking to me now, then? I can hear you're still in the bar.'

Greg excused himself from the company and, taking his pint with him, walked over to the relative privacy of the doorway. 'Denis, don't ask me to explain the vagaries of the mobile telecom system. There was no signal earlier. What do you want?'

There was a pause at the other end.

'Denis? What is it?' Greg was starting to worry.

'I thought you ought to be the first to know,' said his agent eventually.

'Oh my God, has somebody died?' Greg wracked his brains to try and think about whom it would be that Denis was chosen to break the news, Greg had no family and all his current friends lived in Maldon and surely wouldn't get hold of Denis to tell him.

'I'm getting married.'

This was probably a bigger shock to Greg than if someone had died. 'What?' he said.

'I'm getting married,' replied his agent. 'I thought you'd be pleased.'

'Oh, I am, Denis. Who's the lucky girl?'

Greg heard his agent's impatient snort. 'Don't be ridiculous, Greg.'

Greg knew his agent was gay and that he'd had several short-lived affairs with various clients in the past but never anything that could be called permanent. 'Who's the lucky chap, then?'

'Anton,' said his agent.

'Who's Anton?'

'You've met Anton, haven't you?'

'I don't know anyone called Anton, Denis.'

'You know, we met him at that after-show party in the West End. You came to the first night with me?'

'No, I didn't, Denis. When was this?'

There was a slight pause. 'Er...March, I think.'

'What? Two months ago?'

'About then, yes.'

'So you're marrying a man that you only met two months ago?'

'Yes. And it's not a marriage actually. It's a Civil Partnership.'

Greg took a sip of his pint. 'How old is Anton, Denis? Just out of interest.'

'Twenty-five,' muttered Denis.

'Twenty-five!' exclaimed Greg. 'He's less than half your age!'

'So?' Denis sounded indignant.

'Are you sure about this, Denis?'

The few people left in the bar were gradually leaving. Greg waved his glass at the barmaid who raised her eyebrows, looked at her watch and mouthed 'last one'.

'I've never been so sure in my life,' replied Denis.

Greg moved over to the bar and paid for his drink. He smiled at the girl serving him. She was less than half his age.

'Well, I'm pleased for you, Denis. When is the momentous day?'

'Sunday.'

'What Sunday?'

'This Sunday; the day after tomorrow and I want you to be the best man.'

Greg nearly choked on his lager. 'How long have you known about this, Denis?'

'Since yesterday. There was a cancellation at the Registry Office and we just grabbed it.'

'Give me a brandy, Hettie,' Greg begged the barmaid. 'A large one.'

'Bad news?' she said pouring the drink.

'Sort of.'

'I'm supposed to be closing.'

'I won't be long.'

She smiled at him. He felt like a hypocrite. Here he was chastising his agent for cradle-snatching while the same thing was currently going through his own mind. She gestured for him to hurry up.

'Look, Denis, I've got to go, they're closing the bar. I'll ring you in the morning and, of course, I'll be honoured to be your best man. Let's face it; I'll probably be the only man there.'

'Greg?'

He held the phone to his ear again. 'Yes, Denis?'

'There's something else.'

'What? Please don't tell me you're pregnant.'

Hettie looked a bit shocked as she handed Greg his change. He mouthed 'my agent' and pointed to his phone. She smiled, 'Oh that's nice', she mouthed.

'I'm selling the agency.'

'What?'

'I'm selling the agency. Anton and I are moving to France.'

'What?' Greg reiterated.

'Anton is French and wants to get back to his roots.'

'And what happens to my career whilst you're off having your little jeu d'amour?'

'I'm not having a jeu d'amour, Greg; it's not a game. I'm...well...I'm in love.'

Greg almost choked again. Hettie pointed to her watch.

'Does this mean I don't have an agent anymore?' he asked.

'No it doesn't,' replied Denis. 'I've handed everything over to Helen Clarke.' Helen Clarke was Denis' assistant. She used to be an actress but when her child arrived and she became a single mother, twenty years ago, she'd had less time and inclination for the insecure life an acting career offered, so had gone from just helping Denis out occasionally to being his full-time assistant. Greg had always found her to be very competent but she'd never actually run an agency before.

Hettie tapped her watch again and Greg motioned he wouldn't be long. 'Look, Denis, I really do have to go. I will talk to you tomorrow. Oh and congratulations.'

Greg switched his phone off and turned to Hettie. 'How are you getting home, Hettie? I have a taxi booked.'

Hettie smiled and got her coat.

*

Sunday lunchtime saw Greg dressed in a suit brandishing a carnation that somehow had been dyed green, standing next to his agent and his young French 'husband' or 'wife' - Greg wasn't sure about the casting - ready to sign the register agreeing that the two men were legitimately in a Civil Partnership. They were due to emigrate to a small village in South-West France called Bourrouillan in about two months' time.

Anton seemed a very amiable chap and was very pleased that Denis' oldest friend, Greg, had blessed their union. Greg, having been assured by Denis that Helen Clarke would be a more than competent agent and that his career was in good hands, was looking forward to taking up the offer extended by the newlyweds that he must come and spend some time over in France once he'd finished his current TV series.

They had a reception in a pub in Central London – a bit showy for Greg's liking - but there was a free bar so he wasn't that put off. Hettie had agreed to be his guest at the wedding and the two of them were staying at a hotel nearby. On Denis' advice, she'd managed to drag him away before he became too drunk.

Greg didn't see his erstwhile agent before he left for France. He'd been busy filming – and seeing quite a lot of Hettie. Over the next five years he was to visit the small

French village just once, but spent a happy fortnight in the company of Denis and Anton. His relationship with Hettie had come to an inevitable end, and after he'd finished the TV series he hardly saw her.

He'd watched from a distance as Denis and Anton's relationship grew, with a certain amount of envy. He'd resigned himself to never being capable himself of having a permanent relationship. When he'd visited France that once, he'd sat in a couple of bars in the town of Nogaro near to Bourrouillan making eyes at the French girls but they just looked at him as though he were some sort of dirty old man and moved away. He was feeling old. He was forty-two and still trying to behave like a teenager. 'Time to grow up Driscoll', he'd told himself. A girl in skin-tight jeans had floated to the table next to his and sat down. She'd looked at Greg and smiled. 'Plenty of time to grow up later,' he'd thought and smiled back.

**

CHAPTER ONE

MALDON 2013

Greg Driscoll sat at the side of the salt marshes just high enough to be out of the water and yet not quite on dry land. An avocet swooped down and plopped into the shallows about ten feet from him. It may have not been an avocet, Greg didn't know. Although he had spent many, many hours sitting in this very spot, he couldn't really tell a sooty tern from a sandpiper. What's more, he didn't care; he just liked watching them. The avocet, or whatever it was, started digging with its bill. Digging for what? Worms? Insects? Whatever it was looking for it evidently found it, ate it and took off into the grey Essex sky, presumably to look for more.

Greg looked across the mudflats. The tide was coming in, slowly at first but Greg knew that before long, the water would be lapping his boots. The causeway to Northey Island, where the Vikings had been invited to come and slaughter, was gradually disappearing under the murky Blackwater. Greg liked Northey. It was a birdwatcher's paradise, with hides scattered across the small island and, even though Greg was not a twitcher, he liked to watch the birds soaring about the skies without a care in the world. He envied them their freedom. There was a house of some sort on the island, though Greg didn't know whether anyone actually lived there. He knew the island belonged to the National Trust, or the RSPB or something. Maybe there was a warden living in the house? That would be a good job. Hardly ever a visitor; a whole island to oneself; adventures to be had. What if he owned the island? What would he do? Turn the house into an Arts Centre; create great works of art, paintings, dramas, musical soirees; invite all the great and good; make loads of money… and then what?

Money was not a motivation for Greg. Not anymore. It wasn't that he had any. He still needed enough to pay for food, alcohol and cigarettes. Oh, and council tax of course. That was all. The tide was speeding up, the causeway long gone and muddy pools were forming all around where Greg was sitting. A tiny crab crawled from one pool, had a look around and decided it was safer to stay underwater. Several seagulls were wandering along the mudflats, minding their own business, picking up bits of food, scavenging. Greg watched them. He liked seagulls. They didn't bother him as they did the tourists. He didn't have bags of chips for them to steal. As he watched, one of the bigger gulls suddenly fluffed up his feathers and stalked towards the flock out on a small promontory which the tide had formed a few yards from Greg. The other birds flew into the air as the bully approached, landing behind the aggressor, who feasted at the other birds' table, then, still fluffed up, he turned and made towards them again, squawking loudly. Once more the others flew to a different part of the spit and carried on their feeding. Was it a game? None of the other birds seemed particularly worried by the bully. He set to them again, backwards and forwards, to and fro until, after a while, he gave up and joined the others in their feast. They didn't try to chase him away; they just seemed to ignore him as if to say 'You can be as aggressive as you like but if we ignore you, we know you'll get tired'.

Greg smiled. He'd known a lot of people like that gull. Maybe he should have taken the same approach with them. Ignore them and they'd go away. Trouble is, they never did.

A dog barked sending the birds into a panic. They flew across the river, safe in the knowledge the dog was on a lead and not able to follow. Bully bird turned and squawked, laughing at the dog.

'C'mere, you little bastard!' The shaven-headed, human equivalent of the bully bird, on the other end of the lead, pulled the dog away from the flats and thrashed it with the leather. 'Siddown, you bastard!' The dog growled, took a look at his master, resisted his natural instinct to attack and sat on the dank grass. 'Roight! Oi won' tell you agin! C'mon!' Shaven-head pulled on the lead and the dog, confused as to why it had had to sit in the first place, jumped up and continued along the footpath at the top of the sea-wall. Greg, like the seagulls, ignored them.

The tide was full, the muddy pools submerged under the river, the seagulls' promontory now just defined by a few blades of seagrass, ebbing and flowing with the waves. Greg looked back towards Northey, now an island proper, completely cut off from the land. He imagined the Viking ships moored on the banks; many men with shields and swords and spears, waiting for the tide, waiting to fight, waiting to plunder, waiting to gain. And they had gained. Over a thousand years ago they had gained. They had come and taken what was not theirs to take. They had taken life, lives, many lives. And what had made them go away? Dane geld! Money! The Saxons gave them money so they would leave and they left – for a while – and then they returned, again and again. Not just to Maldon but across the country. Give us some money and we'll go away! Just like bully bird. And, just like bully bird, they eventually gave up the game, took over the country and installed Cnut as king!

Greg liked Cnut. He felt like him sometimes, sitting here vainly trying to stop the tide. Not that he believed Cnut ever tried to turn the tide. He was of the view that Cnut was demonstrating that no matter how strong, how powerful one was, nature (or God, if you want) would always be stronger and more powerful. Greg often hoped he was descended from the Vikings, even though his name was from Irish descent. The Vikings, though, had been in Ireland, so there could be some Viking blood lurking somewhere. Vikings were sensible people with sensible names. Forkbeard, for example. You knew exactly what Sweyn Forkbeard looked like - and Harald Bluetooth. It seemed unlikely though. Most Viking descendants inherited some characteristics - blonde hair, height, strength – and Greg had never really possessed any of these. He drank a lot; that was a Viking trait surely.

The sun was starting to dip and the wind was more noticeable as twilight descended. Greg pulled his army-surplus greatcoat about him and, looking once more to his beloved Northey, stood up and started back towards the Hythe Quay. A mother with two young children saw him walking along the path and grabbed her youngsters close to her. Greg smiled and said 'hello.'

'Come along, girls. Stay by me. Don't want to mix with that sort'

Greg smiled again and said 'Bye.'

'Greg Driscoll?'

The voice came from behind Greg, the way the family had gone. It stopped Greg and sent a shiver down his spine.

He suddenly felt very cold. He couldn't move. For the first time in many years he felt fear.

'Greg? It is you, isn't it?'

Greg stood still. He was starting to shake. He felt, rather than saw, the person walk round to face him. He didn't need to see. He didn't want to know who it was. He had a horrible idea of whom it might be but it couldn't be her. He wouldn't believe that.

'Hi. Long time, no see.'

Greg felt his legs shaking. He tried to move, to run. Nothing. Slowly, oh so slowly the light faded, the ground spiralled, Greg felt his face hit the mud and then he felt nothing more.

*

There was quite a buzz around Greg Driscoll as he regained consciousness. For a moment he didn't know where he was. He'd felt a hand slap his face and had vaguely heard a voice calling his name. He opened his eyes to see Wendy Jenkins staring at him.

'Fuck me! Thought you were a goner!' he heard her say.

Wendy Jenkins was his post lady and had been a good friend almost since he'd first moved to Maldon. 'Drink this,' she said, thrusting a brandy glass with a large measure of spirit in it into his face. He backed off and took the glass in his hand. It shook a bit so he brought his other hand to join it to help steady the glass before taking a sip of the liquid. The room started to come back into focus.

'What am I doing here?' he asked, confused.

He was in what used to be known as the 'Members' Bar', a small room at the front of The King's Head. Time was he knew everybody who drank in there. Anyone who wasn't recognised was made to feel so uncomfortable that they soon left and went through to the larger bar on the other side of the pub. Since the advent of all-day opening, however, the 'Members' Bar' had just become part of the pub in general – they even allowed children in during the day!

He looked around him. There were quite a few people in the bar but he only knew Wendy.

'It's alright! He's not dead!' yelled Wendy to anyone who happened to be listening.

The landlord, a man in his thirties called Gareth, looked over the bar. 'Tell him to get his feet off my furniture, then,' he said.

Greg was lying on a long bench next to the wall that separated the 'Members' from the rest of the pub. He flipped his feet to the floor and sat up. His head was spinning.

'What happened, Greg?' said Wendy. 'You look like you've seen a ghost.'

Recollection flooded back into Greg's mind. He studied the other people in the bar. She wasn't there. 'Do you know, Wendy? I thought I did. I was out there on the sea-wall, so how did I get in here?'

'Better ask Alan. He found you.' Alan was Wendy's husband. He used to do something in the City but had been made redundant when the crash came and now did odd-jobs for people. 'He was wandering around on the sea-wall,' Wendy continued, 'although what the fuck he was doing there, I don't know. He was supposed to be meeting me in here. Anyway, he staggered in with you in his arms and said he found some woman trying to pick you up. Literally, I mean. Pick you up from the floor where, apparently, you'd fainted.'

Greg shivered. 'Where is he, then?' he asked looking round.

'Outside on the terrace with the woman. She was pretty shook up.'

'She's here?'

'As far as I know, unless Alan's run off with her. She is quite attractive, I noticed.'

'I don't want to see her,' said Greg, firmly, downing the rest of the brandy.

'Why? Do you know her? Who is she?' Wendy was surprised with the vehemence of Greg's response.

'A ghost, Wendy.'

'She didn't look like a ghost to me. Alan certainly didn't seem to think so.'

Gareth came through from the other bar. 'Get me a Kronenbourg, Gareth, please,' ordered Greg.

'Feeling better, then?' said the barman.

'Not really,' he replied and turned to Wendy. 'Do you know this woman's name?'

'Ginny? Something like that.'

'Ginny?'

'Something like that, I wasn't listening, really.'

Gareth put Greg's pint on the bar. 'Three pounds fifty,' he demanded. Wendy paid him the money and brought the glass over to Greg.

'Did I ever tell you why I first came to Maldon, Wendy?' he said gulping down a quantity of lager.

'Only about a hundred times,' replied Wendy. 'I still see you looking over, longingly, at the old station.'

Greg sat contemplating for a moment.

'You were chasing some villains and your girlfriend was killed in the old station. Is that right?' Wendy pretended to yawn.

'Close,' said Greg. 'The girl that died was called Jenny. Jenny Gulliver.'

'Yes, I remember.' Wendy paused for a second. 'And the relevance?'

'The girl I saw on the sea-wall, who tried to pick me up and who you say is called something like Ginny, and is now sitting outside this pub with your husband...' he paused, unable to say the next words for a while. 'She is Jenny Gulliver.'

'I thought you said she was dead.'

'She is, Wendy.' Greg started to shake again.

'How can you even think that?' Wendy put her hand on his arm.

'She always wore a scent that smelt of orange blossom. I could smell that before I even saw her. I just knew, Wendy!'

Wendy looked sceptical.

'How's the patient?' Alan came through to the 'Members' Bar'.

'I think he'll survive,' answered Wendy, still looking at Greg. She was worried he'd maybe knocked his head when he fell. He certainly seemed to be talking rubbish.

'I'm sorry I gave you a shock, Greg.' The woman had followed Alan into the bar.

Greg looked at the woman standing in front of him. She didn't look like a ghost; not that he'd ever seen one before. 'Are you who I think you are?' he managed to say.

'Who do you think I am?' she replied.

Her name stuck in his throat. Wendy answered for him. 'He thinks you're someone who's dead.' She took in a deep breath but could not recognise any scent that reminded her of orange blossom.

Jenny sat down on a stool opposite Greg, 'Well, I wasn't the last time I looked.' Her hand reached out to him and he let her hold onto his. His heart was pounding in his chest.

'Jenny?' A tear forced its way down his cheek. Jenny gently brushed it away with her hand.

'What's the weather like on the terrace, Alan?' Wendy asked her husband.

'Bit chilly, actually; that's why we came in.'

'Well, it looks alright to me. Let's go and check.' Wendy stood up.

'No, it really is quite...' Alan couldn't finish his meteorological observation as Wendy grabbed his arm and pulled him out of the bar.

'I didn't know if you'd remember me,' Jenny said to Greg, her eyes not leaving his.

He studied her face. It was fuller than it had been twenty years before but the features were more or less the same. Her eyes, her cute nose, her beautiful lips. Her hair was a slightly different colour to the one he remembered. It was redder than the burnt golden Pre-Raphaelite shade it once was. She saw him looking.

'It's dyed these days, Greg. It went quite grey after...well...after what happened.'

'What did happen, Jenny? I held your body and took you from the station. I waited at the hospital. I was with you when you...when you died.' He lied about being there; he was in Cathy Brown's bed – the nurse who had tried to help him through his trauma.

Jenny smiled at him. 'Not me, obviously.'

'But it was you, Jenny. I was holding you.'

She shrugged her shoulders. Neither person knew quite what to say. Greg was confused; she seemed so calm.

'I don't seem to have a drink,' she said breaking the silence. 'Unless you'd like me to go?'

'No!' said Greg quickly. He didn't want her to go. Not now. He had to know more. He stood up, his legs still trembling. 'I'll get them,' he said, waving to Gareth who was talking to a customer at the other side of the bar. 'Sparkling water?' he asked Jenny.

'Not likely,' she replied. 'G and T please.' She smiled at him.

The last time they had been drinking together she'd had one glass of sparkling wine and drank water for the rest of the evening.

Gareth spotted Greg waiting to be served and came over. 'Feeling better now?' he said.

'I'm not sure to be honest. Get me another Kronenbourg and a gin and tonic and I'll let you know.'

Greg brought the drinks back to the table. He noticed Jenny had a scar on the side of her neck that he didn't recollect seeing before. 'You're still very beautiful,' he said.

'For someone who's dead.' She laughed. Greg smiled sadly. 'So when was this that I supposedly passed away?'

'Twenty years ago.'

'Twenty years ago I was in Germany.'

'I know and you were conned into swallowing drugs and importing them as a mule into the country.'

She frowned. 'Why do you think I would do that?'

'You didn't have a choice. They'd done it to me too.'

'Who?'

'Rob Vanderlast and Wiersma!' Rob Vanderlast and Han Koolhaven ran what Greg had thought was a film company. They had booked Greg for a commercial to be filmed in Holland. It was supposedly for a Supermarket chain run by a German called Pieter Wiersma but it turned out to be a front for a drug-running gang. Jenny Gulliver had been cast shortly afterwards for a commercial to be shot in Germany by the same company.

'Don't be silly,' giggled Jenny.

'It is silly, isn't it?' Greg looked at his first love sitting opposite him, full of life. She looked down at the table.

'You don't know what happened, do you?' she whispered.

'What do you mean?'

'To me,' she said. 'What happened to me. I thought you might have heard.'

Greg looked at her quizzically.

'I've had a pretty awful time, Greg.' She took a handkerchief from her handbag and blew her nose.

'Would you like to go somewhere else?' asked Greg.

'Can we talk about something else and just have a few drinks. For old time's sake, if nothing else.'

Greg nodded his head. He needed to know more but it seemed it would have to wait.

'So, what have you been doing, Greg?' Jenny said.

'For twenty years?' he smiled. 'Not a lot, really.'

'Your friends seem nice.' Jenny took a sip of her drink.

'I'm not sure nice is the description I'd choose to describe Wendy. Coarse, probably or nosy, definitely. Either of those is more fitting. Talking of which, where are they?'

'They went outside. I think they thought we wanted to be alone.'

Some time ago, being alone with Jenny was all Greg longed for but now he felt awkward. He wanted to know why she was here, why she wasn't lying in a grave. He supposed he should be happy but somehow he felt cheated.

Alan came back into the bar, followed by Wendy. 'My wife seems to think I should stay out in the freezing cold so you two can talk,' he said. 'I'm quite happy to sit somewhere else but I'm not staying outside. The tide's going out and bringing a bloody gale with it.'

Greg looked at Jenny. She laughed. 'Please come and join us, Alan. I haven't thanked you properly for helping me with Greg. Let me buy you a drink.'

Wendy was standing like an old fishwife with her hands on her hips.

'What would you like, Wendy?' Jenny asked her.

Wendy paused, her lips pursed. She looked at Greg, who smiled. 'Have a drink, Wendy. You know you want to!' he called across to her.

'I'll have a white wine, then,' she said, 'and he'll have a half of bitter.' She indicated her husband.

'I'm sure you'd rather have a pint,' Jenny said to him quietly. He grinned and the two of them sat down with Greg.

They talked about Greg's career over the last twenty years; his spell in 'Gone for a Song', which Jenny had heard of but never seen. Alan kept bringing up Greg's 'Community Shakespeare in the Park' production of 'A Midsummer Night's Dream', which had been the pinnacle of Alan's acting career – a career that Greg consistently pointed out that was an amateur career – and was something that Greg would never be persuaded to repeat. None of them mentioned Helen Wilson, the girl who'd played Titania in the production. She had been the Town Clerk and she and Greg had started a relationship; they'd fallen in love, Greg had thought. Shortly after the production she had been killed in an explosion. Greg thought of Helen a lot. There had been nothing that could have been called a lasting relationship since then. Jenny was interested in Wendy's life as a deliverer of communications (Wendy's description of her job) and Wendy was more than happy to elaborate. Alan was vitriolic about the banking industry but whenever anyone asked about Jenny's life she would only say she'd been living and working in Germany for the last twenty years, without going into detail and skilfully diverting the conversation topic away from her.

'Stop staring at Ginny, Greg. You're embarrassing her.' Wendy nudged him ribs. 'You haven't heard a word that's been said, have you?'

Greg turned to his post lady. 'Her name's Jenny, Wendy,' he said.

'It's OK, Greg,' said Jenny hurriedly.

Greg had been staring at Jenny, trying to work out how the girl he'd seen lying in a coma in a hospital bed dying, could possibly be sitting across from him in his local pub now.

'I ought to go,' said Jenny suddenly.

'Why?' Greg was worried he'd upset her; he couldn't let her go again.

She shrugged her shoulders. 'Maybe I shouldn't have come here. I've unwittingly thrown a bit of a bomb into your lives, I think.'

'Why did you come here?' asked Wendy.

Jenny looked at her, not sure whether she could trust this woman who seemed very protective of Greg. 'I came looking for my past, Wendy,' she said holding Wendy's stare.

'And how much of your past was actually spent here in Maldon?'

'Apart from my apparent death, none of it, Wendy. Have I upset you?'

Greg nudged Wendy. 'Leave it,' he said.

'It's OK, Greg.' Jenny smiled. 'Wendy is curious and so am I, to be honest.' She turned to Wendy. 'I knew Greg some twenty years ago in London before he came to Maldon and I've thought about him every day since I last saw him, believe me. It's taken a bit of time but, at last, I've managed to track him down. I'm sorry if I've caused a problem.'

'How did you track him down to Maldon?'

Jenny held her hands out. 'The internet is a marvellous invention,' she said, turning to Greg. 'There's several pages on you, Greg.'

Wendy carried on. 'Why did you want to track him down?'

'I don't know. I suppose I wanted to see him again.'

Wendy looked at the girl sitting opposite her – the one Greg had told her was dead. What was she doing here? Who was this girl who had died and yet not died? Something didn't appear to be right but she couldn't say what. He obviously thought this girl had come back from the dead for him. She looked back at Jenny. 'Well, welcome to Maldon, Ginny.'

'Shall I get another round,' offered Alan.

'Not for me, thanks,' said Greg. Wendy and Alan looked at him in astonishment. It was virtually unheard of for Greg to refuse a drink, especially if someone else was buying.

'Jenny, my house is literally across the road. Have you time for a coffee?'

Alan snorted. 'Coffee? I'd watch out if I were you he rarely stops at coffee!'

'Fuck off, Alan.' Greg was quite aggressive.

Wendy hadn't seen him like this for a long time. 'Calm down, Tiger. Alan was only joking.'

'I know, I'm sorry, Alan. I just need to talk to Jenny.' He looked at her. 'If that's OK, of course.'

Jenny smiled and said. 'Of course. I'd like to see your house.' She took his hand and, saying goodbye to the others, led him out of the pub.

*

Greg and Jenny were sitting at the small table in his kitchen. They'd ordered a pizza to be delivered to the house but they hadn't eaten a lot; most of it still lay in its cardboard box on the table-top going cold. There was also a half-drunk bottle of Scotch.

'I'm still not sure I understand,' said Greg.

'It's taken me a long time to come to terms with it.' Jenny smiled. It was a sad smile, not the happy smile that had lived in Greg's memory all these years. He downed the rest of his glass and held the bottle up to Jenny. She shook her head.

'And nobody knew you were there?' He half-filled his glass.

'Why would they? Nobody knew who I was. The only people I thought would send out distress signals were you and Denis but I know now that you both thought you'd seen me die. At the time I was distraught. I even thought you were maybe part of the whole set-up.'

'How could you?'

'I was locked up in a cellar, unaware of anything. The only company I had, apart from the bastard who was keeping me there, were the machinations of my brain - and when you're incarcerated everything becomes exaggerated; your whole life is unreal – and worthless.'

Greg took Jenny's hand in his. 'I'm sorry,' he said.

'It wasn't your fault, Greg, I know that now. I'm sorry you were grieving for my death rather than what I was actually going through.'

'Do you think Han and Rob could have had something to with this? Rob was definitely involved in the drugs ring.'

'I wouldn't have thought so. This wasn't anything to do with drugs. I was picked up from the hotel by a car. I thought it was a taxi to take me to the airport but it never went anywhere near an airport. He drove me to a small town in the middle of the country.'

'Didn't you realise?'

'Not at first. I didn't know where the airport was and once I started to ask questions, he stopped the car and put something over my mouth and nose. It smelt musty. The next thing I knew, I was waking up in this cellar.'

Greg took another large swig of whisky. 'Did he...?'

'Rape me? Oh yes, many times.'

'Oh God! How awful.' He held Jenny's hand tighter.

'It becomes a way of life, Greg, you get used to it; it becomes the norm.'

'Didn't you try to escape?'

Jenny laughed. It seemed a bitter laugh to Greg and he realised he'd asked a stupid question that he shouldn't have. 'Sorry,' he said again.

'I never went out. Well, I was allowed into a sort of yard at the back. It had huge hedges all round it with a wire fence behind and he was always with me when I was there.'

'It must have been terrible.'

'Like I said, it was just the norm; you become resigned to your situation. The cellar itself wasn't all that bad, really. It was more of a bedsit. A bed, a comfortable chair, a table, a small kitchen area with a cooker and a fridge, a small bathroom with a loo and a shower. There was even a television screen. I couldn't get any programmes on it, though. It was attached to a DVD player on which he liked to show films.'

'What porn?'

Jenny laughed again. 'No, funnily enough. They were mostly documentaries about space travel or racing cars; what I'd have called 'boy's stuff'. Occasionally he'd bring down a movie but they weren't to my taste either.'

'And he kept you there for years and nobody knew?'

'Ten years, Greg. I didn't know it was that long; you lose track of time. The only indication of whether it was night or daytime was the small amount of light coming from a tiny mottled-glass window set high in the wall. I couldn't see out of it. I was sometimes aware of feet walking past and, at first, I'd shout, hoping the passers-by would come and help me but they couldn't hear and I gave up bothering after a while. You're in a sort of bubble where your own world carries on oblivious of whatever's happening outside. I learnt to cut and style my hair – he bought my clothes and food for me to cook and eat, sometimes alone, sometimes with him as company. He'd bring candles down and we'd play out this romantic scenario.'

'So how did you...'

'How did I finally get out?'

Greg nodded.

'One day he went out – he went out often, of course, he wasn't a prisoner – but this day he didn't come back. I don't know how long he was away - at least four days, I could tell that from the light in the window. I was running out of food; I had to ration myself. I didn't know if or when he'd be back.' She paused. 'I thought I was going to die, Greg.'

He stood up and came round the kitchen table. He took her in his arms and hugged her, tears falling from his eyes onto her shoulder.

She pulled away from him and poured herself a drink. 'Anyway, I didn't die. I heard someone knocking on the door above me – the front door – they were hammering and hammering. I was very scared. Then they were at the door to the cellar. I could see an axe or something sharp smashing through the wooden door. I think I called your name, Greg. I knew it wasn't you but I felt so alone, so frightened, I just tried to think of something that made me happy.'

Greg's tears were flowing in torrents, his shoulders hunched and shaking as he sat at the table. Jenny put her hands on them and massaged. 'It's OK, Greg, believe me. It's all OK now.' She sipped her whisky, one hand still on his shoulder. 'The axe wasn't for me. The door splintered and some people in helmets and uniforms came down the steps to me. They were armed and they looked round the room, while a middle-aged woman took my hands and spoke to me in German. I didn't really understand her.'

'Didn't your kidnapper speak German to you?' Greg said quietly.

'Hardly ever, he spoke perfect English nearly all the time I was there. It turned out this middle-aged woman was some sort of social worker. Apparently my captor had tried to pick up some other girl over in Belgium and been nabbed by the police. It had taken some time to get the truth from him but it seems he confessed eventually. He didn't know what he'd done wrong and was full of remorse. I almost felt sorry for him; he'd been my only companion for ten years, after all. I was not his only prisoner, though. It came to light that he had two or three bolt-holes all over the place, all with a slave immured in some sort of lock-up. I was taken to what they called a 'safe-house' and interviewed by an English speaker. It was so strange, Greg. I felt more imprisoned once I'd been released than when I was in my cellar.'

'Why?' Greg looked up at her. His eyes were red-raw. Jenny sat down and took his hands.

'Greg, I hadn't seen anyone but him for all those years. I was overwhelmed. I wanted to go back to my security.'

'But you were free from that.'

Jenny sighed. 'Yes,' she said, looking Greg in the face. 'I was free but I didn't feel free. It was question after question; things I didn't have the answers for. I didn't know I'd been there for that long. I was a complete wreck.'

'So did you...I don't know how to say this...did you recover?'

Jenny smiled. 'What do you think? Do you think I'm recovered?'

Greg looked at her smiling face; it seemed radiant, barely distressed. It must have been hard for her to go through that whole scenario again for his benefit and yet she appeared quite serene. 'I suppose so,' he said.

'It took years of counselling, I can tell you. The people who eventually looked after me were terrific. So much so that I joined their team. There's a lot of abused women in this world – and men too – sadly.'

'But why did you stay in Germany, after all that had happened?'

'It wasn't Germany's fault, Greg. In fact it was Germany who helped to sort it all out for me.' She paused. 'By the way, I'm not Jenny Gulliver anymore. I think it might be fortuitous if everyone continues to think that she is dead because she is, Greg. To anyone but you I'm not her anymore. I'm now called Virginia Hoffmann. I have a German passport and everything.'

***

CHAPTER TWO

Jenny Gulliver stayed in Greg's spare room for a week before they finally agreed that they should try and rekindle a twenty-year old love affair that had never really had a chance to start. It had been Jenny who had suggested it. Greg had not dared to approach the subject for a number of reasons: much as he longed for her he knew she wasn't the same girl he'd known in London; she was a woman of forty-three who'd been abused; he didn't know how she'd react to him wanting a full-on relationship; she could be damaged physically as well as mentally. He just didn't know. He didn't know anything about these things. They'd never slept together back in London and he was scared that during all these years he'd built up that intimate moment into something so beautiful that it could never be achieved. Was it that? Or was he just scared - scared that she wouldn't like him, that she wouldn't feel the same. He'd lost her once; he didn't want to lose her again. And yet it was Jenny who had looked him up on the internet and sought him out. She must feel something; she didn't run a mile, she stayed. But stayed in the spare room.

'I seem to have moved in,' she said one day as they were having dinner. Jenny had insisted on cooking, saying she'd become quite a culinary expert during her time in

Germany. 'Is that alright with you, Greg, me being here? I don't want to outstay my welcome.'

'It is what I want, Jenny. It's what I've always wanted.' He smiled. 'Anyway, strictly speaking it's your house.'

Greg had bought the small fisherman's cottage next to the Hythe with money he'd inherited from Jenny's will when she, supposedly, died. They'd discussed the legal implications of her death not actually having happened and Jenny didn't care about the loss of her not inconsiderable fortune, which had been disposed of by her solicitors.

'I don't want the money, Greg,' she'd said. 'It was my parent's money. My father killed himself accumulating it and then my mother drank herself into an asylum spending it. I expect she's dead now as well. It's all gone, Greg, I can't have it back even if I wanted to, not after all this time. I'm just glad it helped you and that you put it to good use by buying this fabulous cottage.'

'But legally it's not mine, surely,' he protested.

'Legally it is yours, Greg. Legally Jenny Gulliver is dead and you bought this with money you received in good faith. No-one can take it away from you, not now.'

She'd kissed him just after this. It was the first time they'd kissed for two decades.

'It's just, I was thinking,' she said as she cleared the dinner plates. 'If you want me to stay here for a while...' she stood by the sink, plates still in her hand. 'If I'm going to stay, I'd like to be a bit closer to you.'

Greg didn't know how to respond. 'What are you suggesting?' he said.

Jenny put the plates into the sink and threw her arms round Greg's neck, soap bubbles dripping down his back. Her lips met his and they kissed passionately, her hands moving over his body, tearing at his clothes. He responded by removing her t-shirt and bra. Less than a minute later they were naked on his carpet making love.

That evening, Jenny Gulliver, now Virginia Hoffmann, moved into Greg's room and they started to re-ignite the life they had missed out on twenty years previously.

*

Denis Young's reaction, when Greg finally phoned to tell him, had been incredulous. He warned Greg about unscrupulous people who spent their lives stalking famous celebrities. Even after Greg had reminded his erstwhile agent that he was neither famous nor a celebrity, Denis was still convinced that this woman was out to cause him trouble.

Greg didn't care what Denis thought and told him so. Jenny wanted to meet – they'd never met when he took her on as a client at his agency. She'd had a job offer and he'd sorted it out for her, mostly as a favour to Greg. They were supposed to finalise all the details when she returned from Germany. The trouble was, when she came back, she'd ended up dead, as far as he knew. Now Greg was telling him she'd risen, Lazarus-like and wanted to meet him; not only meet him but come and stay at his place in France.

Throughout the years of their marriage, Denis had talked a lot about Greg. He'd told Anton of many exploits but especially about the circumstances that led to the death of Jenny Gulliver. Anton wanted to know all the details of the drug-runners and the sham film-makers.

Interestingly, Anton had brought the subject up again quite recently. Following his brief flirtation with the entertainment industry – happily curtailed by his marriage and subsequent emigration – he had taken up an interest in journalism, writing as a freelance for some local newspapers, mostly on a no-fee basis. Although his speciality was mostly concerned with provincial goings-on, a story about a small-time villain ending up in a bad way, following an association with some major drug barons had reminded him of Denis' story about Greg and Jenny. He'd done some research on the internet and come across a newspaper interview with Greg Driscoll from a time soon after Jenny's death. Greg had appeared to be obsessed with the young actress and talked a lot about her in the article – quite understandably, she had just suffered a terrible and fatal ordeal – and went into some intimate details; her beautiful hair colour; how much she laughed; how she always wore a scent of orange-blossom. There was a picture of Jenny, and Denis had cried when he saw it. The newspaper article had been in an English publication from the Greek Island of Corfu, designed to be read by the ex-pat community, and was concerned with the death of a well-known German supermarket giant in a boating accident, who'd turned out to be 'not all he seemed'. Denis had never seen it and, even though he'd been Greg's agent, knew nothing about Greg having ever spoken to the paper. He said he would have to have a word with Greg when he came over next but Anton was quick to point out that it had been a long time ago and sleeping dogs should be left to lie.

So when Denis had told him of Greg's phone call, Anton was excited about the possibility of not only Greg but also Jenny – who they'd thought was dead – coming to stay. He reassured Denis that everything would be alright and said how lovely it would be to see Greg again and, unexpectedly, Jenny Gulliver. Denis still felt nervous but agreed that they could come and stay.

*

Greg and Jenny – whom Greg had to try to remember to call "Ginny" now – flew from Stansted Airport to Biarritz, about a two hour drive from Denis and Anton's house, deep in the French countryside. They hired a car and drove, at first, along the motorways before the surrounding area turned to fields of vines and maize and the roads became lined with avenues of Birch trees, standing tall and protective, as they approached Bourrouillan.

'Well, hello! Look at you! You look fab, darling!' Anton kissed Jenny on both cheeks before repeating the action on Greg's. 'You don't look so bad either.' He turned to Denis. 'I still don't know how you let him get away, Den.'

It always amused Greg that Anton used the abbreviated form of Denis' name for his partner, something he wouldn't allow anyone else to do – he'd always insisted on being called Denis.

It was a warm spring evening and they went out onto the terrace where Anton fussed around getting gin and tonics for everyone while Greg and Jenny sat on loungers by the pool.

Anton was a tall man, now thirty years old, but looked in his early twenties. He had a thin waist and wore jeans that were slightly too tight, in Greg's opinion. His upper body was muscly without being out of proportion. He wore his dark hair long and, on this occasion, had pulled it back from his face with an Alice band, showing off his golden tanned face. Greg grudgingly had to admit he was very handsome. Denis was scrutinising Jenny as they sat with their drinks.

'Denis, stop looking at Ginny that way,' said Greg, 'you'll embarrass her,'

'It's OK, Greg,' she said. 'He thinks I'm a ghost too.'

Denis mumbled an apology. 'It just seems very weird; it's like a part of my life didn't happen,' he said.

'It did happen, Denis, I'm sure,' said Jenny, holding onto Greg's hand. 'Just not in the way you thought it did.' She smiled at him.

'Let me show you the grounds, Virginia.' Anton grabbed Jenny's arm and whisked her off across the terrace. The lawns swept down to a large lake about a hundred yards away. Greg and Denis watched the two of them run hand in hand down the slope towards the water.

'Do you want a beer?' asked Denis.

'Thought you'd never ask,' replied Greg. He sat and looked across the lawns while Denis went to the fridge. He could see Anton and Jenny. They were laughing and seemed to be having a good time. He wasn't sure whether he felt jealous or not. There was no reason to be but something didn't feel quite right. They'd only just met and yet were behaving as if they were old friends.

Denis came back with a can of Kronenbourg and a glass. He saw Greg looking at Anton and Jenny. 'You don't have to worry about Anton, Greg, you should know that.'

'I wasn't worried, Denis.' He took the can and left the glass on the table. 'Do you think they've met before?'

'What? Jenny and Anton? I don't see how they can have done, if what you've told me is true.'

'What do you mean?'

Denis looked down at his gin.

'Denis, what do you mean?' Greg repeated.

'How can you be sure that girl is Jenny Gulliver?'

'What?'

'It just seems strange to me that twenty years after she was supposedly buried, she suddenly turns up very much alive.'

'I told you what happened, Denis.'

'I know what you told me but someone died in that station in Maldon. Who was she if she wasn't Jenny Gulliver?'

Greg realised he hadn't really considered who that person was. He'd been so caught up in Jenny's resurrection that the poor girl he'd held in his arms had become some phantom – someone who hadn't really existed.

Denis carried on. 'You said this Jenny didn't want anyone to know she hadn't died – wanted to keep up the fallacy – but what about the girl who did die? Did she have any family? Shouldn't we find out who she was?'

Greg thought for a moment. He didn't know what to do. 'Jenny didn't want any legal complications. If we start probing into the past of the dead girl then it's bound to come out that Jenny didn't die. Besides it was twenty years ago. Maybe any family she had wouldn't want it all dragged up. I mean, they must have accepted that the girl was missing.' Greg was floundering. What was the right thing to do?

'So you just want to ignore it!' said Denis accusingly.

Greg looked over the lawns. He tried to focus on Jenny. She was Jenny, of that he was sure, but Denis was right. Who was the other girl? Where did she fit in? Apart from the now definitely deceased Marjan Smits, no-one else who knew her had seen Jenny other than him. He'd always believed the girl who'd died was Jenny. He'd known her better than anyone, but now she was back and he was convinced this was the same person. 'Perhaps I should talk to her about it,' he said.

'Yes, perhaps you should.'

Anton and Jenny came running up the lawn to join them.

'It's so beautiful, Greg. You should come down and have a look.' Jenny was beaming, her face reddened by the exertion of running up the hill back to the terrace.

'I will sometime,' he replied. Jenny looked excited. 'What were you and Anton talking about?'

'Oh, the scenery, that sort of thing,' she said rather evasively.

'What's for dinner?' butted in Anton. 'I'm starving!'

'Fois Gras followed by cassoulet,' said Denis proudly. 'All local produce, of course.'

'Apart from the salt?' Greg laughed. He'd brought Denis his regular supply of Maldon Salt. Ever since he'd seen several TV chefs extolling the virtues of the Blackwater River salt and realised it came from where Greg now resided, Denis had refused to use any other seasoning in his cooking.

'I'd better check on it. Half an hour alright?'

Greg and Jenny nodded their agreement.

'Anton, set the table,' Denis ordered. 'We'll eat Al Fresco, I think.' He went towards the kitchen.

'I hope you've got insect repellent,' said Anton going to fetch the cutlery.

*

Greg and Jenny's room was in what had been a derelict barn when Denis and Anton had first bought the place. It had now been turned into rustic-looking, yet modern, living accommodation with two double bedrooms, two bathrooms – one en-suite –a kitchen area, which was incorporated into a living room with comfortable seating and a television. The doors from this room led out onto another terrace that surrounded a second swimming pool.

'Have you met Anton before?' Greg asked Jenny as she stood with a towel wrapped round her, having stepped straight from the shower.

'No, why?'

'You just seemed to get on very well, that's all.'

'You're not jealous, Greg Driscoll?'

'No,' he replied quickly.

'I should think not.' She went towards Greg and let him help to dry her. They kissed and she dragged him onto the bed.

'We'll be late for dinner,' he protested meekly.

*

'I think I said half an hour,' said Denis, arms folded, as they joined their hosts on their terrace.

'Sorry, needed a shower,' said Greg. 'We're only a bit late.'

'Well, I just hope the dinner's not ruined, that's all.' Denis went off to the kitchen in a huff.

Anton poured some white wine. 'It won't be ruined, you can keep cassoulet cooking for hours.' Greg noticed him wink at Jenny.

They sat down to dinner at a candle-lit table under a wooden gazebo at the end of the garden. Greg couldn't believe it was still so warm. He could see why Denis preferred it here to damp old London. Denis presented them with plates containing a small slice of pate and some thin toast that curled at the edges.

'Are we on rations?'

'I think you'll find that's plenty, Greg,' informed Anton.

He was right. The pate was a rich Fois Gras and by the time Greg had finished eating it he was more or less full. Jenny didn't even manage to finish hers, although Denis and Anton had cleaned their plates and were ready for the cassoulet.

'Can we have a bit of a break?' said Greg taking out his cigarettes.

'You can go and smoke away from the table, please.' Denis picked up the empty plates and went back to the kitchen. Greg stood up and walked a few paces towards the swimming pool. There was a frog – or a toad, he didn't know which – swimming around in the pool. He watched as it tried, unsuccessfully, to get itself out. Anton was pouring red wine into fresh glasses. He brought one over to Greg, handed it to him and, picking up a net on a long pole, plunged it into the pool giving the amphibian a chance to free itself. It happily hopped into the net and Anton transferred it out into the flowers.

'Denis can't stand them,' he said. 'He can be such a wuss sometimes. Do you like the wine?' Greg nodded as they headed back to the table. 'It's grown over there.' Anton pointed to the rows of vines that adjoined the property. It was quite a heavy wine but Greg managed to down a couple of glasses before Denis returned with a terracotta rustic pot filled with his speciality cassoulet and some hunks of home-made bread.

'You've become quite domesticated, Denis,' smirked Greg. 'What happened to the City boy who thought Maldon was 'the back of beyond'? At least we have a few shops.'

'I never said Maldon was 'the back of beyond'. I said it was a Godforsaken place and I stand by that. I don't know why you insist on living there.'

The banter continued late into the night. They all joined in and there appeared to be four empty red wine bottles on the floor, by the end of which, Greg and Anton had consumed more than their fair share, Denis and Jenny having resorted to gin and tonics.

Jenny nudged Greg as his head started to droop. 'Come on, you. Time for bed.'

Greg sat up and tried to protest but decided acquiescence was probably better. His head was heavy with the grape and sleep did seem like a good idea.

'You go on ahead,' said Jenny. 'I'll help clear up.'

He didn't argue and tramped up the stairs in the barn. It was an hour later that he woke suddenly to realise he was still alone in his bed. There was a bright moon shining through the open curtains and he stumbled over to close them before going to find out where Jenny was. He couldn't say he was worried about her; he just suspected he was missing out on some more late-night revelry. The moonlight illuminated the wooden gazebo at the end of Denis and Anton's part of the house and he could vaguely make out two figures deep in conversation. He rubbed his sleep-filled eyes and tried to focus, squinting through the window. The candles were still burning on the table next to the two people and in their flickering light he could see Jenny's auburn hair dance and sparkle quite clearly now, as she sat under the gazebo. He quickly threw on some clothes, left his room and started down the stairs towards the garden. Jenny met him halfway.

'That was sneaky,' he said.

'What?' Jenny looked surprised.

'Getting another drink in without me? Was that Denis? Don't believe what he says about me.'

Jenny smiled. 'No, it was Anton.' She went past him and into the en-suite bathroom.

'Oh,' said Greg and followed her into the bedroom. He looked through the window before closing the curtains. Anton was still there sitting under the gazebo. He appeared to be smoking a cigarette, something that he was sure Denis would not approve of. He smiled to himself. After all these years Denis seemed to have been tied down by someone who appeared to take no notice of his directives. Maybe that was the answer to a long-lasting relationship – letting your partner be themself.

Jenny came out of the bathroom and collapsed on the bed. 'I don't think I can keep this up for a whole fortnight, Greg.' She smiled at him, puckering her lips. Greg left the window and joined her in the bed. Within five minutes they were asleep in each other's arms.

*

'Greg! Do you not have your phone switched on?' Denis was hammering on the bedroom door. Greg wearily crawled out of bed and threw on the dressing-gown Denis had thoughtfully left in the room for him. It was made of silk and had a pattern that could have been flowers, Greg wasn't sure. Jenny turned over and pulled the duvet round her.

'What time is it, Denis?' groaned Greg as he came out of the door. Denis was pacing along the corridor.

'It's nearly eleven o'clock,' he said, looking at his watch.

'Well, you're an hour ahead of us so it's barely ten o'clock to my body. Why are you waking me up?'

'I've had Helen Clarke on the phone from the office. She has an interview for you.'

'I'm on holiday!' protested Greg, going down to the kitchen and switching on the kettle.

'I know,' Denis followed him down the stairs. 'But this could be really good.'

Greg threw a couple of tea bags into a pot and grabbed a couple of mugs. 'Do you want tea?'

'Did you hear me, Greg? Helen has an interview for you.'

Greg poured the boiling water into the teapot, and putting another mug under the coffee machine, turned to Denis. 'You are no longer my agent, Denis, so why are you flapping like an old hen?'

'I'm not flapping,' replied Denis. 'And I do still have an interest, you know.'

'In what? Me or the agency?'

'Both. I still have shares in the agency but I also think this is a good opportunity for you. It's the same team that did 'Gone for a Song'. It's a new drama serial and they've asked for you specifically.'

'Then they can wait 'til I've finished my holiday.' Greg poured tea into one of the mugs, took his coffee from under the machine, added milk to them both and went to take them upstairs.

'I've booked you on a two o'clock flight to London, and they'll see you at five-thirty. They're even sending a cab to pick you up at Stansted.'

'Cancel it!' Greg started up the stairs.

'I think Denis is right, you should go, Greg.' Jenny came down the stairs and took her mug of tea with her into the kitchen. She was wearing a dressing-gown that matched Greg's.

'How long have you been listening?' asked Greg.

'Long enough. Besides you were both yelling so loudly I would think the whole of South-West France knows what's going on.' She grinned.

'But we're on holiday I don't want to go running back to London. It's probably raining there. If they're so keen to have me they can wait a week or two. They know what I can do; I've worked for them before.' He sat down next to Jenny at the kitchen table.

'Look, Greg, it's lovely being here with you and Denis and Anton but you've got to keep your career going, you know. There's not that much work around that you can just pick and choose when you're seen. If they're so keen to get you back, they must want you, sure, but they could always find someone else. You're not irreplaceable.'

'I am.' Greg pulled a face.

'Only to me.' Jenny kissed him on the lips. Denis turned away. 'You could be back tomorrow.'

'And we'd be more than happy to look after Ginny.' Denis came over to the table. 'I'll run you over to Biarritz Airport, if you like and pick you up again tomorrow.'

Greg looked at his erstwhile agent and then at Jenny. 'Why are you so keen to get rid of me?' he asked.

'We're not,' assured Jenny, taking hold of his hand. 'I just don't think you're ready to retire yet.'

Greg sighed. 'I'd better go and ring Helen, then.'

'It's OK,' said Denis. 'I've told her to tell them to expect you. She's e-mailed me all the details. Get dressed and you can read them on the plane.'

'I've a feeling I'm being bullied.' Greg stood up.

'Just make sure you get the job.' Jenny kissed him again and, grabbing his hand, dragged him back up the stairs.

'We have to leave in twenty minutes so no hanky-panky,' yelled Denis as they disappeared.

Half an hour later, Greg was sitting in Denis' car trying to read a synopsis for a drama serial about a group of friends who'd met at University in the 1980's and how their lives had, or had not, met their expectations.

'It's a bit old-hat, isn't it?' he said turning a page.

'It's a formula that's proved successful in the past,' replied Denis.

'In the past, yes,' thought Greg. There'd been lots of series about friends who'd grown up, grown apart and come back together to find they didn't have those same things in common that had drawn them together all those years ago. But did people still want to watch that these days? Haven't we moved on? He looked at the details Helen had attached to the synopsis. They did seem keen to have him on board but he had to convince the money men he was right for the part, although with the film company behind him and his amazing charm, that would just be a formality surely. It would be good to be working again, there wasn't a lot of money coming in and Jenny didn't seem to have any income.

Denis drew up outside the small airport at Biarritz and, checking Greg had his e-ticket and his passport, let him go into the departure area.

*

'Are you sure he doesn't suspect anything?'

'Doesn't seem to. I didn't think I'd get away with it but he seems to believe me.'

'Denis always said he was gullible, especially when it came to women.'

***

CHAPTER THREE

'I thought you were on holiday with your floozy?' Wendy Jenkins was sitting in The King's Head when she saw Greg walk into the members' bar.

'I am on holiday,' he replied. 'Unfortunately some bigwigs at a film company thought I should fly home for a five minute interview.'

Greg had arrived at the offices of the film company to be greeted warmly by the producers and the director of the proposed drama serial, both of whom he knew from 'Gone for a Song'. There were a few men in suits sitting round a table in the meeting room and Greg was introduced to them. The suits said they'd seen his work and were more than happy for him to play the part the producers had him in mind for him. They were going to fund the filming and they hoped it would be a great success.

Greg had wanted to ask why he'd had to break into his holiday to be told this but didn't have time. Apparently the suits had other business to do and they shook his hand and left the room. The producers went with them, leaving Greg alone with the director, Phil Woodford.

'Well, that went well,' said Phil. 'How have you been, Greg?'

'I've been fine, Phil, thanks. What I don't understand is why I had to fly back from France for a two minute chat where I didn't even get to speak.'

'I know. Sorry about that. They've insisted on meeting everyone. Don't ask me to try and understand the workings of the minds of money people. I really appreciate you coming over.'

'When can I see a script?'

Phil handed Greg an envelope, 'This is a draft of the first episode. Don't let anyone else see it.'

'Thanks,' said Greg. 'Fancy a pint?'

'Can't, mate, sorry. Business calls, you know?'

Greg didn't know and didn't really care. He'd always got on well with Phil during filming but couldn't say they were actually friends. He'd never spent any time with him socially and wasn't too disappointed that he'd turned down the offer of a pint. They'd shaken hands and Greg had made his way back to Maldon and straight to The King's Head.

'She's not my floozy, Wendy, as well you know.'

'Oh yes,' she replied. 'She's the ghost of your past, isn't she?'

'Shall I go and sit somewhere else?' Greg was getting tired of Wendy's constant ribbing about Jenny. He didn't understand why she didn't seem to like her.

'It's up to you, Greg. If you want to ostracise all your old friends then that's your choice.' Wendy downed the remains of her wine.

Greg picked up her empty glass. 'You're right, Wendy. Please accept my sincere apologies and allow me to replenish your libation.'

'If you mean you'll buy me a drink, I'll accept.' Greg went to the bar. 'I'll have a large one,' she yelled after him.

He went to the bar. Natalie, who for some reason Greg couldn't fathom liked to be called Tallie, was behind the bar.

'Where's Gareth?' asked Greg.

'He is allowed a night off, you know. If I'm not good enough for you, you know what you can do,' replied Tallie.

'You're more than good enough for me, Tallie, you know that. I think Gareth should have more nights off so we can be graced with your beautiful presence more often.'

'Kronenbourg, is it?' Tallie did not seem impressed.

'And a large white wine, please.'

Greg took his pint and Wendy's wine back to the table. 'Have I really been neglectful?' he said.

'I wouldn't know. We never see you anymore.'

'I'm sorry, Wendy.' Greg sat opposite her. 'It's really weird, you know. For twenty years I've thought Jenny was dead and now she's here as if nothing has happened.'

Wendy sipped her wine. 'Is she just the same, then? As she was twenty years ago, I mean?'

'Well, she's twenty years older, of course but...yes, she is really. Why?'

'I don't know. It's like you say, it's weird. Anyway what was this interview about?'

Greg told her a bit about the new drama serial, how it was the same people who'd done 'Gone for a Song' and that he'd been offered the job.'

'That's great,' said Wendy. 'Who else is in it?'

'I don't know. Does it matter?'

'Might do if I've got to watch it.'

'You don't have to watch it, Wendy, if my talent isn't enough for you.'

Wendy had been fiddling with her phone all through their conversation. Greg still hadn't got used to the fact that fiddling with your phone whilst conversing was the norm these days. He found it extremely rude and irritating. 'Am I boring you?' he said pointedly.

'No, of course not. Why?' Wendy didn't even look up from her phone; her thumbs were working overtime on the keyboard.

'Because you seem to be more interested in that piece of technology in your hand than what I'm saying.'

Wendy put her phone on the table. 'Do try and join the twenty-first century, Greg. I took in everything you said. You're going to do a new TV show, you don't know who else is in it and I'm very happy for you.'

Greg looked at Wendy's phone. 'It's sort of a secret at the moment,' he said. 'You haven't...'

Alan bounced through the door and slapped Greg on the back. 'We have a TV star in our midst again. Will he still speak to us lowly mortals, I wonder?' he yelled to the pub.

Greg looked at Wendy who shrugged her shoulders.

Ian Stewart followed Alan into the bar. He was another of the community players who'd appeared in Greg's production of 'A Midsummer Night's Dream'. He had become another of Greg's close friends over the intervening years. He was a very tall and large man who worked contentedly in a local wood yard, quite happy to be told what to do as long as he didn't have to engage his brain.

'TV star, TV star!' he bellowed, leaping up and down and pointing at Greg.

Fortunately the few people in the members' bar chose to ignore him and showed only embarrassment or annoyance at having their quiet evening disturbed.

'Thanks, Wendy,' said Greg. 'Remind me to check if you have your phone with you next time I tell you anything in confidence.'

'I always have my phone with me. Anyway, social media is a good thing. You should try it. Oh no, sorry. The clue's in the title, isn't it? Social. That means communicating with people, doesn't it?'

'When I was young, Wendy, the 'social' was a hand-out you got when you were out-of-work, which, as an actor, I was – quite a lot. That's why I avoid things with social in the title.' He grinned and accepted the proffered pint from Alan.

The four of them chatted and drank for the rest of the evening. Greg was to catch a plane back to France at 10.30 the next morning and had a cab booked for 8.30am. This didn't deter him from staying until closing time however, nor from having a nightcap or two of whisky when he finally staggered back across the road to his house.

He sat in his chair and switched the television on. There wasn't anything he particularly wanted to watch and he flicked through the TV guide, settling on some music channel he'd never heard of, but was playing stuff from the 1980's that he recognised, so he let it play. He decided something to eat might lessen the expected hangover – he hadn't used to get hangovers but as he grew older they tended to rear their ugly heads and hang around more and more. He stood up and wandered through to the kitchen at the back of the house. His hand was on the light switch when he realised the outside security light had come on – it had a PIR sensor and lit up when anyone came near the house. He went to the window and peered out. He couldn't see anyone and the timer on the light switched it off, leaving the small yard in darkness. He switched the kitchen light on and searched the cupboards for something to eat, grabbed a packet of chocolate digestives and went back towards the lounge. Switching the kitchen light off, he became aware of the yard being brilliantly lit again. Putting his biscuits down on the kitchen table, he opened the back door and went out into the yard. There was no sign of anyone. He wasn't particularly worried. Maldon was hardly a hot-bed of crime. If he'd still been living in Hackney, he'd have locked all the doors and probably hidden under the duvet. But here...? He'd never had any trouble, often leaving the house unlocked. A quick scan of the yard convinced him there was no-one there; it was probably a cat or a fox that had set the light off. There was a small gate at the end of the yard that led to a path and the street behind the house which Greg never used and he spotted it was swinging open. He wandered down and closed it, leaning over and peering through the gloom down the path. He wouldn't have been able to see anyone if they had been there. Grabbing his biscuits as he returned to the kitchen, having made sure he had locked the back door, he went back to his chair in front of the TV.

The curtains in the living room were open, he rarely closed them, and he became conscious of being watched, a face at the window, looking at him. He waved, assuming it was Wendy or someone, stumbled to the door and flung it open.

'I've got to be up early!' he said to no-one. He looked up the street and, through the dim lighting, saw a person fleeing along the quay – a female person, not Wendy, judging by the dress or skirt flying out behind the retreating figure. He smiled. Must be a fan, who, having overheard the conversation in the pub, wanted to check out the TV star. He closed the door and went back inside. Before Jenny had returned he would probably have invited the girl in and given her a drink; but not now. He thought of Jenny out in France and had an urge to ring her, see how she was but, looking at the clock, he realised it would be past one o'clock in Bourrouillan and, even if they were still up, he might not make himself too popular. He poured himself another scotch and sat back in his chair.

*

The hammering on the door woke him. He was still in his chair and the television was still blaring. It was light outside. Greg checked his watch. 8.30! 'Shit!' he said to himself and went to the door.

'Won't be a minute,' he said to the waiting taxi-driver.

Greg's body informed him he had slept in the chair as it shot pains across his shoulders and down his back. His head told him he'd finished off the bottle of scotch. He switched off the TV and grabbing his jacket, checking his passport and e-ticket were still in the inside pocket, joined the driver in his cab.

'Heavy night?' observed the cabbie.

'Not really,' lied Greg, his head now throbbing. He hadn't even had time for a coffee and felt, and obviously looked, dreadful.

Grateful that the cab-driver deemed it unnecessary to ask any more questions, he endured the journey to Stansted, paid the fare and headed to the nearest coffee franchise in the terminal, managing to down a couple of double espressos before being called through to the departure lounge.

Denis was waiting for him at the small Biarritz airport as Greg came through the gate for EU residents. He didn't have any luggage so, not having to wait, followed Denis out to the car park, lighting a Marlboro as soon as he was out of the main building.

'You're not smoking in the car; you know that.'

'I'm not in the car yet, Denis.'

'I'm just saying, that's all. You look like shit, by the way.'

'Thanks.' Greg stood by the car finishing his cigarette.

'How was the interview?' Denis was sitting in the car with the door open.

'Waste of time,' replied Greg.

'But it sounded like it was a formality. Didn't you get the job?'

'Of course I got the job. I just don't know why I had to go all the way to London to be told.' He threw his cigarette end away and got into the car. 'How's Jenny?'

'Fine,' was all Denis replied.

'Why does no-one like her?' Greg was curious about the lack of enthusiasm shown by his friends towards Jenny.

'I do like her,' said Denis. 'Anton seems to like her a lot,' he added. 'I've hardly seen either of them since you left.'

'Oh beware, my lord, of jealousy; it is the green-eyed monster which doth mock the meat it feeds on.'

'I'm not jealous. Don't be ridiculous.' Denis' hands gripped the steering wheel tighter. Greg grinned and decided that closing his eyes and having a snooze was probably a good idea.

Jenny came running towards the car as Denis pulled up the gravel driveway by the side of his house. She grabbed Greg as soon as he opened the door and hugged and kissed him as though he'd been away for a month rather than a day.

'How did it go?' she asked.

'How do you think?' he replied, grinning. 'Apparently I'm going to be a TV star again.'

She gave him another kiss. 'You smell like you had a good time last night.'

'What on earth do you mean?' he grinned.

'How was Wendy?' said Jenny, folding her arms.

Greg faked looking hurt. 'What makes you think I saw Wendy?'

'Well, you were obviously in the pub so I assumed she'd be there.'

'She was actually, with Alan and Ian.'

'Oh dear, must have been a very late night, then. Did you actually get any sleep?'

'Of course I did.' Greg grimaced and stretched his back. 'In the chair, unfortunately.'

Anton put his head out of the front door. 'Do you two want lunch?'

'Do we want lunch?' Jenny looked at Greg.

'I think I have an appointment with my masseuse, don't I?'

'We'll wait, Anton, thanks,' yelled Jenny, pulling Greg towards the barn. 'We'll be a bit busy for a while.'

Anton raised his eyebrows and put his head back inside. Denis sighed and went into his house.

*

The remainder of the holiday was spent enjoying fine home-cooked food and drinking wine from grapes grown in the next field. Jenny and Anton had gone off for long walks, much to Denis' annoyance but, as Anton pointed out, he had asked him to join them. As far as Greg was concerned, walking through the fields may be a pleasant way of relaxing for some people but even with the pleasure of Jenny's company, it seemed to him a waste of energy and he was more than happy to sit by the pool in the company of Madame Alcohol. Besides, he'd had several phone calls to handle from Helen Clarke regarding the new series. She had procured him a very good deal financially as well as headline billing. There were some interviews arranged already for his return to the UK and Denis decided it was still his job to make sure Greg understood everything. It appeared that Denis was missing his old job.

'Getting fed-up with retirement, Denis?' asked Greg as Denis continued to fuss around him.

'No, why?'

Greg looked up from the beer he was drinking. 'You really were a very good agent, you know.'

'All in the past, Greg, all in the past. Another beer?'

Greg had nodded and Denis had strutted off like a peacock to the fridge.

On the night before they were to fly back to Stansted, Greg had booked a table at a restaurant in a small town called Estang, a few kilometres from Bourrouillan. It was a small family-run restaurant-cum-hotel-cum-bar next to a bull-fighting stadium. Denis had been there once before, some years ago, when Greg had last been over. He'd been repulsed by the knowledge that people still held bullfights in 'this day and age' and had refused to return to Estang on that premise. Greg had booked the table without Denis knowing. He'd remembered that the meal they'd had before was particularly good and this was to be Greg's treat as a thank you for Denis and Anton's hospitality, as well as to celebrate his new TV series.

Greg tried to cover Denis' eyes as they strolled past the bull-ring and received a friendly slap in the face for his trouble.

They were seated at a table in a back room where two or three other groups were also eating. A couple of men waved at them as they entered.

'Someone you know?' Greg asked.

'Not me,' replied Denis. 'You know I never come here.'

'Friends of mine,' said Anton.

Denis had a closer look at the men. 'I don't know them,' he said, frowning.

'You don't know all my friends, Den,' he replied giving Denis a kiss on the cheek.

Greg noticed Jenny smile and wave at the group. 'Do you know them?' he asked.

Jenny's face turned a shade of pink as she replied. 'I think we met them on one of our walks, didn't we, Anton?'

Anton nodded.

An aperitif arrived at the table, a mixture of Armagnac and sparkling wine, and they toasted Greg's new job, reciprocated with a toast to Denis, Anton and La Belle France. Greg was aware of Anton not raising his glass to the last toast.

'Have I said the wrong thing?' he asked. 'Is it not called La Belle France?'

'It's not the Belle France I grew up in,' said Anton, looking over his shoulder.

'Oh come on, you left when you were five,' retorted Denis.

'I know but it's just not the same anymore.'

'The world keeps turning, Anton,' said Greg.

'Yes it does and the people keep turning with it, mostly from the Middle East, it seems.'

'What do you mean?' Greg was confused.

'Well, you look around and you don't see many French people these days.' Anton was talking much louder than was necessary, as if he wanted the rest of the room to hear what he was saying.

Greg looked around. 'Are these people not French, then?'

'Oh these are,' replied Anton. 'The other sort wouldn't come in here. They don't spend the money we give them.'

Greg was feeling extremely uncomfortable. 'Are you talking about refugees?'

Anton laughed. 'Refugees? They're not refugees. They're just coming here and doing our jobs for little money. But in their currency it's a lot more than they could earn at home and that's where they send their money - back home. They don't spend it here,'

'That's a bit racist, isn't it?'

'You don't understand, Greg,' said Denis. 'There's a lot of people can't get jobs because of the immigrants.'

Greg was astounded. 'Aren't you an immigrant, Denis?'

'Not that sort of immigrant.'

'What sort then?'

Jenny took hold of Greg's arm. 'Let's leave that subject,' she said.

Greg stood up. 'I'm going for a smoke,' he said.

'You haven't ordered,' said Jenny.

'Order for me,' he said. 'I don't seem to have much of an appetite anymore.' He went outside.

He stood looking at the bull-ring as he lit his Marlboro and thought about the brutality to the animals that occurred there, that Denis so abhorred and he contemplated the difference between the way the Matadors – or whatever they were called – treated the bulls and the way they'd just been discussing immigrants. He supposed Anton would quite happily throw them into the ring and let the lions loose on them as the Romans did with the Christians they had felt threatened by. He couldn't understand. Anton was intelligent. Was he really that easily brainwashed by the sort of tabloid press they had in Britain? He assumed the same sort of crap came out of the media in France too. What surprised him most was Denis. His leanings had always been towards humanity and helping the helpless. He now seemed to have signed up for bashing the foreigners, even though he was exactly one of those self-same incomers. He stubbed his cigarette out in an ashtray on a table and immediately lit another. He didn't want to go back inside just yet; he knew he had to calm down first.

He felt a hand on his shoulder. 'You OK?' asked Jenny.

'Did you know Anton was so racist?'

'He's not really.'

Greg turned to face her. 'It sounded like it to me.'

Jenny held his face and kissed him. 'This is a celebration of your new job. Let's not spoil it because of a few stupid comments.' She paused, looking Greg in the eyes. 'Please,' she added.

Greg looked at Jenny's pleading face and smiled. He kissed her cheek. 'I don't want that topic to be raised again,' he said.

'I'll make sure it isn't,' she said and took Greg back inside.

The topic was not raised again. They ate their meal, drank some wine, talked about Greg's new job, thanked

Denis and Anton for their hospitality again and generally had a good time. Greg, however, could no longer view Anton in the same light as he had previously.

Denis gave Greg and Jenny a cooked breakfast early the next morning. There was not a lot of conversation and a tense atmosphere was palpable. Greg wanted to ask about Denis' change of attitude regarding immigration but Jenny had pleaded with him again not to broach the subject. Anton was conspicuous by his absence.

'He sleeps late usually,' explained Denis. Greg wasn't convinced. 'Don't be strangers,' said Denis as they went out to the car. He gave Jenny a peck on the cheek and Greg a quick hug.

'You know where I live, Denis,' said Greg sniffily and started the car.

They drove off in the direction of Biarritz. Jenny just commented on the scenery and what a beautiful part of France this was. Greg tried to feel same joy but it was hard. This part of France was somehow tainted for him now. He didn't even know if he'd be back.

As soon as they'd dropped the car off, Greg went straight to the bar in the terminal.

'Bit early, isn't it?' said Jenny.

'It's nearly lunchtime.'

'It's eleven o'clock. They won't let you on the plane if you're pissed.' Jenny sat at a table. 'I'll have a coffee, please.'

Greg ordered two coffees and a large cognac.

'How long have you known Denis, Greg?' said Jenny as he brought the drinks to the table.

'I don't know. Twenty-five, thirty years or so, why?'

'Is it worth throwing all those years away because he has a different opinion to you about something?'

Greg sipped his coffee. 'You don't understand, Jenny. His attitude has completely reversed. I think he's just trying to agree with his boyfriend.'

'Husband,' corrected Jenny. 'Is that such a bad thing?'

'Do you agree with him, then?'

'About immigration? From the point of view that they are human beings, who need some sort of help, I can't condone what Anton was saying but it doesn't really affect me at the moment.'

'Does that matter?'

'From an humanitarian point of view, I hope I'd have some compassion and try to work out some sort of solution. I think immigration should have some sort of control probably but I don't know enough to understand how that could be put into practice.'

Greg finished his coffee and threw back the cognac. 'Do you want another coffee?' he said getting up.

'I don't think there's time,' she replied.

Greg went to the bar and ordered another cognac. He really wanted a beer but Jenny was right, they were calling their flight over the Tannoy.

'Look,' said Jenny, as Greg returned to the table, having downed his brandy at the bar. 'I don't understand politics like you do but you're right, they are human beings just trying to make their way in the world like everyone else. You're a good man Greg Driscoll and I love you for it. Perhaps we should try to do something to help rather than look on the black side. There, now I'm agreeing with my boyfriend.' She laughed and kissed Greg.

Greg felt a warmth run through him. She'd never actually called him her boyfriend before. It sounded strange but somewhat wonderful. He kissed her again.

'Come on, you. We'll miss the plane,' she said, dragging her case towards the small room marked Departures.

***

CHAPTER FOUR

Jenny seemed to take up the cause of helping refugees quite seriously. She said that, although most immigrants needed help, the refugees were those who needed it the most. Greg wanted to know how she was going to define the difference.

'That's the challenge,' she said. 'I suppose the most important thing is to work out why they feel the need to migrate and what they are leaving behind.' She was studying pages of information on the internet on Greg's laptop. Greg was looking at the scripts of his new TV series.

They'd been back from France for a few weeks and Greg's time had been taken up with interviews for both the TV and the radio as well as a two-page spread in a national newspaper. Rehearsals were due to start the next day with a read-through of the first episode. Greg was quite excited and not a little nervous. He'd discovered that an actress called Trudie Carling was also cast in the show. Trudie Carling had recently been voted as 'the most glamourous woman in Britain' by some trendy magazine and, although Greg had never seen her act, he was intoxicated with the pictures he'd seen. She certainly was very beautiful.

'You're a bit worried about playing opposite Trudie Carling, aren't you?' Jenny had been watching Greg as he read his script. A frown had appeared in his face as he was reading.

'No,' he said, looking up.

Jenny moved over to his chair and grabbed the script from his hand. 'Oh my God! You've got to kiss her.'

'I'm an actor, Jenny. I've had to kiss lots of beautiful women.'

She knelt by his feet and pouted her lips. 'Should I be jealous?' she purred.

Greg leaned over and kissed her. 'Probably,' he said, 'but she is half my age and I'm not sure I still possess the charm I used to.'

'Don't you believe it!' Jenny pulled him onto the floor and Greg didn't look at his script again for another hour.

*

The read-through went very well. There were a couple of people who had been in 'Gone for a Song' with Greg and after the reading they all adjourned to a nearby hostelry. Greg seemed to be particularly popular with some of the younger cast members who had evidently marked him out as the most important actor in the series, having done most of the pre-publicity. Trudie Carling also showed him a lot of attention and Greg sat back and bathed in the admiration.

His taxi dropped him off outside his house. Even the taxi-driver had recognised him from the papers and asked for his autograph. Greg went straight into The King's Head. He'd sent Jenny a message to say he was on his way.

Jenny had walked into the pub to be greeted by Wendy and Alan. She'd sat with Wendy as Alan went to buy her a drink.

'You smell nice.' Wendy had noticed an aroma floating round Jenny.

'Greg bought me some perfume in France.' She'd held out her wrist for Wendy to smell.

'Hmm! Orange Blossom. Nice.'

Greg swaggered into the bar, stood by the door and posed.

'Anyone you know?' said Wendy to the others, pointing at Greg.

'Not me,' said Jenny. 'Looks to me like someone whose ego has been boosted beyond its limits. Not attractive at all.'

They all turned their backs on the famous TV star.

Greg bought himself a pint and went over to join them. They were sitting at a small table by the window next to the chimney breast.

'I could have stayed in the West End where I was appreciated, you know,' he said.

'Did somebody speak?' said Wendy.

'I don't think so, Wendy,' replied Jenny.

'I've just been having a drink with the lovely Trudie Carling.' Greg sipped his pint.

Alan couldn't resist. 'What's she like?' he blurted out. 'Is she as gorgeous off-screen?'

'Oh, far more gorgeous, Alan.' Greg took out his phone and showed him a picture he'd taken in the pub.

'Cor!' said Alan.

Wendy gave him a playful punch. 'What's she got that I haven't?'

Greg and Alan looked at each other and smiled.

'Read-through went well, then?' Jenny gave Greg a peck on the cheek.

'Yeah. I actually think this could be a good series. They've finally decided on a title. It's going to be called 'Once in a While'.'

'What a shit title,' muttered Wendy.

'It's not great, is it.' agreed Greg.

'Sort of catchy, though,' Jenny observed. 'Easy to remember.'

Wendy punched Alan on the arm again. This time it was little less playful. 'Give Greg his phone back, you dirty bastard.'

'Looks like you were getting on well,' he said, handing Greg his phone back and rubbing his arm.

'I suspect she's got a crush on me.' Everyone laughed a bit too loudly and it was Jenny's turn to punch Greg on the arm.

'You've got a very high opinion of yourself,' she said. Greg smiled smugly.

'Do you fancy her?' asked Wendy.

'She has been voted the Nation's most glamourous woman and yet I hardly noticed her,' replied Greg. 'I only have eyes for one woman.' He pouted his lips and moved his head closer to Wendy.

'Fuck off!' she said.

'I think you'd better go and get the drinks in, Greg.' Jenny pulled him from his seat and led him to the bar where he bought a round. Jenny took Wendy's and left Greg to bring the rest back to the table.

'You'll never guess who I saw today,' said Alan taking his pint. 'Kate Freeman.'

'Who?' said Jenny.

'I thought she was locked up.' Wendy took a slug of wine.

'She was in a hospital, Wendy,' explained Greg. 'Kate was in the community play I directed, Jenny. She had a few problems.'

'A few problems?' yelled Wendy. 'She killed her father and then accused Greg of raping her!'

'Shush!' Alan looked round to check the bar was still empty. Jenny was looking at Greg, frowning.

'She had serious problems, Jenny. Her father had been sexually abusing her for years and she just snapped one day. It was after the last night party of the community play and...well...it was all very difficult but not her fault.'

Wendy snorted. 'I didn't think they'd ever let her out. Where did you see her, Alan?'

'On the sea wall,' he replied. 'I think it was her anyway, she'd changed a bit, all her hair cut off, put on a bit of weight.'

'Well, I hope I don't bump into her. I'd give her a piece of my mind.'

'I think her mind has enough problems, Wendy, without having a piece of yours as well.' Greg smiled. 'She's been in care for ten years, so presumably they think she's safe to be back in the community.'

Wendy snorted again.

'Has everyone eaten?' said Jenny, changing the subject.

'We've got something in the slow-cooker,' Wendy informed.

'Shall we get a take-away, Greg? I'm starving.'

'Sounds good to me, Jenny.'

'I'll give the Indian a ring.' She went outside to try and get a signal on her phone.

They left The King's Head shortly afterwards and Greg and Jenny took delivery of their curry and sat in the kitchen to eat.

'Does this Kate Freeman thing worry you?' said Jenny between mouthfuls of Chicken Dhansak. She tore a naan bread in half and handed some to Greg.

'No, why should it?' he said scooping some curry onto the bread.

'How far did the rape accusation go?'

'What do you mean?'

'Were you arrested? Did it go to court?'

'I was sort of arrested and it didn't get as far as court. Pass the pilau.'

Jenny handed him the container of rice. 'Where was she locked up?'

'She wasn't locked up, Jenny. She was in a hospital and I don't know where it was. Some sort of secure unit, I suppose. She was in Chelmsford for a while, I had to go and visit her.'

'Why?' Jenny had stopped eating.

'The policewoman who was dealing with her thought I might be able to help to get to the truth. She had a crush on me.'

'What? The policewoman?'

Greg spluttered on his food as he thought of DS Mhairi Collins having a crush on him. 'No, definitely not. Kate had a crush on me. She said she killed her dad because he wouldn't let her see me.'

'Heavy.'

'Yes, it was at the time but it was a long time ago. Get on with your curry.'

After the meal they had a relatively early night as Greg was to start rehearsals proper for 'Once in a While' the next morning.

*

Greg was three weeks into rehearsals when Jenny suggested a trip back to France.

'I can't go to France, Jenny, I'm rehearsing.'

'I know,' sighed Jenny. 'It's just that I feel a bit on my own here. I thought it would be nice to go and see Denis for a short break.'

'And Anton?'

'Well obviously. You're not jealous, are you? He's gay.'

Greg smiled. 'Of course I'm not. I'd love to go out there again but I really can't.'

'I know. I'm just dreaming I suppose.' She put on a sad face. Greg noticed her nose didn't crinkle the way it used to. Getting older seemed to take away all the good things. He'd been aware of her getting a bit bored recently. He'd been full of the TV series and was forgetting that Jenny had been an actress herself and was probably missing the joie de vivre of a theatrical company. Here she was in a quiet town in Essex where he knew everyone but she was still a relative stranger. It hadn't occurred to him that she might be lonely and a bit insecure.

'You could go on your own, if you want,' he suggested. 'I'm sure Denis would pick you up from Biarritz.'

'Oh I couldn't go on my own,' she said. 'Could I?'

'Well, Denis and Anton know you. If you want a break, I'm sure they'd make you welcome.'

Jenny gave Greg a hug and kissed him. 'Won't you miss me?' she purred.

'What when I'm spending all day with the glamourous Trudie Carling? Of course I'll miss you.'

'I hope I can trust you, Greg Driscoll.'

'I'm sure Trudie Carling has a boyfriend built like a brick shit-house. Even if I had any inclinations towards her,

I'd probably end up a pile of broken bones before I could get as far as 'would you like to go for a meal!'' He smiled at Jenny. 'So I think you're safe, my darling.' He gave her a kiss as if that were proof.

'I'd trust you anyway,' she said.

Greg spent any spare moment he had the next day phoning Denis - who had tried to sound enthusiastic about Jenny's impending visit - and booking plane tickets. He'd called in at a travel agent's during his lunch break, bought a load of Euros and that evening presented Jenny with her plane ticket and a wallet full of cash.

'I've arranged for a cab to pick you up in the morning and take you to Stansted. Denis will be at Biarritz airport to meet you and you're staying for ten days. OK?'

Jenny looked at him quizzically. 'Are you trying to get rid of me?'

'I am sacrificing the pleasure of you being with me to allow you a few days of relaxation and good company. Besides we start recording on Monday, so I'll be around even less than I am at the moment. It's not fair on you, darling.'

Although Greg was supposed to be studying his script that evening, he didn't and the two of them were in bed by nine o'clock.

***

CHAPTER FIVE

'You miss her, don't you?'

'Who?'

'Your girlfriend.'

'She's only been away for four days and she's back in less than a week. I'm sure I'll cope.'

Greg Driscoll and Trudie Carling had been recording a scene for 'Once in a While'. They were the only two people in the scene. The storyline had brought their two characters together. She was playing the daughter of one of Greg's character's old friends from University and their budding relationship had caused tension and friction amongst the previously happy group. Greg had queried the believability of Trudie's character falling for his but had been convinced that it served the dramatic direction the writer wanted. The upshot was that they had just shot a scene on a closed set (meaning only people essential to the recording were allowed) where their characters had made love for the first time.

Greg had never done a scene that involved him removing his clothes before and was more than a little nervous about it. Especially in front of someone as attractive as Trudie Carling! When it came to shooting the scene, however he found that Trudie – even though she had shot many similar scenes – was just as anxious as he had been.

'It's always a bit worrying,' she'd said. 'You're exposing yourself to the few people in the studio but always terribly aware that several million people will see it on the telly.'

'Well, you don't have to worry, surely. Especially if you're in a scene with an ugly git like me.'

She'd stroked his arm. 'You're not ugly, Greg. In fact I think you're rather attractive. I won't have to do much acting in this scene.' She'd pecked his cheek.

They had been standing just off the set wearing dressing gowns over their nakedness, waiting for the crew to get the lighting right and for the cameras to set up the shots. They'd already recorded the undressing part of the scene which, Greg had to admit, was a lot more comfortable than he'd expected. Trudie, however nervous she'd said she was, had shown her experience and guided Greg through the initial embarrassment he'd been feeling. He'd soon forgotten that anyone was watching as he kissed and fondled the beautiful actress who was removing his clothing. He'd almost been disappointed when Phil yelled 'Cut' and the dressers rushed forward brandishing the dressing gowns.

'Do you have a boyfriend?' Greg asked the now fully dressed Trudie as they sat in a bar near to the studio.

'Why do you ask?' she replied.

'I never see you with anyone round the studio or anything.'

'There's a couple of people I see but, to be honest, I wouldn't call either of them a boyfriend. They're just friends who happen to be boys.'

'Do you...?'

'Sleep with them? Yes, I do, Greg. This is the twenty-first century, you know. Women are allowed to do that sort of thing now.' She sipped her gin. 'Don't tell me you're shocked!'

'No. Not really.' Greg was embarrassed more than shocked. If he'd been younger, he'd probably have been jealous.

'That's what I love about you, Greg Driscoll. 'You're so old-fashioned. I suppose you don't think women should be allowed to buy you a drink, either.'

'Ah, when it comes to buying drinks, I'm all for equality.'

Trudie came round the side of the table and kissed him on the lips. 'Another pint?'

'Please.' Trudie went to the bar. Greg watched her as she crossed the floor. It was a quiet pub in a backstreet, frequented mostly by people from the studio, which meant they were rarely accosted by members of the public; most of the locals knowing them as ordinary people. A man sidled up to Trudie at the bar. Greg saw him indicate in his direction and she nodded. The man took another look at Greg, shook his head and went back to his drink.

'What was that about?' asked Greg as she handed him his pint.

'What?'

'The bloke at the bar.'

Trudie looked over at the man and waved her fingers. 'He wanted to know if you were my boyfriend.'

'And you nodded?'

'It makes life easier Greg, believe me. I hope you're not insulted.' She pouted in a sad way. She still looked beautiful. Greg smirked.

'Just surprised,' he said.

She moved over to him again, took his head in her hands and kissed him again. 'He's looking over. Pretend you're with me, please. I really don't want to be bothered by him right now.'

'Do you know him?'

'I've seen him before but he's never spoken to me until tonight.'

Greg put his arm round her and kissed her. A light flashed and the man left hurriedly.

'Shit!' said Trudie. 'He had a camera.' She went and sat at the other side of the table again.

'I suspect lots of people take photos of you, Trudie.' Greg smiled and held out his hand.

'I was being stupid,' she said, her eyes welling up with tears.

'What's the matter?'

'I have to be so careful all the time, Greg. I sometimes feel I can't do anything without someone wanting to know what I'm up to.'

'He's just a fan, Trudie, taking a photo on his phone.'

'Yes, you're probably right,' she said, blowing her nose. She looked up and smiled. 'You're so good, Greg. I wish I had your experience. Tell me about Ginny?'

'What do you want to know?' He was a bit surprised by the sudden change of subject.

'Everything. How you met; how long you've known her; what she's like; when I'm going to meet her, Everything.'

Greg thought for a moment. How much did he want to tell this girl? She reminded him of when he'd first met Jenny. A pretty young actress still in love with the glamour and the lifestyle of being in the theatrical profession: so similar and yet so different. In the short time Trudie had been in the business, Trudie had achieved success and fame, something that had eluded Jenny. Even so, it seemed to him that, like Jenny, this famous actress still had...what was it? Respect for him? He hoped not, that just made him feel even older than he was and he had to accept that Trudie had done more work in the last few years than he had done in his whole career! 'Well,' he said eventually. 'I first met Ginny when she was about your age. She was an actress like you and we were in a play together.'

'And you've been together ever since? How romantic.'

Greg smiled. 'No. We didn't see each other for the best part of twenty years.'

'Blimey!'

Greg laughed, she sounded so quaint.

'And then you got back together?'

'Yep.'

'How?'

'You're very inquisitive. It was quite by chance, really. We sort of bumped into each other and, I suppose, realised what we'd been missing.'

Trudie sat back in her seat, tears starting to well again. 'I think that's the most romantic thing I've ever heard,'

Greg tried not to look condescending. 'I know, they should make it into a movie, shouldn't they. You'd be a shoe-in for Jenny.'

'I thought her name was Ginny.'

'That's what I said.'

'Do I remind you of her?'

'In a way, yes.' Greg gave her a hug. She lifted her head and looked into his eyes and their lips met for the third time that evening.

The bell rang for last orders at the bar.

'Want another?' asked Greg.

'Do you mean a drink?'

'Yes, I do, Trudie,' admonished Greg, grinning.

'No.'

'You're right. I've probably had enough for the time being and I was supposed to ring Ginny but they're an hour ahead of us in France so it will have to wait till morning, I guess.' He was enjoying his evening. It was the first time he'd spent any time alone with Trudie and he felt very relaxed in her company. She smiled at him.

'You could come home with me, if you like.' She held his stare. Greg looked away.

'Twenty years ago, Trudie, I can't think of anything I'd rather have done'

'Yeah, but I was only five then; it wouldn't have been so much fun.' She giggled.

Greg shuddered. 'I'll see you in the studio tomorrow.'

Trudie Carling stuck her bottom lip out. 'I'm not in tomorrow,' she said. 'You're doing the scenes with my screen dad where he gives you a bollocking for deflowering his precious daughter.'

'Good job I'm going home, then.' He gave her a peck on the cheek and went to find a cab.

*

Greg had checked his phone in the taxi on the way home. He was a bit disappointed to see Jenny hadn't called him and there was nothing on his answerphone when he got home. He looked at the clock, it was just past midnight. He suspected that Jenny and the boys would still be sitting out on the terrace in Bourrouillan, drinking the local wine, even though it was after one out there. He felt envious. It would be very pleasant to be sitting there looking at the moon smiling over the lake at the bottom of the garden. He poured himself a nightcap of Scotch and sent a text off to France.

Half an hour later there had been no reply so he assumed they had all gone to bed after all. He'd spent that half hour thinking about Trudie Carling. It amused him that she'd asked him to go home with her. If it hadn't been for Jenny he probably would have done but he knew he would have regretted it the next morning. She was very lovely but so much younger than him. It would have seemed wrong. It would have been wrong. What was going on? Perhaps he was discovering morals in his old age. He downed the remains of his whisky and went to bed.

***

CHAPTER SIX

'You dirty bastard!'

Greg had just come through the door to the studio canteen to be greeted with jeers and lewd gestures. Bolly, one of the crew was already partaking of his subsidised breakfast and sitting with Michael Abbot, one of the cast.

'Sorry. I had a shower this morning,' retorted Greg, sniffing his armpits on his way to get a coffee.

'On your own?' Bolly leered at Greg. Greg thought he was a chippy or a sparky or something, he didn't really know and hadn't had much contact with him before. 'You lucky devil,' he added, making another lewd gesture with his arm.

'This is why we actors rarely mix with you lot,' said Michael. 'We have a bit more decorum than you.' He looked at Greg. 'What's she like, Greg. In real life. Is she as good as I imagine when I'm alone in my room?'

Greg brought his steaming mug over to the table. 'Anyone going to let me in on the joke?'

Bolly thrust a copy of the Daily Mirror in front of Greg's face. 'Dirty bastard,' he reiterated.

'Oh for fuck's sake!' Greg could feel the anger boiling up inside him instantly. He grabbed the paper and looked at the picture on the page. It was of him and Trudie in the pub the night before. Greg had his arm round her and they were kissing. Above the picture was the headline *"CHARMING CARLING WITH HER NEW (OLD) MAN"*

'What!' yelled Greg. He could feel the others looking at him.

'You wouldn't be able to keep it secret for long, mate,' said Michael. 'Not with her publicity machine behind her.'

'There's nothing to keep secret,' protested Greg. 'We just went for a drink after the shoot.'

'After you'd been screwing.' Bolly was leering again, showing his bad teeth. Greg wanted to punch him.

'Read the article,' said Michael, pointing to the column beneath the picture. 'If you can call it an article.'

Greg looked at the paper again. Under the photograph he read: *"Tasty Trudie Carling was seen out with a new (old) man last night. The two of them had just finished filming a steamy bedroom romp which, by the looks of it, didn't require much acting at all. In fact we have it on good authority (from someone who was there!) that they actually made love in front of the cameras. "They actually SCREWED" said our source. What we here in the editing room can't understand is why? Why would such a luscious lass as Trudie Carling waste her time with an old man like Greg Driscoll? (Answers on a postcard) Our correspondent saw them leave a pub together shortly after taking this snapshot. They got into a taxi and drove off into the night, presumably to rehearse more randy rompings which we will soon hopefully see on our screens in their new series 'Once in a While'. Seems to us once in a while is not enough for this couple of copulators. Got to admire the old man's stamina!"*

'Fucking hell!' Greg slammed the paper down on the table.

'You're going to say it's not true, aren't you?' said Bolly looking disappointed. 'I wanted all the gory details.'

Greg stood up and put his head close to Bolly's. His face was flushed and contorted. Michael grabbed his shoulders and made him sit down again.

'Cool it, Greg.'

Greg grabbed the newspaper and took his anger out on that, tearing it to shreds.

'Oi! That's my paper,' said Bolly.

Michael threw a fifty pence piece at him. 'I'll pay you for it.'

Bolly took the money and left the table muttering something about actors' sex lives.

'I assume it's not true, then,' said Michael.

'Of course it's not bloody true! I have a partner who I'm more than happy with. Why would I jeopardise that for some child?'

'A very attractive child, though.' Greg glared and Michael put his hands up in apology. 'Have you told her yet?'

'Who?'

'Your partner.'

'No, she's in France, fortunately. At least she won't have seen this shit.'

Michael took out his phone, brought up his social media app and showed it to Greg. In column headed 'Trending' he read 'Trudie Carling's new (old) man'.

'No-one needs to read a newspaper for their news these days. Spreads like wildfire over the internet.'

'Shit! I'd better ring her.'

'I would and quick,' said Michael. He stood and left Greg surrounded by the debris of his lewd night of passion that had never occurred. Greg took out his phone and switched it on – he never left his phone on whilst at work as he wouldn't be able to answer it anyway. The screen burst into life. '3 missed calls' it read. He didn't need to check who they were from. Jenny had evidently seen the news already. He touched the screen and connected to her.

'So that's why you were so keen for me to go away.' she said as soon as she answered.

'Jenny, it's not true,' he protested.

'What? You and the most glamourous woman in Britain? I knew I shouldn't have left you on your own.'

'Jenny, please, you have to believe me. I've only just found out about this myself.'

There was a long pause at the other end.

'Jenny?'

Spluttering laughter broke the silence. 'Of course I believe you, Greg.'

'I don't know how it happened, Jenny. We went for a drink after work, that's all. Oh shit!' Greg suddenly remembered the man at the bar the night before and the photo he took with his phone. 'I think I've been set-up.'

'By whom?'

'Trudie Carling. There was a man in the pub. Trudie told me she thought he was trying to chat her up and wanted me to pretend to be her boyfriend or something to put him off. He took that photo.'

'And you were quite happy to oblige, I notice.'

'I thought I was doing her a favour. Believe me, Jenny, there's nothing going on between me and Trudie Carling.'

'I know there isn't, Greg. Trudie could have her choice of any man, so why would she go for mine?'

Greg paused. 'You're sounding a bit like a cheesy country song, now.'

Jenny laughed. 'Look, I trust you Greg Driscoll. But you are in for a hard time. They won't leave this alone: I've been there. The German press constantly bothered me after my ordeal and the British papers are a lot worse. Be careful what you say and do, won't you.'

Greg hadn't had time to consider the consequences that were about to overtake his life. 'Well, I won't be going to that pub anymore, I can tell you. Or socialising with little Miss Carling.'

'What does she have to say about it?'

'I don't know, she's not in the studio today. She knew that as well – she knew exactly what she was doing – and I've been set-up just to give that girl publicity.'

'Sounds possible. I wouldn't go round saying that, though. Think before you engage your brain, Greg.' Jenny was silent for a moment. Greg didn't know what to say. 'Anyway,' she said at length. 'I'm having a lovely time out here, thanks for asking.'

'I'm sorry Jenny, I've had other things on my mind.'

Jenny laughed, 'I know, I'm only teasing.' Greg heard someone shout Ginny's name. 'I have to go. Anton is driving me up to Northern France somewhere. He's tracing his ancestry or something.'

'Have a nice time.' Greg desperately wanted to join them on their jaunt. 'Oh and Jenny?'

'What?'

'Thanks. I love you.'

'I know,' she replied. 'Got to go. Bye'

Greg's phone went dead. He switched it off and put it back in his pocket.

'Ah, Greg. Good.' Phil Woodford came over to where he was sitting.

'Sorry, Phil. Am I late?'

'No, no...um...need to have a chat.' Phil looked Greg in the face. 'My office?'

Greg sighed. 'Aren't we shooting in half an hour? I haven't been to make-up yet.'

'I've re-arranged the schedule for today. I thought it best.'

*

'So are you going to sack me?' Greg sat down in Phil's office. He was angry and spoiling for a fight now.

'Oh God, no.' Phil looked worried. 'That would be far too expensive.'

'What?'

Phil smiled. 'We'd have to start shooting all over again – re-writes and the lot. The series starts airing in less than three months, you know.'

'So why am I sitting here and why have you changed the schedule?' Greg folded his arms and tried to relax. He failed. He was more tense than he'd been for years and was trying not to explode. He knew there was going to be trouble and he knew it was none of his making – although deep inside he knew he'd been stupid agreeing to kiss someone with the profile of Trudie Carling in public.

'Well,' said Phil, looking at the newspaper in front of him. 'Firstly I need to know if there's any truth in these rumours about you and Trudie. I know it's none of my business...'

'No, it's not any of your business.'

'Well,' Phil looked up. 'It sort of is, in a way.' There was a silence, neither person wanting to make the next move.

Eventually Greg slammed his hand down on the table. 'Of course it's not bloody true, Phil!' he yelled. 'She's half my age for fuck's sake!'

Phil Woodford held his palms up in the air. 'Ok, Greg, I'm not accusing you of anything. It's just that it's a situation we have to handle carefully.'

'Too right you do!' Greg was still shouting. 'I want to know how it happened. Who was the bastard who lied to the press? Their man on the inside?'

'No-one talked to the press, Greg. There was not a soul on that closed set that I don't trust implicitly.'

'The paper said...' started Greg.

'Papers make it up, Greg. Surely you know that?'

Greg sat back in his seat. 'We didn't...you know...on the set.'

Phil laughed. 'I know, Greg. I was there, remember. I've shot loads of those sorts of scenes and I've never known anyone who's 'done it' on a shoot even if some might pretend they did.'

'So how...?'

'They make it up. It sells their paper.' Phil looked down at the article again, 'The thing is, we have to find the best way to use this, now.'

'Meaning what?'

'Well...we...um...haven't started the big push on publicity yet and this could, sort of, change things.'

'In what way?' Greg was starting to feel uneasy.

'Well, all publicity is good publicity. The series name is out there without us even trying yet.' Phil held up his hands again. 'Look, don't shoot me, I'm only the director. The producers want a meeting with you and Trudie this afternoon. I've called her in for two o'clock and I need you both to be there. She's as angry as you, by the way.'

Greg laughed sarcastically. 'I bet she is. She knew the bloke who took that snapshot, Phil. I was set up. My only hope is that you weren't in on it.'

Phil looked worried, 'I hope you don't think...'

'I don't know what to think, Phil. A load of free publicity for your series.'

'Our series, Greg. We're a family here.'

Greg ignored the remark and carried on. 'A load more publicity for the star of your show. Fantastic. My life and relationship ruined. Fucking shite! Yes, I think that's what I'm thinking at the moment.'

'We can talk to your partner, if that would help.'

'No, that wouldn't help.'

'So, two o'clock, then.' Phil stood and offered Greg his hand, He left without shaking it.

*

Trudie Carling looked a mess as she entered the production office of 'Once in a While'. Her face was puffy and her eyes bloodshot, her hair unwashed and uncombed. She was accompanied by a man in a linen suit that looked like it needed the cleaners.

'Hello, Gene.' Phil shook the man's hand. 'Do you know Greg?' The man shook his head without looking at

Greg. 'Greg Driscoll, Gene Waters of Waters' International Management.

Phil Woodford was standing behind his desk. The producers, Janet Milner and George Norris were seated next to him. Greg was on the opposite side of the desk. Gene Waters nodded in his direction without making eye contact. He held out a chair for Trudie to sit on and placed his between her and Greg before turning to Janet and George.

'So how do we handle this, then?' he said, seating himself. 'As you can see my client is very upset and unless it is handled with extreme percipience, we may have to discuss whether it is worth my client being in your series and whether we allow anything to be broadcast.'

Janet Milner looked at Trudie. 'I'm really sorry about this, Trudie. I have to say none of this came from the production office. We are investigating who may have sold the story.'

Greg was astounded. He knew exactly who was responsible for the newspaper article. She was currently sitting at the table looking sorry for herself.

'We can only agree to using this as publicity if it relates directly to the series and if Mr Driscoll is heavily supervised as to what he is and what he is not allowed to say.'

'What?' yelled Greg, rising to his feet.

'You can't just say what you want in this situation, Greg,' said Janet. 'It could damage the whole series.'

'What about Trudie?' He indicated the co-star of the episode. 'Is she being supervised as well?'

Trudie Carling blubbed loudly and took out a handkerchief. Greg looked at her with contempt. She's good, he thought. She's very good.

'I don't think my client wants any more hassle, Mr Driscoll. She won't be talking to the press.'

'But she knew the bloke in the pub who took the picture.'

'I did not!' Trudie glared at Greg.

'You said you'd seen him before,' he protested.

'I didn't know him, though. You don't understand what it's like to be me, Greg.' She blew her nose and let her eyes turn on their taps again.

'I'm beginning to understand, believe me,' he muttered.

George Norris handed her a clean handkerchief from his pocket. 'Sit down, Greg. I can write a denial from the production team, if you'd like.'

'That's the worst thing you could do,' thundered Waters. 'It'll just create more and more newspaper inches.'

'Isn't that what you want, Mr Waters?' Greg was still standing. 'More publicity for your client irrespective of who gets caught in the cross-fire?'

Gene Waters looked at Greg and sneered. 'I assume you're not referring to yourself, Mr Driscoll. You already have a reputation for interfering with members of the opposite sex.'

'I beg your pardon?' Greg slammed his fist into the table and leaned over the agent.

Gene Waters was not to be intimidated. 'I understand you were sacked from a previous series for touching up your co-star.'

'Well you understand wrongly.' Greg's face was very close to Waters'.

'Greg, sit down,' Phil pleaded.

Greg looked at his director, then at Trudie, who by now was sobbing, cradling her head in the crook of her arm on the table-top. Waters was still glaring at him. Without another word, Greg grabbed his jacket from the back of his chair and stormed out of the room.

*

'Do you want me to come home?'

It gave Greg a warm sensation to hear Jenny call his house 'home'.

'No, darling. I'd stay out of it, if I were you. In fact, I might come and join you.'

'But you're in the middle of filming.'

'After today, I might not be,' sighed Greg. He was now regretting losing his temper instead of pleading his innocence.

'They're not likely to sack you, Greg. It would cost too much.'

'That's what Phil said. The thing is I don't know if I want to do it anymore. All anyone seems interested in is protecting poor Miss Carling. They mustn't upset the star of the show. Or her agent.'

'You're the star, as far as I'm concerned.'

'Yes but you're not the producer, are you. They wanted to write a denial.'

'Let them, then,'

'Mr High-and-Mighty Waters wouldn't let them. Besides they'd probably just destroy me.'

'They're not going to destroy you, Greg. It's all about publicity. It'll soon blow over when something more exciting happens.' Jenny paused. 'Perhaps I should come back anyway.'

Greg smiled. He did want to be with her right now. He wanted her to hold him, comfort him, love him. He felt very lonely and in need of love. 'No, stay there, Jenny. It would just be selfish of me to drag you away. How are things out there?'

'They're great, actually. I think even Denis has accepted me as a friend.'

'You are honoured.'

'And Anton is showing me all over the countryside.'

'Just the white Anglo-Saxon Protestant countryside, presumably.'

There was silence at the other end, followed by a heavy sigh. 'Greg, most people in France aren't Anglo-Saxon and very few are Protestants. This is predominately a Catholic country, although I must say there's a lot of tokenism. Not that many under the age of fifty seem to actually practice Catholicism.'

'You know what I meant.'

'Don't be too down on Anton, Greg. It's just the way in these rural places. I suspect Maldon's not all that different.'

Greg thought about the many conversations he'd overheard in the 'members bar' at The King's Head and had to agree. 'Just be careful, Jenny, that's all.'

'Actually, I'm trying to get him to see the difference between economic migrants and genuine refugees. He just lumps them all together.'

'Like most people, I suppose.'

'You could help, Greg, if you want.'

'I think I've enough trouble to deal with at the moment, Jenny, thanks.'

Greg heard Jenny sigh again. 'Yes,' she said. 'Sorry. Try not to worry. It will all blow over before you know it. You're not important enough for them to make much money out of, which is all they're interested in.'

'Oh thanks!' Greg pulled a hurt face then realised that Jenny couldn't see it. 'You are right as always, my darling.'

'I know, I've been there. Don't give them anything and they'll soon lose interest. Actually, I was going to ask you if it would be alright to stay a little longer than I'd planned. You're probably right I should keep out of the way 'til this blows over. I don't want them to start digging into my history.'

'Oh God, no. That hadn't occurred to me.' Greg felt deflated. He was looking forward to her returning in a few days and now he'd been the one to suggest she kept out of it. He could see her point though. Someone would be bound to look into her past if she was seen with him. 'I suppose I'm going to be busy, anyway, if I haven't been sacked. They seem to want to work us as hard as they can for their money. It's like being in a soap opera again. You stay there, as long as Denis and Anton don't mind, and I'll try and nip across if I get a couple of days off.'

'I love you,' purred Jenny.

Greg wanted to giggle like a child. 'Now, stop that or I'll make you come back right now and prove it,' he said.

'Do you love me?' she said.

'Let me think,' he said, rubbing his chin. 'I do, I do, I do.'

'More than Trudie Carling?'

'That's not even remotely funny.'

The two of them laughed nevertheless.

***

CHAPTER SEVEN

Greg cooked himself what he called a 'kiddie tea'. Sausage chips and beans. He'd had a call from Phil Woodford checking he was OK and, sort of, apologising for Gene Waters. Greg's studio time had been cancelled the following day as Trudie Carling was 'not up to it' so they would catch up on Friday. Greg suspected they were just keeping him away from the studio. The company's publicity machine would be working overtime to get the best publicity for the series out of the story of Trudie Carling and her 'old man' lover. Greg's anger had diminished since he'd spoken to Jenny. She knew more about the way the press worked than he did. His only previous spat with the newspapers was when he was written out of 'The Market', the cheap daytime soap that he'd done at the very start of his career. He'd been accused by the actress he was playing opposite of 'touching her up', which Gene Waters had been quick to point out. Unfortunately she was the producer's daughter. Greg had never really got on with producers ever since. But, sure enough, the papers had soon forgotten about the incident. Then there was the time when Jenny died and he got mixed up with drug gangs and the like but that blew over too. And anyway Jenny didn't die. If the papers found that out he dreaded to think what they'd make of it. That might not blow over quite so quickly.

The one thing that still worried him about Jenny's 'death' was that he still had no idea who the girl was who was buried in her name. Jenny didn't want him to find out; she didn't want to risk the consequences so he'd tried to forget it, but every now and then, his conscience pricked him. Who was she and where had she come from? He pushed the guilt to the back of his mind and went over to The King's Head.

'You couldn't wait, could you?' Wendy was sitting in the alcove.

'No, I was thirsty. Want a wine?' Greg went to the bar.

'I didn't mean that,' said Wendy, her face taut and pinched.

Greg brought his pint and Wendy's wine over to the table. 'What couldn't I wait for, then?' he asked already knowing the answer. 'To see my favourite post lady?'

'To leap into bed with her,' Wendy's face contorted into a snarl.

'I'm very fond of you, Wendy, but I know you're married.'

'Not me, you jerk. Trudie Carling.'

'It's all lies, Wendy. I haven't leapt into bed with anyone. If you are referring to this morning's tabloid rag piece of fiction, it's all bollocks!'

Wendy put a newspaper in front of him, open at the inside pages and Greg found himself looking at a picture of himself, naked in bed with Trudie Carling.

'That's a scene from the series I'm doing, Wendy.' He turned to the front page. 'Where did you get a copy of the London Evening Standard, anyway?'

'You can pick them up in the supermarkets in Chelmsford, which I did, and I don't mind telling you I'm extremely disappointed.'

'It's not a great paper, is it?'

'In you, Greg Driscoll. Disappointed in you.'

'It's called acting, Wendy. It's what I do.'

'That's not what it says.'

Greg turned back to the article. It read very much like the morning's story stating that someone on the inside had leaked pictures of *"Greg Driscoll and Trudie Carling actually making love on the set of Once in a While – the new series due to be on our screens in a matter of weeks. We can't wait!"*

'It's acting, Wendy,' Greg repeated.

'Tell that to Ginny or whatever her name is.' Wendy put her little nose in the air.

'I have and she believes me.'

'She's more stupid than I thought, then.' Wendy stood up.

'Where are you going?' Greg was a bit confused.

'I suddenly don't like the company,' she said and went to the door.

'Wendy? I bought you a wine'

She turned at the door. 'Give it to one of your floozies,' she sneered and left.

Greg didn't bother following her. He'd had enough for one day. All he wanted was a quiet drink. He was just glad that the bar was empty and no-one had witnessed his altercation with Wendy.

Greg downed his pint. Tallie was the barmaid on duty. She was chatting to someone in the other bar, so he rattled his empty glass on the bar to attract her attention.

'I don't serve people who do that,' she said, taking his glass and re-filling it. 'I'm not sure I should be serving you anyway.'

'And why would that be?'

'I'm not sure women are safe in your company.'

'I know, I'm a beast, really. I was trying to keep it secret but you just can't trust the press these days. My house is a veritable bordello.' He handed Tallie a five pound note. He detected a slight blush in her cheeks as she took the money. He smiled sadly and took his change. Tallie went back to her chat in the other bar.

As he returned to his seat, the door opened and a figure, covered up in some sort of Artic looking apparel, followed a large golf umbrella into the 'Members' Bar'.

'Is it raining?' called someone from the other bar rather pointlessly.

'It's chucking it down,' replied the stranger, shaking her umbrella in the doorway. She threw the hood of her coat back to reveal a shock of crimped blonde hair. She looked over at Greg and smiled and he reciprocated before returning to his pint. Wendy had left her Evening Standard and he turned to the crossword page.

'This is a lovely pub,' he heard the girl say to Tallie. 'I'm surprised it's not packed to the roof.'

'You should see it on a hot day during the school holidays,' Tallie replied.

'I can imagine.' She pointed through a window in the other bar. 'The view out there must be fantastic when it's not raining.'

She had what Greg called a pseudo-posh accent, like someone who was trying to sound as though she wasn't really common. He continued with his crossword.

'Mind if I join you?' The blonde sat down before he could answer. She was sipping at a tall glass containing a colourless liquid and a slice of lime with a curly straw sticking out of the top of the glass. 'Ah,' she sighed. 'Nothing like a nice vodka to chase away the blues.'

Greg looked up and smiled again.

'I seem to know you. Do you live round here?' said the stranger.

He looked at her. He didn't recognise her at all. 'Yes,' he replied warily. 'I live in Maldon.'

'It's a lovely pub.'

'Yes it is.' When it's quiet, thought Greg.

'Your local?'

Greg sighed. He really wanted to be left alone. 'Yes,' he said.

'Lucky you.' She sipped her vodka again. 'Do you need some help?' She indicated the crossword puzzle.

'Not really, it's the easy crossword, I'm just filling in time.'

'Waiting for someone?'

'Um...sort of,' lied Greg.

He went back to his puzzle. Who was this person and why did she seem determined to interact with him. He raised his eyes and looked towards her. She was sipping her drink through the curly straw. She was extremely attractive, Greg had to admit, a thought he tried to push to the back of his mind; he was in enough trouble. She caught his eye and smiled over the top of her glass.

'Charmaine,' she said putting her glass on the table. Greg noticed the long slim fingers with nails painted a deep scarlet.

'Greg,' he replied politely.

'I know. You're Greg Driscoll.' She looked at him through long dark lashes.

'Oh dear,' sighed Greg.

'I saw you in a play in London,' she continued.

'You don't look old enough to have seen any of the plays I did in London. I haven't been on the stage for years.'

'They were right. You are charming, aren't you?'

'And who are they that give me such credit?'

'Oh, you know, people.'

'Yeah, I'm sort of off people at the moment.'

Charmaine drew the remains of her vodka through the straw. 'Yeah, me too. Can I get you another drink?'

'Depends,' said Greg.

'Ooh, on what?' she replied fluttering her eyelashes again and smiling, showing her perfect teeth.

'On why you're here and why you want to talk to me and who's paying for the drink.'

'Well, I'm paying for the drink, for a start and I'd like to talk to you because there's only the two of us in the bar and I thought it would be rude to ignore you but, if you'd prefer, I could sit over there on my own.' She pointed to the long table by the wall. 'Or over there,' pointing to the long table under the front window, 'or I could just stand at the bar like some old lush.'

Greg smiled at her. She didn't smile back. A red flush had appeared on her cheeks. 'I'm sorry, I'm a bit sensitive at the moment,' he said. 'I'll gladly accept a pint of Kronenbourg from you and the pleasure of your company as long as we can talk about you and not me. Talking about me would be very boring for both of us, I'm afraid.'

She smiled again and went to the bar. She had completely shed her Arctic protection and Greg watched her black skin-tight jeans make their way to Tallie at the bar. A light blue sweater, probably cashmere, covered her shapely upper body and she tossed her hair as she walked sending it shimmering and cascading over her shoulders. Greg folded up the Standard carefully. There was slim chance, he supposed, that Charmaine had not seen a newspaper today, but he doubted it. His biggest fear was that she was a journalist sent to seduce him into giving her an exclusive story on Trudie Carling. He would have to be on his guard.

*

'I'm not sure he's the best choice, Virginia.'

'I know what I'm doing.'

'All that newspaper coverage could ruin everything.'

'The bigger the profile, the better. Trust me.'

***

CHAPTER EIGHT

Greg woke with a pounding headache. He looked round the room and realised, thankfully, he was alone in his bed. But something didn't feel right. He closed his eyes against the bright sunlight permeating his thin curtains and turned over. The bedroom door opening made him jump.

'I got you black coffee for two reasons. One, there was no milk and two, the state you were in last night, I thought you'd be needing it.'

Charmaine was wearing the dressing gown he had bought Jenny just a few weeks before – and very little else. Greg's heart thumped. What had he done? Well, he could guess the answer to that but desperately didn't want to believe it. Charmaine put the mug of coffee on the bedside table and perched on the edge of the bed.

'At least it's not raining,' she said, smiling radiantly. She certainly didn't seem to have a hangover.

Greg was silent. He wanted to ask what she was doing here but assumed it would be a stupid question...

Charmaine put her hand under his chin and made him look at her. 'Oh dear,' she said. 'Perhaps you should lay off the whisky. You look terrible.'

Greg felt terrible and it was nothing to do with whisky.

'Look, I'm going to have to go soon, I just want to thank you for letting me stay the night. I really didn't fancy driving home in all that rain,'

Greg looked at her. Her hair was wet but still had that crimped look he'd found so attractive in the pub the night before.

'I took the liberty of having a shower,' she said running her hand dreamily through her damp hair. 'I don't suppose you have a hair-dryer, do you?'

'Um...I think there may be one in that drawer,' replied Greg pointing to the chest of drawers by the window. Charmaine walked over to the window and pulled the curtain back enough to peer out. 'Lovely morning.'

'Did we...um...did we..?' Greg stuttered.

Charmaine laughed prettily. 'No we didn't, Greg Driscoll. What sort of girl do you think I am?'

Greg heaved a sigh of relief. 'I'm sorry, I didn't mean...'

Charmaine was at the bed again and she leaned over and kissed Greg on the lips. 'Shut up,' she smooched. 'I know you didn't. You're a very sweet man, Mr Driscoll.' Greg thought she was looking at him sadly as she described him. She stood up and started drying her hair. 'I'm really looking forward to your new series,' she shouted over the noise of the dryer. 'Any chance I could have your number in case I'm over this way again? I'd love to meet up with you and Ginny when she gets back.'

Greg heartrate increased again. What had he told this girl about Jenny? 'That would be nice,' he said.

She switched the hair-dryer off and tousled her hair. She looked very beautiful as she flashed her lashes at Greg. 'So?'

'It's...er...written on the dial, I think.'

Charmaine laughed again. 'The dial? What century are you living in?'

'Oh, yeah.' Greg laughed. His head hurt. He told Charmaine his landline number.

'Don't you have a mobile?'

'It's never on. I'm in the studio a lot. Also, I don't actually know the number as I never ring myself.'

Charmaine smiled. 'The landline will do fine. I'll go and get dressed.' She left the room.

Greg had to confess to feeling a certain amount of disappointment as the lithe body walked away from him. He leapt out of his bed and threw on some clothes. Downing the black coffee he went downstairs to re-fill the kettle. He heard Charmaine moving around in the spare room that she must have slept in. She sounded like she was talking quietly to someone on her phone.

He sat at the kitchen table trying to re-boot his memory. He remembered being in the pub with Charmaine. They'd talked about her – she was a PA or secretary or something for a managing director of a company in Harlow in Essex. She'd come to Maldon to take some pictures of the Thames barges for her firm's catalogue but the weather had been so bad she'd given up and taken refuge in The King's Head. The two of them had stayed in the pub until closing time and Greg had vague memories of suggesting she'd had too much to drink to drive back to Harlow, especially in that weather.

He looked at the empty bottle of Famous Grouse whisky standing on the draining board. He was pretty sure it had been at least half-full. No wonder he had a headache. He looked through to the living room. At least that was relatively tidy. These things worried him nowadays. Time was, he wouldn't have given a second thought as to whether people considered that he lived like a pig. Maybe he was growing up, starting to fret about such trivialities. Hearing Charmaine coming down the stairs reminded him that he still behaved like a moronic teenager. He stood up and met her as she descended. 'Black coffee?' he offered. 'There's no milk, I'm afraid.'

'I know there isn't,' she replied. She checked her watch. It looked expensive to Greg. Must be a good secretary, he thought. An unjustified jealousy against her boss suddenly swept over him. 'I could have a quick one, I suppose.'

Greg grinned and fetched a clean mug.

Twenty minutes later, his headache waning, Greg Driscoll helped Charmaine into her Artic jacket and gave her a peck on the cheek. She picked up the holdall she'd dumped on the sofa. Suddenly Greg realised what had been wrong in his bedroom when he woke. That bag was on a chair by the window. Why was it in his room if she'd slept in the spare? She walked to the front door and opened it wide.

Flashlights caught Greg and Charmaine as they stood in the doorway. As his eyes cleared he focussed on about a dozen photographers in a phalanx outside the door. Charmaine gave him a kiss. 'I'm sorry,' she said, waved and ran off to where she'd parked her car the night before.

The door of The King's Head opened and Gareth strode out towards the cameramen.

'Come on! Bugger off! This is private property.'

A few tried to argue it was a public road but once Gareth told them they could argue that with the police who were on their way, they gradually packed up their gear and dispersed. They'd got what they came for.

Gareth crossed over to where Greg stood like a rabbit caught in headlights at his front door. 'You look like shit, mate,' he said.

'Thanks.'

Gareth took Greg back inside his house and closed the door. 'What did you think you were doing?'

'I wasn't doing anything, Gareth.' Greg went through to the kitchen and filled the kettle once more.

'Got a hangover?' Gareth stood at the kitchen door leaning against the lintel.

'No,' lied Greg.

'You should have.'

Greg took a mug from the draining board. 'Coffee? It'll have to be black. As well as not having a hangover I don't have any milk.'

Gareth sat at the kitchen table. 'How much was she? I hope she was worth it.'

Greg stopped mid-pour. 'I beg your pardon.'

'How much? She looked pricey to me.'

'She wasn't a prostitute, Gareth.'

The King's Head landlord raised his eyebrows.

'She wasn't,' insisted Greg.

'Checked your wallet?'

'I don't have to.' Greg checked the wallet in his back pocket anyway. Fortunately it still had money in it. He didn't know how much he'd taken to the pub the night before and couldn't remember how much he'd spent but there were still notes in his wallet. He made sure his bank cards were still there before showing Gareth the contents.

'Someone else must have paid, then.'

'She wasn't a prostitute, Gareth.' Greg slammed the coffee mug onto the table, spilling some on the Formica top.

'She was certainly high-class.' Gareth picked up his mug, being careful not to drip coffee onto his trousers. 'Did you know she was spiking your drinks?'

'What?'

'Every round she came up for she ordered a pint for you and a vodka for her, insisting that the tonic was not poured into it. Then she slipped the vodka into your pint and just drank tonic water herself. I've seen it before, Greg, when I worked in the Midlands. We had a couple who used to come in, sit at the bar, waiting to be picked up by some unsuspecting idiot, spike his drinks so he didn't know what he was doing and then take him off to the hotel next door. Must have cost the mugs a fortune.'

'Isn't it illegal to do that?'

'What?'

'Spike people's drinks?'

'Only if anyone sees it happening.'

'So why did you let her do it to me?'

'I wasn't there, Greg. It was Soozie who'd spotted it, by which time you were pissed anyway and being taken across the road.'

Greg thought for a moment. 'Anyway you're wrong. She slept in the spare room.'

'Really?' Gareth took out his phone and opened an app. After a second or two scrolling he showed Greg a grainy picture on his social media page. Greg's heart sank. Posing in front of his face was a naked Charmaine in his bedroom hovering over his prostrate body.

'Fuck!'

'That's what it looks like, yeah.'

'But I'm asleep!' yelled Greg. 'Look!' He pointed to the screen.

'I'm not sure how many people will believe that. She is quite tasty, isn't she?'

Greg slammed the phone onto the table. The landline rang in the living room.

'You didn't give her your number, by any chance, did you?'

Greg glared at Gareth as the answerphone kicked in.

"Beep...Hi Greg. This is Jeremy Kilmer from The Daily Express. Could you ring me back? I'd like to do a story on you. I can pay good money. Thanks." He left his mobile number.

Gareth grinned. 'I wouldn't answer your phone for the next few days if I were you.'

'I don't understand what's going on,' said Greg. He put his head in his hands.

'You've been set up, mate.'

'Obviously. But who by and why?'

'Heard from your friend Trudie?'

Greg's mobile rang. 'You didn't give her your mobile as well?'

Greg looked at the screen. It was Phil Woodford. 'Hi Greg. I'm going to have to get you in for another meeting, I'm afraid.' Greg's director sounded irritated. 'I told you not to say or do anything, didn't I?'

'I didn't do anything, Phil. I've been set up.'

'I need to see you at noon. Make sure you're here.' Phil Woodford hung up.

'Great!' Greg put his phone on the table next to Gareth's.

'In the shit?'

'I'd better not be. This is not my fault!'

Gareth gave him a sideways look, finished his coffee and stood up. 'Careful who you talk to, Greg. If I'd been in earlier last night I'd have tipped you off. Soozie wouldn't have known what was going on.' He went back to the pub, closing Greg's front door behind him.

Greg sat alone in his kitchen, aware of a wave of despair sweeping over him. He wanted to cry; to crawl back under the duvet; to be hugged and comforted by Jenny, if she were here. Jenny! What if she's seen...well of course she would have done. He grabbed his phone from the table and punched in Jenny's number,

'Hallo Casanova,' she answered.

'Jenny, you know I've been set up, don't you?'

'Again?'

'Yes, I know it probably doesn't look like that but...'

'Greg, I tried to warn you. I know what the press can be like. They'll make up anything for a story to sell their shit.'

The phone in the living room rang again. Greg let the answerphone deal with it.

'But you know I didn't do anything, don't you? Have you seen the picture? I'm asleep. Look closely. I was drugged, Jenny.'

'I know, Greg. I've told you, you don't need to worry about me. As long as the newspapers don't look my way.'

Greg was surprised at Jenny's reaction. He was relieved that she believed he'd been set up but she appeared more worried about her being caught up in it than what he was going through. 'I have to go to another meeting at the production office today.'

'Good. Let them sort it out. You have to stand up for yourself, Greg. Don't let the bastards grind you down.'

Jenny's language was unusual. She didn't often swear and yet that was the second time in a matter of seconds. 'Are you alright?' he asked.

'I'm fine, Greg. Missing you, of course but it's all OK over here. Denis and Anton are perfect hosts.'

Greg sighed. 'Oh God, I wish I was there with you.'

The phone in the living room rang again.

'You're very popular today,' said Jenny.

'Bloody newspapers! That's the third one in the last half hour.'

'Perhaps you should talk to them.'

'Not bloody likely. I'm in enough crap as it is.'

'What time's your meeting?'

'Twelve.'

'I'd better let you go, then. Stand up for yourself, Greg. I'll see you soon, I hope.' Jenny blew a kiss down the phone and disconnected.

Greg sat at his kitchen table. Speaking to Jenny hadn't made him feel any better. He checked the clock and ordered a cab for eleven.

*

Trudie Carling seemed to have recovered from her trauma and was sitting dressed in tight jeans and a low-cut

V-necked tee-shirt, smiling happily and chatting amicably to her agent. They were in one of the offices at the studio with Phil Woodford, Janet Milner and George Norris. Greg strolled into the room and sat next to Trudie. She put her hand on his leg.

'How are you Greg?' she whispered.

'How do you think?'

Gene Waters leaned over and spoke in a loud voice. 'Well, Mr Driscoll, I think you owe my client an apology.' Greg held his stare silently. 'For accusing her.'

'I don't think I accused her of anything.'

Trudie Carling moved her hand on Greg's leg. 'It's alright, Greg. I don't need an apology.'

'So what's all this about, Greg?' The voice came from across the table. Greg turned and looked at George Norris. 'Why did you do it?'

'I didn't,' replied Greg. 'I was set-up by someone.'

'Again, Mr Driscoll?' Greg looked at Gene Waters. He had a smirk on his ugly face that Greg desperately wanted to wipe off.

A realisation suddenly came upon him. 'I don't suppose you'd have any idea as to who would do such a thing, would you, Mr Waters?'

The big man smiled. 'I hope that's not any sort of accusation, Mr Driscoll.'

'Of course not, Mr Waters. At least I seem to have taken the heat off your client for the time being, though, haven't I?' It was Greg's turn to smile.

Trudie looked quizzically at her agent. Had he set Greg up? She turned back to Greg, who shrugged and removed her hand from his leg.

'The thing is,' said Janet Milner, 'What are we going to do about it?'

'Keeping Mr Driscoll out of the pub might be a good starting point,' suggested Gene Waters.

Greg laughed.

'I think we need to be serious about this,' Janet Milner continued, opening a folder in front of her. 'The thing is, Greg, a certain amount of publicity won't do us any harm but this is all a bit sleazy, really. We have to be careful.'

Greg leant back in his chair. 'Do you know, if I'd spiked a woman's drink, gone back to her house and taken pictures, deliberately made to look as though I was screwing her, I'd be up on a rape charge by now – quite rightly – and yet, even though that's exactly what this girl did to me, I still seem to be the villain of the piece. What I'd like to know is who set me up?' He glared at Waters.

'Whatever the situation, Greg,' said Norris, 'we have to protect the programme at all costs.'

'Of course we do, George. I don't matter one iota.' Greg folded his arms.

'You do, Greg, of course you do but I'd like to ask you if you could just let this die down quickly. Don't try and start an argument with the National Press, whatever you do. I can see you're quite angry about it. Just keep quiet, please, for God's sake.'

'God's or yours?'

'Yours, Greg. If you ignore this and keep out of trouble, it will blow over soon enough without doing any damage.'

Greg shook his head in disbelief.

Trudie put her hand back onto Greg's leg. 'George is right, Greg. I know, I've been there. Trying to protest your innocence will just make you look guilty.'

Greg patted Trudie's hand condescendingly. 'Thanks,' he said.

'So.' Janet closed her folder. 'We're agreed that we ignore this little hiccup and carry on with the same release date as if nothing'd happened.'

'What's in that folder?' asked Greg.

'It's the publicity folder, Greg, nothing for you to worry about.'

'Depends what it says about me.'

Janet Milner opened the folder and handed Greg a sheet of paper. 'This is what we're releasing to the press tomorrow. As you can see it makes no mentions of your peccadillos.'

Greg scanned the sheet. It was a standard press release for the series. He handed it back as everyone stood up to go.

'So we're back on schedule from tomorrow, please,' announced Phil. 'Oh, Greg. Can I have a quick word?'

Greg sat down wearily as the others left the room.

'Well?' said Greg as Phil closed the door.

'What do you think happened last night?' Phil sat on the chair next to Greg.

'What I think happened, Phil, is that someone wanted to protect their client by making me look like a reprobate.'

'Gene Waters?'

'Trudie seemed a lot better, I thought.'

'But surely...'

'I know, it's ludicrous, isn't it? I hadn't really considered it before I saw the two of them sitting there looking so smug. They'll probably release a load of crap about how I've cheated on her next.'

'Are you sure about this, Greg?'

'No. I'm not sure about anything, but someone paid for a high-class whore to spike my drinks, take photos of herself poised naked over my comatose body, and also arranged for a load of paparazzi to be outside at the very moment she left my house. I don't know who would do that.'

'I'll have a word,' said Phil.

'Oh, don't bother on my account, Phil. Don't want to jeopardise the series – or its star!'

'You're just as important to this series as Trudie – probably more so from an acting point of view.'

Greg looked at his director and raised his eyebrows.

'I could give you the weekend off, if you'd like. I'd have to rearrange the schedule again, though.'

Greg laughed quietly. 'No, it's fine, Phil. I'll be here in the morning and I'll keep out of the pub for the rest of the day, don't worry.'

'Greg...'

'It's fine, Phil,' said Greg firmly, holding the door handle. 'See you in the morning.'

*

Greg didn't keep out of the pub. His cab home dropped him off at the door of The King's Head and, not bothering to cross the road to his house, he went straight into the 'Members' Bar'. Gareth was standing with a glass in his hand. 'Kronenbourg with a splash of vodka?' he asked, smiling innocently. Greg gave him a steely look before Gareth handed over an unblemished pint of lager.

'This one's on me, mate,' he said. 'How did it go at the studio?'

'I think I have an idea as to who set me up. He told me to stay out of the pub.'

'I'm glad you took no notice.'

The door opened and Greg's heartrate involuntarily increased... Wendy stood at the door. 'I may owe you an apology,' she said.

'A pint of untampered Kronenbourg will do,' he replied, holding his arms out to embrace his friend.

'Gerroff!' she said pushing him away. 'There are some sluts in this world, aren't there?'

'There certainly are, Wendy, and thankfully you're not one of them.' She cuffed him playfully round the ear as he went to sit at the long table.

Greg left the pub at nine o'clock. Several other people had joined them throughout the evening – none dressed for the Arctic fortunately. Gareth had obviously spread the word and friends had rallied round giving Greg their support. It gave him a warm feeling. No prostitutes had come into the pub as far as anyone knew and there were no paparazzi around. Greg went home, threw a ready meal in the microwave and was in bed, alone, by eleven o'clock.

***

CHAPTER NINE

Jenny arrived back from her extended trip to France in early July. It came as a huge relief to Greg. Throughout the trauma with Trudie and Charmaine, he'd felt terribly alone. Much as Wendy and the others had shown their support, there had been no-one at home to give him any sort of succour. Now Jenny was back, she took to the task as though it was her main purpose in life, spoiling him, cooking him delicious meals, cleaning the house and, most of all, giving her love to him.

It seemed that George Norris and the others had been right – the press had soon lost interest in Greg Driscoll's voracious sexual appetite. It turned out that a minor Royal had been caught with his pants down which was deemed to be far more in the public interest than the affairs of a minor actor. He didn't take on Gene Waters either, though he was convinced he'd been the one to organise the prostitute and the paparazzi. Greg would not have been surprised if Waters had arranged the Royal misdemeanour as well – except for the fact that Trudie Carling didn't receive any publicity from it!

'Once in a While' was back on schedule, meaning a few late nights for Greg and Trudie in order to catch up. They'd both found it awkward at first but, at lunch on the first day back, the two of them talked about how they were feeling. Greg convinced himself that Trudie really had had nothing to do with the stories in the press and even that the incident in the pub was as much a surprise to her as it had been to him. He was less convinced by her loyal protestation of Gene Waters' lack of involvement – particularly concerning the prostitute business – but he let it go. He needed to be professional or the series would go to pot and, in some way, he could see that the programme was maybe more important than their little lives. Of course, none of this had anything to do with the fact that Trudie Carling was back to being her beautiful and charming best as she sat opposite Greg in the studio canteen.

Jenny seemed to be becoming obsessed with the migrant situation in France. She talked of very little else. She said she'd spent time trying to convince Denis and Anton that the people in Calais were refugees and they were different from economic migrants. They weren't here to 'take their jobs'. Greg listened with a mixture of interest and despair as she told him of the conditions the people were being forced to live in and he found himself promising to do something to help as soon as he'd finished 'Once in a While'.

The programme aired on schedule and Greg and Jenny sat on their own in front of the television in his lounge. They were holding hands. Greg was feeling unusually nervous. He didn't know how the series would be received. He hadn't seen the edited programme. It was the actor's lot to be left in the hands of the director and editor. It was up to them which 'take' they would use, irrespective of whether the performer thought it was their best performance or not.

'You're about to come into this scene, aren't you?' Jenny gripped Greg's hand.

'How do you know?'

'Your pulse just got faster. Are you nervous?'

'No,' lied Greg.

Jenny smiled and kissed his cheek.

The first episode was received with universal acclaim. Greg's worry was the next one, where his character's relationship with Trudie Carling's sees them ending the episode in bed together. He was pretty sure the press would resurrect the stories from the previous month, which, of course, they did but the series was more popular than the scandal and, once again, the stories faded into insignificance.

In the 'Members' Bar' the occupants were constantly asking Greg what was going to happen next. Greg, pretending to be irritated actually revelled in the fame and glory.

The filming finished a couple of weeks later and, much to the joy of the producers and the main cast, 'Once In A While' had already been commissioned for a second series.

The wrap party was held in a West End restaurant and, although the production company had supposedly booked the whole restaurant for the private party, there seemed to be a lot of extraneous people, whom no-one appeared to know, hanging around taking photographs. Greg made sure he steered clear of Trudie Carling and, even though the bar was free, he managed not to drink enough to disgrace himself. Jenny had refused the invitation to join him as his guest. She'd said this was his night and she'd only feel in the way. Greg had become quite angry, saying he needed her there which was just met with derision. It had almost turned into a full-scale row. It had made Greg feel insecure; they hadn't really argued at all before, not as badly as this. Was he being selfish? He just wanted to share his night with the woman he loved. He'd backed down when Jenny pointed out that she didn't want to be in the spotlight. She'd been there and didn't want her past being brought to the fore again. He promised her he wouldn't be late or drunk. And he wasn't. He'd been more than happy to leave the party early, hugging and kissing everyone in the expected theatrical farewell style and telling them he was looking forward to seeing them all on the next series, due to start later in the year.

The taxi dropped Greg off in time for him to enjoy his own private wrap party at The King's Head attended by his friends and, best of all, Jenny.

*

A couple of days after the party, Greg and Jenny sat in their living room discussing the future. Greg now assumed that Jenny was a permanent fixture in his life here in Maldon. It was a selfish attitude with no thought given to where Jenny might want their relationship to go. It had, however, become the norm for him and he was happy for it to continue.

Jenny, on the other hand, wanted to know what the two of them wanted. She didn't want to be just the girlfriend of a famous TV star.

'You're not talking marriage, are you?' said Greg nervously and totally missing the point.

Jenny laughed. 'Oh God, no! I just like to feel that I have a purpose in life.'

'Oh,' Greg felt a bit disappointed. Even though he didn't really want to get married, this was a definite refusal. 'Like what?' he queried.

Jenny sighed. 'You're quite insensitive, really, aren't you, Greg Driscoll.'

'You're not pregnant?'

Jenny laughed again. 'Look, you are doing fine, you have a job, a purpose. You're getting on with things. I just feel like your skivvy, sometimes.'

'We could get a cleaner. I can afford that. I've got work offers coming in and I'm definitely in the second series.'

'I don't actually care whether you can afford a cleaner or not.' Jenny virtually spat the words at Greg. 'I need some direction in *my* life. I don't enjoy just sitting back in your reflected glory, thank you very much.'

Greg was quiet. 'I didn't realise...' he started.

'I know you didn't. That's the problem.' Jenny showed him an article in her newspaper. 'Look. Look what's happening in the real world. The situation in Calais is getting worse by the day. There are hundreds in this camp. There'll be thousands before long. I want to do something positive about it. People are arriving every day, desperate people, coming from all over the world. The French don't want them there so they're deliberately not helping them.'

'That's awful,' said Greg handing the paper back to Jenny.

'Don't you care?'

'Of course I care. I don't see what I can do about it though.'

'There's a lot you can do.' Jenny was shouting now. 'Don't you understand these people need help?'

Greg thought for a minute. 'I suppose I could use my new-found celebrity status to raise awareness. You know, organise a charity thing or something – as long as I don't have to do anything energetic.' He chuckled smugly.

'It's not about you or your celebrity, Greg. It's about these refugees. They haven't got a clue who you are and I don't expect they'd care if they did. I think we should go over to France.'

'Ok. It'd be good to see Denis and Anton again, though I bet they don't agree with you about the refugees.'

'I don't want to go on holiday! I mean we should go to Calais.'

'And do what?'

Jenny paused for a moment. She sighed and went to sit next to Greg. 'What these people need immediately is food. They're starving and the authorities can't, or won't, help them. Maybe we could take a food parcel over or something.'

'A food parcel? How many refugees are we going to feed with a few tins of beans?'

'It's something, Greg. These people are corralled in an enclosure. No-one can get to them easily and all they're getting is the bare minimum at the moment. We could slip in regularly with some provisions; make their lives a bit better, save some lives, even. There's children there – orphaned children who need help.'

'Perhaps we should take a van or something? I'm sure I could borrow one from someone.'

'They wouldn't let you in, Greg.' She put her hand on his leg. 'It's a good idea, though. The problem is the respective governments are trying to pretend it's not happening.' Jenny stood up and went into the kitchen. A second later she was back carrying a huge rucksack, with a metal frame about four feet high.

'I saw that,' said Greg. 'I was going to ask you about it.'

'I bought it yesterday. If we can fill this with useful things for the refugees, you know, food, clothing, that sort of thing, it could be carried on the ferry. No-one's going to question someone going on a camping holiday.'

Greg looked at the bag. 'You'd never be able to carry that if it's full,' he said.

'That's why I need you,' she said, giving him a kiss on the cheek.

'I'm not sure I could carry that.'

148

Jenny smiled. 'But you're my big brave knight in shining armour and you could be the same for these poor people as well.' She beamed at him.

He smiled back at her and lifted the rucksack onto his back. 'It's not too bad, I suppose for a big strong knight like me.'

Jenny hugged him.

*

The ferry was busy. It was a warm September day and several groups of people, mostly old people, Greg noticed – spending the 'grey pound' - were heading to the continent. The schools had gone back, he was pleased to discover, so there were hardly any families armed with buckets and spades, but there was a rowdy group of young, strangely dressed men who were apparently on their way to a rock concert in Paris.

Greg and Jenny sat in a quiet part of the ship's bar, Jenny drinking coffee, Greg a pint of Stella Artois. It was 10.15am. At Greg's feet was the large rucksack holding food, covered with blankets and children's clothes bound for the refugee camp.

'I feel like I've been carrying a house on my back,' said Greg, stretching out his shoulders. 'It's bloody heavy. How much food is there in there?'

'That'll be the tins,' replied Jenny. 'You're the one that suggested beans. I suppose I could carry it for a bit, if you want.'

'Don't be silly. I'm a knight in shining armour, remember? It would be going against my code of chivalry. Besides there's another half an hour before we reach Calais. I may have recovered by strength by then.' He lifted his pint.

'Don't overdo that, Greg. Nobody's allowed in the camp so we have to keep our heads down and not attract attention.'

Greg sat and looked out at the channel. 'I don't understand why they won't let people help. Surely if we tell them we're on a humane expedition, they won't object.'

Jenny shook her head. 'Security's really tight. We have to make sure no-one sees you.'

The rock fans came en-masse into the bar loudly singing something they obviously thought everyone should share with them. No-one joined in and, in the typical British way, pretended nothing was happening. The group assembled themselves round a couple of large tables not far from where Greg and Jenny were sitting. The singing increased in volume as copious amounts of canned alcohol, obviously not bought on the ferry, was poured down their throats.

'Oi!' yelled a fat man with a beard, wearing a plastic helmet with horns, like the Vikings didn't wear. 'Aren't you on TV?' He pointed in Greg's direction. 'You! Aren't you on TV?' he repeated unnecessarily.

Greg nodded and said, 'yes,' quietly.

'You're in that one with that Trudie Carling, aren't you?'

Again Greg nodded. Two or three of the group approached the table where Greg and Jenny were sitting.

'What's she like?' leered the bearded man. 'Is she a goer? I bet she is, isn't she? Is she a goer? Eh?'

Greg wondered why this man thought it necessary to repeat everything he said. 'She's a very nice young lady,' he replied.

'Must be a good job, yours,' said one of the other Vikings. 'I could do that, just sitting and looking at her all day.'

'And snogging her,' joined in another.

'And the rest!' They all laughed. 'I bet you did lots of rehearsal for that bed scene. I know I would have done.' More laughter.

'We need to go to the duty-free shop,' said Jenny, standing up.

'We don't get duty-free, love. We're in the EU aren't we? I say, we're in the EU.' He sat down uninvited at the table.

'I know we don't,' said Jenny gently. 'We have to get a souvenir for our children.

Greg looked at her with surprise. He stood up and heaved the rucksack onto his back. 'Sorry boys. Have to go.'

'Bloody hell! What you got in there?'

'Trudie Carling,' yelled one of the Vikings to guffaws of laughter and shouts of 'You dirty bastard!' as Greg staggered after Jenny towards the duty-free shop.

'Don't attract attention, please, Greg,' said Jenny as they settled in some seats far away from the bar area.

'It's not my fault,' he protested.

'I know but we must keep a low profile.'

Greg dumped the rucksack on the floor and stretched again.

'Careful!' Jenny said quickly. 'We don't want to ruin the food, having carried it this far.'

'I don't suppose they'll mind a few bent tins,' grumbled Greg. 'Anyway, I don't know why we couldn't just buy all this stuff in Calais rather than me cart it all the way over.'

'Because the people of Maldon have generously given it for the refugees. They don't want us to buy it over in France; they want it to be their gift, to feel like they're doing something. Don't be so ungrateful.'

'They don't have to carry it,' muttered Greg.

The loudspeaker informed all drivers to return to their vehicles and all foot passengers to remain in their seats until informed that they should start to disembark.

'Come on,' Jenny stood up, taking control again.

'Shouldn't we wait until we're told to disembark?'

'Not likely. You'll be caught up with that load of Trudie Carling groupies again. Let's get to the staircase so we can get off as soon as we land.'

'Dock,' smirked Greg.

'What?'

'We dock, not land. We're on a boat not a plane.'

Jenny gave Greg a playful slap and helped him hitch the rucksack onto his back. The top of the bag reached about eighteen inches above his head and covered his back almost to his knees.

*

'Going camping?' said the bright young customs officer as Jenny handed over both their passports.

Stopping Greg making a sarcastic reply, she quickly answered, 'yes.'

The officer just glanced at Greg's documents but studied Jenny's with a deal of scrutiny. 'Virginia Hoffman?' he said, looking up.

Jenny nodded.

'German?'

'I am a German citizen. That's why I have a German passport. I was born there. My father was in the Royal Air Force and was stationed there.'

'Whereabouts?' There was a long line building up behind them and Jenny could hear the singing of the Vikings getting louder as they joined the end of the queue.

'Bruggen,' she replied. 'It doesn't exist as a base anymore.'

The customs officer was distracted by the rock fans. 'Better get on, then. You don't want to get caught up with this lot. Every year they come over. It's like a pilgrimage. Pain in the proverbial.' He handed back the passports and Greg and Jenny went through into the Port of Calais. They found a cafe and bought coffee.

Greg was thankful to relieve the strain on his back by placing the rucksack on the floor by the table. There were few people in the cafe; just a couple of dock-workers in fluorescent orange jackets and a family with two small children who were apparently defying the ban on taking children out of school during term-time, and who seemed to think it was not irritating to let their noisy offspring run round the cafe shouting and yelling.

'Right. You know what to do?' Jenny said in a low voice.

'I do,' whispered back Greg. 'I go through the woody bit and into the camp away from the road. I put the rucksack down in the middle of the camp and I leave the same way I came in. Should I camouflage my face?'

'This is not a game, Greg.'

'Sorry, tell me again why you're not actually coming in with me?'

'Just one person is easier to infiltrate the security. Don't forget, if you're stopped, you are lost and have gone into the camp by mistake. Plead ignorance.'

'I could be good at that,' smirked Greg.

Jenny sighed. 'I'll be waiting by the side of the road over there.' She pointed through the window to the main dual carriageway, currently taking hundreds of holidaymakers and lorries into France.'

'Yes ma'am.' Greg saluted.

'Be serious, Greg. The authorities won't take kindly to anyone trying to help these people. They want to pretend it's not happening.'

'Well, they're bastards, then. We're just helping people who are fleeing for their lives, aren't we?'

'They don't see it like that so be careful. Are you sure you want to go through with this, Greg?' He hadn't touched his coffee, she noticed and thought his jocular manner was a way of concealing his nerves.

'Of course I do.' He wasn't sure at all.

'Go to the loo, first, Greg.' Jenny indicated the public lavatories at the back of the cafe.

'Right. Don't want to get caught short in the devil's lair.'

The two dockers looked over at Greg and muttered something in French. They had both been engrossed by something on their mobile phones, probably a game or something, Greg thought. He couldn't understand people's obsession with playing games on their phones instead of actually communicating with other people. He was about to give them a wave when he caught Jenny glaring at him. They had a plastic carrier bag with them upon which was the legend 'Duty-Free'. 'Perks of the job, I suppose' thought Greg as he carried on into the Gents.

The two dockers stood up as soon as Greg disappeared and walked past Jenny to the door.

When Greg returned refreshed, Jenny was the sole occupant of the cafe, the family also having exited. She helped Greg with the rucksack again and went towards the door. 'Let's go,' she said.

They walked along the side of the road and parted at a junction, Jenny going into a small clearing and Greg carrying on towards a wooded area a few hundred yards further on. There were a few gendarmes, heavily armed, along the dual carriageway and a couple more leaning against an armoured car, smoking. Greg thought all this security was a bit over the top. He could see a few makeshift tents and shelters in a field a bit away from the road. He skirted round the outside of a wire fence and, pushing the rucksack ahead of him, scrambled through a break in the barrier and on into the cover of the woods.

It smelt damp under the trees, even though the weather had been dry and warm in France. The floor was covered in rotting bits of bark. He touched one of the trees, expecting it to be wet and slimy but it appeared to be as dry as tinder. There was evidence of camp-fires and burnt ashes and rubbish littered any open area in the wood. The musty smell was almost overpowering, reminding Greg why he'd never been the outdoor type. He hadn't been a Boy Scout or anything. He could fathom why anyone would deliberately sleep out in the open air. Or tie knots! What was that all about? He wondered if any of the people he was here to help thought the same. He supposed some of them must do. After all, they hadn't chosen to come and sleep outdoors in this wood. They weren't on holiday.

The rucksack on his back was getting heavier and more cumbersome as he fought his way through the overhanging branches, the top of the metal frame breaking off small branches as he went. He was about to stop and rest when he saw the clearing with the shelters. He looked round for any Gendarmerie and seeing none apparent, went through an opening in the trees, through to a space between the tents. There were some soiled and dirty-looking blankets hung up on rope between the tents and some pots and pans, blackened and bent, along with rubbish bags. Greg decided to put his food-parcel down in front of them. A few people sitting round outside their temporary abodes looked at him without any expectation. He wanted to tell them he was leaving food and blankets and clothes for their children but Jenny's instructions had been clear. He was to leave the rucksack and go. He was not to speak to anyone. He performed his duty, left the bag and headed for the trees. He saw, with some satisfaction, several people approach the bag as he disappeared into the darkness. As instructed, he sent Jenny a text saying 'mission accomplished' and made his way back up towards the road.

'Hey. Stop!'

Greg started to panic. He wasn't sure what his best course of action would be. Should he make a run for it?

Turn and fight his way out? Don't be silly. He stopped and turned round ready to face the music.

'Do you speak English?' said a young man who looked a bit scruffy to be a gendarme.

'Yes,' he replied, still not sure whether to run or not. This chap didn't look armed.

'Greg Driscoll?' The young man had a microphone and behind him appeared another older man with a video camera on his shoulder. The young man grabbed hold of Greg and hugged him. 'I was a runner on 'Gone for a Song'. Remember? Johnny.'

Greg didn't remember but in his relief to discover he was not about to be shot by the French police, just said, 'Yes, of course. Hi Johnny.'

'What are you doing here?'

'I got lost,' replied Greg, remembering Jenny's instructions.

'Not a good place to get lost, mate. There's a camp of migrants just down there. We're doing a documentary. Hey! Can we get your opinion? Interview you?' He turned to the cameraman. 'Start on a two-shot, then go in close on Greg,' he instructed.

'Um...I don't know, Johnny. I ought to be going.' Greg started to leave but the lens was already trained on him.

'So, we have a celebrity here with us in the camp today. Greg Driscoll. What do you think of what's happening here in Calais, Greg? What's the solution?'

'Well, I don't really know the whole situation but they are human beings and it appears they're not being treated any better than...' He didn't get time to finish the sentence before the sky lit up in a blaze of red and orange and a resounding blast split the air. Johnny and his cameraman ran through the trees towards the camp. Greg wasn't sure what had happened or what he should do. He stood there shaking. A hand grabbed him from behind.

***

CHAPTER TEN

'This way,' said a deep Gallic voice, 'Vite! Vite! Greg felt himself propelled into some undergrowth beneath the trees as a troop of gendarmes ran past, guns drawn, heading for where the noise had come from. Sounds of panic and screaming were emanating from the camp.

'What happened?' Greg asked his new companion.

'Come with me,' was all he replied.

'Where to?' Greg tried to resist, not knowing where he was being taken or by whom but the man was strong and dragged him away from the area towards the main road. They arrived at a culvert by the carriageway to be met by another man, wearing a white coat, who forced Greg into a kind of donkey jacket with Police written in large letters across the shoulders. He then took a quantity of gauze stained with something browny-red and held it to Greg's head.

'Come!' he ordered and walked Greg out onto the road leading to the port. 'Do not speak!' he said fiercely.

They wandered along the road as several official-looking people ran in the opposite direction towards the camp.

'Victime! Victime!' shouted the man and hurried Greg past them.

Greg didn't know what was going on. His head was spinning. What had just happened? He was aware of people shouting as he was forced along to the embarking point of the ferries. As they reached the gate, the man tore the coat off Greg's back and pushed him forwards. 'Go,' he said. 'Go. Ferry. Now.'

'No,' Greg turned to face the man. 'I have to find my girlfriend.'

'Ginny Ok,' replied the man. 'She will text. You go.' He pushed Greg again in the direction of the ferries. A Gendarme looked over to see what was going on. 'Go now.' The man disappeared leaving Greg alone. Eyeing the gendarme, he headed to the booth and handed in the return portion of his ticket. The customs officer looked closely at his passport, nodded and let him embark.

Once on the ferry, Greg took out his phone. There was no message from Jenny so he rang her number.

"The person you are dialling cannot take your call at the moment"

He looked around him. A group of people were talking about the explosion. No-one seemed to be aware that there had been a refugee camp in the vicinity. Most people thought it must have been some sort of accident in a fuel depot or something. There didn't appear to be much concern as to whether anyone had been injured, just relief that it hadn't held up their journeys at all.

'Probably someone chucking a fag away,' said someone in a group of young men. 'They all smoke these Froggies, don't they?'

'Yeah,' said another. 'And they're careless. I can't stand 'em.'

'But you'll all come over here and take back cars full of their cheap wine,' thought Greg. He tried Jenny's phone again to no avail. He wanted to get off the boat: go and look for her: find out what had happened, but they had already left the port and were heading out into the channel. He didn't know what to do. Should he go to the authorities? Explain that he needed to find Jenny. She should be on the ferry with him. Maybe she was. He hadn't thought of that. If she'd caught the ferry it might explain why she couldn't answer his calls. There was no signal now they'd left the shore. Maybe she was getting on the ship when he tried to ring and she couldn't get to her phone... But how was he to find her on a ferry full of passengers? There was a map of the boat on a wall behind him. It showed there was an information desk on this deck. He made his way towards it. Surely they would have a list of passengers.

The young woman at the desk smiled a practised smile. 'How can I help you, sir?' she said,

'Er...I'm looking for my girlfriend.'

She smiled again. 'Do you know where you lost her, sir?'

'Yes, Calais. I want to know if she caught the ferry or not.'

'Oh I see, sir. What's her name?'

'Jen...' he started. 'Er...Virginia Hoffman,' he corrected.

The girl looked at her computer screen and then back up at Greg. 'Are you on the television?' she asked.

'Yes, I am,' replied Greg irritably. 'Virginia Hoffman?'

She looked at her screen again. 'There's no-one of that name on my list,' she said.

Greg thanked her, went outside onto the smoking deck and lit a Marlboro. Several of the group who had been complaining about the careless smoking Froggies were in attendance, all with lit cigarettes themselves. One of them flicked his cigarette butt into the sea, carelessly.

Greg pulled his coat round himself to try and shield himself from the cool sea-breeze that had blown up as if to indicate they were heading back to damp old Blighty. He walked past the group to the other side of the boat. Where was Jenny? He wondered if she strayed into the camp when the explosion happened but convinced himself that wasn't possible.

There had been a sign by the information desk saying he could buy some time on the ship's Wi-Fi system. He put his cigarette out carefully in one of the ashtrays conveniently bolted to the deck and went back inside.

'I've got it,' said the smiley girl. Greg's heartbeat raised in anticipation.

'Virginia Hoffman?'

'Oh no, sorry. Have you found her?'

'No.'

'I meant I've got where I know you from. You're in 'Once In A While', aren't you?'

'Yes I am.' Greg was getting impatient.

'I love that series. What's that Trudie Carling like? I don't like her.'

'She's very nice, actually. Look...um...How do I get Wi-Fi on my phone?'

The girl shuffled in a drawer in front of her and handed Greg a small card with some numbers and letters on it.

'What's that?' he asked.

'It's the Wi-Fi code. You're supposed to pay for it but I'll let you have it free.' She smiled again.

'What do I do with it?' he asked, feeling very confused.

'You put the code in your phone and then you hook up to the ship's Wi-Fi.' She looked at him puzzled. Did this man who was a TV star really not know how his phone worked?

'Ah, of course,' he said looking blankly at his screen. He couldn't see an obvious way of putting the code in there.

'Would you like me to do it for you?' offered the girl.

Greg, feeling like he was a hundred years old with dementia, meekly handed her his phone.

'You go into settings, see.' She showed him the screen. 'Then Wi-Fi and, look.' she showed the screen again. 'There's our Wi-Fi. You touch that and then it asks you for the code and you put in these letters and numbers,' she fiddled with the keyboard and a second later. Voila!'

A tick appeared by the ship's Wi-Fi. Greg, still not having a clue what the girl had done, thanked her. 'What do I owe you?' he said.

'Oh, nothing, all part of the service. Unless...'

'What?'

'Could I have your autograph?' The girl had become very bashful all of a sudden.

Greg signed the notepad she'd thrust at him, he didn't ask her name, just put his signature and the girl blushed a deep red. He went back outside.

The smoking deck was quieter now. The group of men had presumably returned to the bar to relieve the French of some more of their lager. He managed to get a signal on the app that said radio and tuned into an English news channel. The reporter was suggesting that the explosion could have been a bomb, planted by some far-right group who were anti-immigration. Greg suddenly realised how close he'd come to being killed. It hadn't actually occurred to him that the explosion could have been a bomb. If he'd been a few minutes later leaving his food parcel, he would have been blown to bits. He sat down on one of the tables screwed to the deck and lit a cigarette. The reporter was saying that the French police knew of the group suspected of planting the bomb but had no information that this was being planned and it could still possibly be some sort of accident. The reporter didn't think so.

The reception on the radio app kept breaking up and Greg switched to a text news app where he could read updates on the situation. They were reporting the same as the radio. A bomb planted by a far-right extremist organisation. Mixed thoughts were filling Greg's mind. Is that why Johnny and his cameraman were there? Were they responsible, or did they know something was going to happen and wanted to be there to film it? They'd been interviewing him at the time. What had he said? He didn't want to be implicated in anything. He couldn't remember - everything had been a bit of a blur from the time he'd left the food until he'd been bundled onto the ferry. Who were those people who had brought him down the road? They seemed to know who Jenny was. Did they know where she was?

His thoughts were interrupted by the loudspeaker blurting out the fact that the ferry would be docking shortly and could all drivers return to their vehicles. Already? It felt like he'd only just got on the ship. He looked out to see the port of Dover approaching them. He put his cigarette out and went inside. He sent a text to Jenny saying he was back in England and was OK and asking where she was. His phone read *"message not sent"*. There was still no message from her. The foot passengers were told to assemble at the top of the stairs and he duly joined the large crowd.

The customs officer took his passport and scrutinised the photograph. 'Greg Driscoll?' he asked. Greg nodded. 'The actor?' He nodded again. He desperately wanted to get away, get back to Maldon in case Jenny had phoned the landline – not being able to get him on his mobile – and there was still a three hour train journey to go.

The officer looked at the photo again. 'Could you step through that door, Mr Driscoll, please?' He pointed to a white door in the side of a portakabin.

'I'm in a bit of rush, actually,' he said

'We won't keep you long, sir. Just through that door.'

The door opened and another officer, carrying a machine gun, beckoned Greg inside. People in the queue behind him were whispering and gesturing. Greg decided his best course of action was to comply with the armed officer's wishes. He went in.

Inside the portakabin was a table behind which sat a man in a crumpled suit, looking like he'd dressed himself in a rush. He stood up and offered his hand.

'Mr Driscoll, please take a seat.'

'I'm in a bit of a rush, I'm afraid,' said Greg, remaining standing. 'What's all this about?'

'We'll try not to keep you any longer than necessary,' said the crumpled suit. 'Sit down, please.'

Greg did as he was told.

'My name's Detective Inspector Thornton. I'm investigating a group of people calling themselves, 'Indigenous'. Have you heard of them?'

'No,' replied Greg.

DI Thornton looked at his notes and then at Greg. 'I'm enjoying your series by the way,' he said.

'Thank you.'

'Trudie Carling? What's she like?'

'She's lovely. In fact I have to get back to London. We have an early morning recording to do.'

'We'll make sure you're back.' He sat back in his chair. 'So, what were you doing in France, Mr Driscoll?'

'I was visiting a friend,' Greg lied.

'And who was that?'

'My old agent.'

Thornton looked at his notes again. 'Would that be Mr Young?'

Greg frowned. 'Why do you have my ex-agent's name?'

'Who lives in Bourrouillan?' checked DI Thornton, ignoring Greg's question.

'What's going on? Is he alright?'

The detective looked up at Greg. 'You tell me. You've just been to see him, haven't you?'

'Yes, I have.'

'In Bourrouillan?'

'Yes, why?'

'How did you get from Calais to Bourrouillan?'

'I hired a car.'

'Really?' He picked up an iPad and touched the screen. 'According to this, it takes over eight hours to drive from Calais to Bourrouillan,' He looked at his notes again. 'And according to this passenger list, you only arrived in Calais at 10.45 this morning and it's now...' he looked at his watch. '3.30pm, which means you were in France for less than four hours. What sort of car did you hire, Mr Driscoll?'

Greg paused, struggling with his story. 'I met Denis, Mr Young, at a point halfway, not actually in Bourrouillan.

The DI looked at Greg over the top of his glasses.

'Ok,' said Greg. 'He met me in Calais, we had a quick lunch and then I had to get back as I'm supposed to be in the studio.' Greg was starting to panic. Why was he being questioned like this? Had he broken some law? Was this to do with delivering a food parcel to some starving refugees? Greg was getting angry now.

'You travelled with a companion this morning. Did she not come back with you?'

'No. As far as I know she's still in France.'

'As far as you know?'

Greg was silent.

'She's German, I believe,' continued Thornton.

'She's a German citizen. She was born there but her parents were English. Why?'

'How long have you known Fraulein Hoffman?'

It still sounded strange when people called Jenny by her German pseudonym. 'A long time,' he said.

'More than a year, then?' Thornton was focussed on his notes.

'Of course.'

'So you met her in Germany, presumably?'

Greg had had enough. 'I'm sorry, can you tell me what this is all about? Have I done something wrong?'

The DI looked up from his notes.

'But you've never been to Germany, have you, Mr Driscoll?' He looked into Greg's eyes. 'And Virginia Hoffman had never been to the UK before February of this year and yet, you claim to have known her for years. Whereabouts did you meet her, then? Maybe the Netherlands?'

Greg was returning Thornton's stare. His heart was pounding and he hoped it didn't show. What was he to do? Should he tell this policeman the truth about Jenny's past? Why did he want to know?

'I'm thinking,' carried on Thornton,' that I must have some wires crossed somewhere. Do you know Anton DuBois?'

'Anton?'

'DuBois, yes. He has some sort of relationship with your ex-agent, I believe.'

'They're married,' said Greg defiantly.

Di Thornton raised an eyebrow.

'They're in a Civil Partnership.'

'And how long has Mr Young known Monsieur DuBois?'

'They've been married for five years.'

'And before that?'

'Am I under arrest?' Greg's anger was beginning to overtake the fear he also felt. He didn't know what was going on but it didn't feel good.

'Of course not, Mr Driscoll. Should you be?'

'What do you mean?'

'Have you committed a crime?'

'Not that I'm aware of. Look, I have to be in a studio in London very early tomorrow morning and I still have to get home. Do you know how long it takes to get from here to where I live?'

'I certainly do. Maybe we should hire that car that whisked you across France in a matter of minutes.'

'We?'

'I'm going the same way. I thought we could travel together.' He smiled and started to pack up his things. 'I'm based in Chelmsford but I'm sure we could detour as far as Maldon.'

'How does he know I live in Maldon,' thought Greg. 'How does he know so much about me and Jenny and Denis and Anton?'

'This way, Mr Driscoll.' The DI led the way out towards a black Mercedes saloon car parked next to the portakabin. 'What happened to your rucksack?' he said opening the car door.

'I left it with Virginia,' lied Greg.

DI Thornton nodded and went round to the driver's side.

'How do you know I had a rucksack?'

Thornton smiled condescendingly. 'Mr Driscoll, in this world of technology, there isn't much we don't know. There's CCTV all over the place. Every time your passport goes under that little light at the customs, all your information is recorded. Almost anything you do, we can find out about if we want to. All a bit scary, really, isn't it?' He started the car and headed out onto the A2 towards London.

*

'It's a fucking disaster!' Anton DuBois was yelling into his phone. Denis Young was watching from the kitchen window. He'd noticed a change in his husband over the last eighteen months or so. At first he'd thought Anton was getting bored. He was a lot younger than Denis and,

174

although he was happy to just wander about the countryside and live a relaxed retirement, he knew Anton must want a bit more excitement. That's why he'd not been too bothered when he started going into Nogaro regularly - to play chess, he'd said. It was hard to take, being told chess was more exciting them staying at home with him but Anton had asked him to go along as well. Chess didn't appeal that much, especially as everyone there spoke French and Denis was still having trouble getting to grips with his adopted language. Jenny coming over to stay had provided Anton with a companion to go exploring with. Denis wasn't jealous of any of Anton's new companions but he was starting to feel a bit neglected.

'I told you not to,' Anton yelled into the phone.

Denis couldn't hear exactly what his husband was shouting but he looked very angry. He went to the patio door and opened it.

Anton looked up at the open door. 'I have to go,' he said. 'I will see you tonight. Find out what the fuck went wrong. You are going to have a lot of explaining to do.' He switched off his phone.

'Rather foul language, Anton,' said Denis as Anton came up the path. 'What's going on?'

'Nothing, Denis.' He gave Denis a peck on the cheek. 'You don't need to worry.'

'Dinner will be about an hour.'

'I may have to forego dinner, I'm afraid, darling.'

Denis pursed his lips. 'Again? Why?'

Anton sat down on the wooden bench by the patio doors and invited Denis to join him by patting his hand on the seat. The sun glinted in the lake on the perimeter of their garden. Denis sighed and sat down.

'You heard about the explosion in Calais, I suppose?' said Anton.

'I did,' replied Denis. 'It's terrible. People were killed. They're saying it was a bomb.'

'More likely some of those immigrants messing about with gas bottles, if you ask me. Serves them right.'

'Anton!'

'Anyway, it seems Ginny was in the vicinity.'

'Jenny? In Calais? What was she doing there?'

'Day trip, you know. Booze cruise, getting some cheap alcohol.'

'Oh God! Is she hurt?'

'No. Bit shook up. She had only just got off the ferry. Anyway, I said I'd go and pick her up. All the ferries are cancelled, apparently.'

'Is Greg with her?' Denis asked nervously.

'No, he's filming or something, I think.'

'Calais is an eight hour drive at least, Anton. Is this a good idea?'

'That's why I have to leave, sort of, now.' He looked at Denis. 'Do you want to come?'

'It's a long way, Anton. Wouldn't she be better going back to Greg?'

'There's no ferries until the morning at the earliest.' Anton shrugged his shoulders.

Denis didn't want to sit cramped in a car for the best part of the night. 'Are you coming straight back?'

'I thought I might book into a Campanile or something and come back in the morning.'

'Well, I do have a lamb in the oven. I could turn it off, I suppose, but it'll be ruined.'

'I'm quite happy to go on my own, Denis. I am a bit worried about Ginny. She sounded very upset.'

'Of course, Anton. Give me a ring when you've met up with her.'

'Sure.' Anton stood up. He took Denis by the shoulders and gave him a kiss. 'You're a good man, Denis.'

The good man Denis watched his husband walk off to the car. He waved as Anton got into the driver's seat and sped off. Something didn't seem right to Denis. He went back inside and phoned Greg. There was no reply from either his mobile or his landline.

Greg felt the phone vibrate in his pocket. He was sitting in the passenger seat of the black Mercedes, Thornton watching the road as he drove. There had been no explanation about what was going on. Greg was desperate to take his phone out of his pocket. He knew it was Jenny. He fingered the phone trying to slide it out without Thornton seeing. The vibration stopped. Greg was in a panic. He needed to know what had happened to Jenny. They were somewhere on the M2 motorway and had just passed a sign saying that there was a service station five miles further on.

'Can I stop for a loo break?' Greg asked.

Thornton looked at him. 'Have a few drinks on the ferry?' he said jovially.

'Yes,' replied Greg. He hadn't had a drink at all on the return journey; he'd been in too much of a panic.

'Sure,' said Thornton, pulling into the inside lane. 'Might get a coffee, if you fancy it.'

'That'd be good.'

The black Mercedes pulled into the motorway services and parked in a disabled spot next to the main entrance. Thornton put a sign saying 'POLICE' on the windscreen and got out. Greg followed him into the concourse and indicated he was heading for the Gents.

'Coffee or tea?' asked Thornton.

'Oh yeah, coffee, white, no sugar, please.'

They went their separate ways. As soon as Greg was in the corridor to the toilets he whipped out his phone and checked the missed call. It wasn't from Jenny but from Denis. He touched the screen where it said call-back and waited for it to connect.

*

'How many killed?' Anton was driving up the A20 on his way to Calais, talking hands-free on his mobile.

'I don't know; there's no details.'

'Well, find out. I'll be another four hours, at least. I'll meet you in the usual place.' He disconnected the call.

*

'Denis, what's happened, is Jenny alright?' Greg tried to keep the panic from his voice, unsuccessfully.

'I was going to ask you,' said his ex-agent. 'You weren't in Calais today, were you?'

'Yes, but I'm back in England now. Jenny was supposed to come back with me but we lost each other. You heard about the explosion, I assume?'

'Yes. What were you doing there? Anton said Jenny had gone on her own because you were filming.'

'How did Anton know?' Greg was confused.

'I don't know, Jenny must have told him. She rang to say she was in trouble in Calais and couldn't get home. He's gone to pick her up and, presumably, bring her here. He said Jenny was on a booze cruise on her own. He was definite about you not being there.'

Greg was silent. What should he tell Denis? He wanted to tell him the truth. Surely he could trust Denis?

'Greg? Are you still there?'

'Yes, Denis. It's a bit awkward at the moment. I'll tell you when I get home. Jenny's not answering her phone to me. I'm worried, Denis.'

'I think they're staying over in Calais tonight. If I hear from either of them I'll get her to ring you. I wish I knew what was going on.'

'So do I, Denis. So do I.' He disconnected and tried Jenny's number again. It went straight to voicemail and he left a message urging her to call him as soon as possible before heading towards the restaurant area. DI Thornton was sitting on a high stool in the corner of the central cafe area. He waved Greg over to him.

'Your bladder must have been bursting,' he observed. 'Hope your coffee's not cold.

'Yeah, sorry,' said Greg, suddenly realising that his bladder was quite full and he hadn't actually relieved himself yet.

Di Thornton joined Greg at the urinals following their coffees. Greg suspected he was making sure he wasn't contacting anyone. Did he realise he'd been on the phone before instead of going to the loo? Greg was feeling paranoiac.

They got back into the Mercedes and pulled out onto the motorway again.

'Must be quite exciting being an actor,' said the Inspector, indicating and pulling out into the overtaking lane.

'It could be worse.'

'I don't suppose any of that rubbish about you in the paper was true, was it? You know... you and the naked girl in the bedroom.'

'No, it wasn't.'

'Shame, she looked like a nice girl.'

'She was a prostitute, Inspector. I was set-up.'

'Yes, I thought that might be the case. Why didn't you report the incident to the police?'

'Because I wanted it to go away. If I'd reported it, the papers would just have carried on making a story out of nothing.'

DI Thornton pulled back into the middle lane as a BMW shot past them.

'Bet he'd have a shock if he knew I was a copper,' said Thornton.

They stayed in the middle lane, even though the inside lane was empty. Greg knew that proper road use meant being in the inside lane as much as possible unless overtaking. It seemed that didn't matter to the police.

'Was that what your agent advised?' said Thornton.

Greg thought about this, Helen Clarke had been very quiet about the whole thing, really, but then, he hadn't sought her advice, either. If Denis had still been his agent he'd have flapped away for dear life. Helen had just asked him if he was alright after the paper came out, and he'd said he was fine. She didn't seem to want to get involved and Greg didn't mind. 'My agent didn't advise me in any way, Inspector. I made my own decision.'

'Oh I see.' He carried on driving for a few miles. 'I'd have thought it would be the sort of thing you'd want to report, though. I know I would.'

'Well, I didn't.' Greg just wanted to get home and try and sort out what the hell had happened today.

'No pressure from the studio?'

Greg closed his eyes.

'Or somebody else's agent, maybe?'

Greg looked at the DI. 'What do you mean?'

'Do you know an agent called Gene Waters?'

'I've met him,' replied Greg.

'Bit of a shit, really, I thought, wouldn't you say?'

Is that what this was about? Gene Waters giving him trouble again. But why? They'd finished this series. Was he trying to make sure that Greg Driscoll didn't appear in series two? 'I really wouldn't know, Inspector.'

Thornton nodded and carried on driving towards Essex.

***

CHAPTER ELEVEN

The King's Head wasn't very busy. Tallie was behind the bar and she started pulling his pint as he entered the 'Members' Bar'.

'Kronenbourg, I assume?' she mooted.

'Looks like I don't have a choice,' Greg replied with a smirk as Tallie put his pint on the bar in front of him.

'I can throw that away if you'd like to go somewhere else,' she said.

'Don't be like that. You know I wouldn't dream of going somewhere that doesn't have such charming barmaids.'

'I know,' she said taking his money.

He sat by the small window. He'd checked his answerphone and there was still no message from Jenny. DI Thornton had dropped him off outside his house – he knew the address somehow – and demanded that Greg visit him at Chelmsford Police Station the next day. He still wouldn't explain for what reason. Greg promised to be there as soon as he'd finished filming but couldn't say what time. This was not strictly the truth as he wasn't filming the next day; they'd finished filming the series a week earlier. He hoped Thornton didn't know this but something in his look and condescending smile suggested he knew Greg was lying. He should have known that in Thornton's technological world, he would know exactly what Greg's commitments to 'Once In A While' were. He tried Jenny's phone again but it didn't even go to voicemail this time – just no reply.

'Thank fuck you're alright! Is Ginny ok?' Wendy came bursting into the bar, followed by Alan. 'Were you there when it happened?'

Alan brought drinks over and sat down next to where Wendy had parked her backside. 'Did you get to deliver the...you know,' he whispered.

Alan and Wendy had been instrumental in arranging for local people to donate towards the food parcel Greg had taken over to the refugee camp in Calais.

'Yes, Alan. Just.' Greg turned to Wendy. 'As far as I know Ginny's OK. She missed the ferry in the confusion so she's with Denis, I think.'

'You think?' uttered Wendy. 'Don't you know?'

'I haven't heard from her directly but I spoke to Denis and it seems she's being picked up by Anton.' He downed the remains of his current pint and lifted the fresh one to Alan before placing it to his lips.

'I saw it on the news,' said Alan. 'Looked like a hell of a mess. I don't understand why anyone would want to do such a thing.'

'They reckon someone left a bag with a bomb in it right in the middle of the camp,' said Wendy. 'There were kids, Greg, innocent little kids.'

'Did it say where this bag was left?' Greg had a sense of foreboding creeping over him.

'Not really. It must have near some trees, I think, because loads of trees caught fire which made the whole thing even worse. Someone was filming it. It's as if they knew something was going to happen, if you ask me.'

'Someone wanting to scare off the migrants, I suppose,' said Alan.

'They're refugees! There's a difference.' Wendy was quite vehement.

Greg was quiet. He hadn't seen a bag or anything where he'd left the food parcel but he'd left it near some trees. He could have been within feet of where the bomb was. He thought back over the events of the morning, trying to visualise what was around where he left the rucksack. There were some blankets; maybe the bomb was behind those. There was so much rubbish and debris all over the place you wouldn't notice a rogue bag lying about. DI Thornton's interest was beginning to make sense. Did he suspect Greg had something to do with it? Had someone seen the film Johnny was taking? Seen him being interviewed? No. Thornton wouldn't have dropped him off at home; he'd have taken him straight to the cells. Greg became aware of Wendy and Alan staring at him. 'What?' he said.

'You haven't heard a word we've said, have you?'

'Yes I have. You said they were refugees and not migrants.'

Alan looked at him and shook his head.

'I said I saw Kate Freeman again today. Tried to speak to her but she just ignored me.'

'Don't blame her,' retorted Wendy.

'How did she look?' asked Greg, grateful the subject seemed have moved on from bombs.

'Same as the last time I saw her. Bit of a mess, to be honest.'

'Poor girl,' sighed Greg ignoring Wendy's snorting. 'I wonder where she's staying.'

'Somewhere where she's kept away from normal people, hopefully,' said Wendy finished her glass. 'Another drink?'

'I'll get it,' said Greg.

'No. I may be only a woman but I can buy my own round.' She pushed past the men and went to the bar.

'I think she's 'out in the community' or whatever it's called,' said Alan.

'Kate?'

'Yeah. I think I've seen her around a few times.'

'Perhaps I should find out where she is, go and see her or something.'

'Don't be so fucking stupid,' Wendy slammed Greg's pint down in front of him. 'Have you forgotten what she accused you of?'

'No, Wendy, I haven't. She was a very confused person back then.'

Wendy sat down. 'You must enjoy it – causing trouble for yourself. Let me know when you're going to go and see her. I'll let the press know. You haven't been in the papers for a week or two.'

*

Greg Driscoll was anxious as he sat in his chair nursing a late-night whisky. He was thinking over what Wendy and Alan had said in the pub. He started shivering as he thought about how close he had come to death.

The outside light in his back yard coming on made him jump. He went over to the window but could see no-one. Either someone had a new cat that was making his yard its territory or there was a fox on the scene. He went through to the kitchen and opened the back door. 'Hello? Anybody there?'

The sound of a slamming gate came from the bottom of the small garden. Greg jumped again. His nerves were a bit raw, even the Scotch wasn't calming him. He went over to the gate and looked out down the path. He could see no-one. It must have been the wind. He closed the gate and secured it with its bolt before going back to re-fill his whisky glass.

*

'Finished filming early, then?' DI Thornton sat behind his desk in his office at the Police Station in Chelmsford.

Greg sat down opposite. 'I didn't have any filming today, Inspector, but I expect you knew that.' He'd decided to come clean with Thornton. There had been no contact from Jenny and he was worried about her. Denis had told him that Anton had met up with her and they were due to be in Bourrouillan later that day. Greg wanted to join them as soon as he'd finished with the police. Surely he hadn't committed any crime by trying to feed some poor refugees. Once he'd explained that, he was convinced that Thornton would let him go and he'd be able to meet up with Jenny. He wasn't going to tell him about her involvement and would make him believe that this was a solo humanitarian mission of his own devising.

DI Thornton was writing notes on a pad in front of him. He stopped and looked up at Greg, his chin resting in his left hand. 'So, Mr Driscoll, tell me again. Why were you really in Calais, yesterday?' He stared deep into Greg's eyes.

Greg looked away. 'I was feeding some refugees,' he muttered.

'And what were you feeding the migrants with?'

'Why can't you call them refugees?' Greg looked up.

'Because we don't know whether they are or not, yet, until they've filled in an official application. What were you feeding them?'

'My rucksack contained a food parcel collected from people in Maldon who wanted to help them.' Thornton was making notes again. 'Anything else in the rucksack?' he said without looking up.

'A few blankets and some clothes for the little ones.'

'Was there any time you left your rucksack unattended, Mr Driscoll?'

'No, Inspector. I know what you're trying to imply but there is no way that a bomb could have been placed in that bag.'

DI Thornton looked up puzzled. 'Who said anything about a bomb?

Greg sighed. 'I heard that they thought a bomb in a bag left in the camp was the cause of the explosion. There was no bomb in my bag and there was no bag in the vicinity where I left it. I can only think the bomb must have been hidden somewhere I couldn't see it or I'd have warned people.'

'Would you? You seem to know a lot about this bomb.'

'Well, that's what you want to talk about, isn't it?' Greg was confused now.

'Not really. Did you meet up with anyone once you arrived in Calais?'

'No.'

'Not your agent's boyfriend?'

'I said no.' Greg couldn't work out where this was going.

'Did you buy any duty-free?'

'You know you can't buy duty-free within Europe.' Greg folded his arms, sitting back in the hard chair.

'So you wouldn't have had a duty-free carrier bag in your rucksack.'

'I said no.'

Thornton pushed an iPad across the table with a photo displayed on the screen. Greg peered at an image of burnt trees and the remains of makeshift shelters still smouldering. In the foreground of the picture was a bent and crumpled metal frame on which was hanging shreds of blue canvas, broken and torn metal cans strewn about it. Greg, with difficulty, just about recognised what was left of his rucksack. Thornton came round to Greg's side of the desk and pointed to a piece of white plastic lying half attached to the metal frame. He moved two fingers sideways and the image expanded, showing an orange letter 't' imprinted on the plastic. 'A duty-free carrier bag, I would say,' he said.

'Could be anything,' said Greg.

'No, it's a duty-free carrier bag. Forensics have done their job, Mr Driscoll.'

Greg didn't know what to say. He could see that it looked as though the explosion could have originated from the rucksack or very near it but he knew there was only clothing and food in it. He looked up at Thornton, who just stared back at him, eyebrows raised waiting for a response.

'I didn't take a bomb into that camp, Inspector. You can't really believe that.'

'Can't I? You say there was no bag where you put your rucksack and yet the evidence says something rather different.'

Greg sat there, scared and nonplussed.

Thornton sat down behind his desk again. 'Now. You're right I don't think you *knew* that you took a bomb in there but it's almost certain that the bomb was in your rucksack.'

'It can't have been!' Greg was exasperated.

Thornton was at his notes again. 'Indigenous?' he said. 'Still deny any knowledge?'

'What?'

'Autochtone?'

'I don't understand what you're talking about.' Greg was aware of his voice getting higher as his throat started to tighten.

'Virginia Hoffman. Have you heard from her yet?'

'No, I haven't but she's safe, I believe.'

''Autochtone', and its English friend 'Indigenous', are right-wing organisations opposed to any form of immigration, Mr Driscoll. Are you sure you've never heard of them?'

'Never.'

'And yet you've intimately known one of their chief officers for years, you told me yesterday.' Thornton looked hard at Greg, He was either a better actor than Thornton thought or he was completely in the dark about what he was talking about. 'Virginia Hoffman is a leading member of a group called 'Indegenen Volker', a right-wing group from Germany. I believe Fraulein Hoffman has been residing with you for the last few months and yet you say you've never heard of any of these groups. You know, I find that rather hard to believe.'

'Ginny's not a member of any of these groups, Inspector.'

Thornton was leaning close to Greg, his elbows on the table. 'I'm afraid she is, Mr Driscoll.

'It must be a different Virginia Hoffman.'

Thornton looked sceptical.

'I'd have known!' Greg was indignant. What was Thornton talking about?

'I suspect you would know, Mr Driscoll. That's why I find it hard to believe you don't.'

Greg sat quietly. This was serious. What was he to say? Tell the truth about Jenny? Who she was? Why did she choose a name that belonged to a terrorist? She couldn't have known.

'Well, Mr Driscoll?' Thornton smiled.

'Look,' said Greg. 'The woman who has been living with me in Maldon and who went to France with me yesterday is not your Virginia Hoffman.'

'That's what it says on her passport.'

'Yes...it's just...' Greg didn't know how to explain.

'Just what, sir?'

'Her name's Jenny Gulliver.'

Thornton looked surprised momentarily. He wasn't expecting this. 'Travelling on a false passport, then?'

'No. Well, no. She wasn't. It's her passport. She had to change her identity. It appears she chose the wrong name.'

'I think you'd better explain.'

'It's a long story.'

'Will you come to an interview room? I'd like to record this epic. I'll get some coffee. White, no sugar, isn't it?'

A constable led Greg to an interview room and Thornton disappeared for about half an hour.

*

'So let me get this straight, Mr Driscoll.' They were sitting in an interview room with a young policeman standing guard at the door, presumably in case Greg made a run for it. DI Thornton was trying to get his head round what Greg had just told him. 'You met this woman, by chance, who told you she was the same person who had died twenty years earlier?'

'I recognised her as such.'

'Did anyone else recognise her as such?'

'No-one in Maldon knew her.'

'What about your agent? He must have recognised her when she went over to France.'

'Yes, he did but...'

Thornton looked over the rim of his coffee mug and raised his eyebrows, a habit that was beginning to irritate Greg. 'But?'

'Well, he'd never met her before, when she was alive...before.' Greg was confusing himself. He wished Jenny was here to explain, although she wouldn't be happy that he was telling the policeman her story. She wanted anonymity now. She'd been through enough. Greg was letting her down.

'Denis Young was her agent, you said.'

'Yes, but he'd only just taken her on for that job, at short notice. They'd never actually met.'

'Unusual.' Thornton swigged back his coffee and poured himself another from a glass jug. 'Is there actually anyone, apart from you, who could verify her identity?'

'The identity doesn't need verifying. She is Jenny Gulliver.'

'I'm afraid I can't take your word for that, Mr Driscoll. I don't know if you're aware but you are in serious trouble here. It's only because of me you're not locked up awaiting trial for terrorist offences. If you refuse to co-operate with me I shall make sure that is exactly what happens to you. Would you like to spend your foreseeable future in a prison, Mr Driscoll?'

'But you've got it all wrong,' yelled Greg. The constable at the door stood to attention.

Thornton stood up and walked over to the young man and spoke quietly in his ear. He was getting fed-up with this actor. He had to regain his composure or he'd end up shaking him. The man must be stupid. Thornton was convinced that Driscoll didn't know what he was doing when he took the rucksack into the camp. He had no form; there was nothing to show he mixed with those sorts of people – except for the Hoffman woman. He'd been in trouble before, his record showed, but he'd always been just a patsy, unwittingly involved. The story about this Jenny Gulliver coming back to life just didn't fit. He'd checked Driscoll's file and the demise of this girl was in there. Jenny Gulliver was definitely dead. Why was he trying to convince him she was the Hoffman woman? There was no point in shouting at Driscoll. He'd probably just burst into tears – he looked close to it now. Thornton stood with his back to Greg for a full minute before he spoke again, calmly.

'If I were a stupid man then I might be convinced by you resurrection story, Mr Driscoll, but I'm not a stupid man and I don't believe you are either.' He turned round and walked slowly back to the desk. 'If you can convince me that the woman you've been living with is the same

Jenny Gulliver who was confirmed dead by the Coroner in 1993, then I'll just have to accept that I'm not the genius I think I am. How do you think you can do that?'

Greg was silent. He'd been thinking. He knew Jenny was Jenny. They'd been intimate; they'd talked about things that only they could have known. She looked like Jenny. Even though Wendy and Denis had both doubted that she could suddenly re-appear after twenty years, they hadn't known her. He'd had his doubts himself at first but you can't deny what's in front of you. She was definitely Jenny. But how could he convince this Inspector?

Thornton leaned over the desk. 'What do you think I should do?' he said.

'Believe me?' tried Greg.

'Against all the evidence. That's not how we work. You're telling me that a girl that you yourself saw die in your arms has miraculously come to life and you're expecting me to believe you?'

'I didn't see her die,' muttered Greg.

'But you were there.'

'Not when she died.'

'Did you go to the funeral?'

'No.'

'Why not?'

'I don't know. I was too upset. I felt guilty. I felt it was my fault.'

'So when she returns, all that guilt is absolved?'

'No...well...I suppose so.'

'So you wanted this woman to be Jenny against all the odds?'

'No! She was...she is Jenny.'

Di Thornton shouted over to the young officer by the door. 'Go and get us some fresh coffee, will you? Now.' The constable went through the door, thankful to leave the room. He thought this Driscoll bloke was either lying cleverly or else was completely off his head. He couldn't understand why the Inspector was wasting his time with him.

The Inspector sat down at the desk and took out a folder from his briefcase. 'Virginia Hoffman doesn't exist, Mr Driscoll.'

'That's what I've been telling you.'

'It's a false name used by a German woman called Gerta Roth – that's probably not the name she was born with either – she's what Arthur Conan-Doyle would have called a master – or mistress – of disguise. You've heard of Arthur Conan-Doyle?'

'Of course.'

'Fiction, Mr Driscoll. That was what he was good at. This is fiction, all this Jenny Gulliver, Virginia Hoffman, Gerta Roth. Except this person is not fictional, she exists and is very dangerous. She is very clever, though, as she seems to have managed to convince you she's your dead girlfriend from twenty years ago.'

'She's not dead.'

'Oh she is, I'm afraid. We have proof of that. What we don't have proof of is her resurrection.'

There was a knock at the door and a female constable came in with the coffee and two clean mugs on a tray. She placed the used mugs on the tray and smiled at Greg.

'He'll give you his autograph later, Julie,' said Thornton dismissing her with a wave of his hand. 'Nice girl, Julie. Watches too much television.' He poured fresh coffee into the mugs, added milk and placed a mug in front of Greg.

Greg looked at it but didn't touch it. He didn't know what to say, what to think, what to do. He looked up at Thornton. 'If your story is true, which it isn't, why would this German terrorist pick on me; live with me for months and become friends with my friends? What could any of that do to help her cause? None of the people she's been mixing with find racist views anything other than intolerable.'

200

'That's what I've been trying to work out. At first I thought it might be about publicity, then I worked out a connection. Anton DuBois.'

'Anton?'

'Tell me,' said Thornton. 'Is your agent the sort of person you would expect to retire to an obscure part of rural France?'

'Are you accusing Denis now?'

'No, Mr Driscoll. It's just that Anton Dubois, born in France but spent most of his life in the UK, is a member of a group called 'France pour le Francais' – France for the French – and, yes, it's affiliated to the other right-wing groups across Europe. None of these groups is illegal, so there is nothing we can do about them until we catch them breaking the law. If these groups have arranged this bombing in Calais – and if we can prove it – we can do something about breaking them up.'

Greg was stunned. He had never been particularly fond of Anton and he had taken a particular interest in Jenny as soon as she arrived in France that first time. He'd also made racist remarks when they went for the meal in Estang. But, no. Denis would know if there was something going on, wouldn't he? Was Denis involved in it too? He wouldn't believe it. Not Denis. Not Jenny. No. This Inspector had got it all wrong.

DI Thornton was going through the folder on his desk. He looked at Greg. 'Han Koolhaven,' he said.

'What?'

'Still in touch?'

'Han? No. I haven't seen him for years.'

'Hmm! Presumably he had seen this Jenny Gulliver when she was alive. He employed her didn't she?'

Greg could see what Thornton was getting at. 'I don't have his number anymore, before you ask me to get in touch.'

'Oh, but we do. Technology. I just wondered whether you'd like to invite him down to your ex-agent's house so he could meet up with his reincarnated employee.'

Greg sat silently.

'Or, of course, we could start legal proceedings against you.' Thornton smiled.

***

CHAPTER TWELVE

Greg Driscoll looked out of the window at the clouds below him. They looked like his brain felt at the moment – woolly and drifting.

DI Thornton had phoned Han Koolhaven's number in Cuijk and passed the handset to Greg. He'd had no choice, as Han answered, but to talk to him.

'Greg! How are you? I was only saying to Ilse the other day that we ought to see you again. It's been too long.' Han sounded genuinely pleased to hear from him.

'Well, that's sort of why I was ringing.' Greg had looked at Thornton, who'd smiled encouragingly. Greg hadn't felt encouraged, he'd felt sick. 'I don't know if you knew but Denis has retired to the South of France – oh and he got married, to a man, obviously – and we were wondering whether it would be too far for you to come and spend a weekend.'

'Sounds a great idea. We could drive there. When were you thinking?'

'Um...this weekend?' Greg heard Han shout something in Dutch, presumably to his partner Ilse. 'You're on,' he said as he came back on the phone.

Greg had given Han Denis' address and had arranged to see them there on Friday evening. Thornton had arranged

Greg's flight to Biarritz and they were to be accompanied by a young Detective Sergeant who'd been detailed to 'keep an eye' on Greg. DS George Wilde was sitting next to Greg reading a book. He hadn't spoken to Greg during the flight and said nothing more than pleasantries before they'd taken off. George Wilde did not want this job. He didn't join the force to be a babysitter. On top of that he was extremely hot. Why they had to go to the South of France in the middle of a heatwave, he couldn't fathom. He couldn't fathom why the South of France was having a heatwave anyway – it was September, for God's sake! DI Thornton was sitting on the other side of Wilde, also reading. The two policemen were booked into a hotel in Nogaro and Greg was to report to them at regular intervals, especially any reaction Han gave on meeting the woman pretending to be Jenny Gulliver. Greg felt like some sort of captive fugitive. Needless to say, Denis Young had not been over-pleased when Greg had told him he'd invited Han and Ilse to his house without even asking him. Greg was under strict instructions not to tell Denis why he'd arranged the rendezvous – nor was he to tell Han. He'd told Denis not to mention to Jenny or Anton that Han was visiting, who had protested that there were no secrets between him and Anton – something that, if Thornton was right, was a very worrying situation. Either Denis knew about this right-wing group his husband belonged to or Anton was indeed keeping secrets from Denis. If Denis did know, then he knew the sort of things the group got up to. Eventually, Greg had managed to persuade Denis to keep the secret and not risk spoiling Jenny's surprise. He felt he was betraying Jenny and Denis and Han. He hoped, more than anything else, that Han would see Jenny and know immediately who she was. He envisioned Jenny rushing up to him and hugging him, although he couldn't be sure the meeting would be one she'd want. After all, the last time she'd seen him, she'd ended up being imprisoned in a cellar for the next ten years.

Greg looked at the two policemen, still engrossed in their books. Greg didn't mind; he didn't want to talk to anyone. The speaker announced that they making their approach into Biarritz and Thornton put his book into his briefcase. Wilde put the table up into the seat in front of him, transferring his book to his lap, without taking his eyes off the page. Throughout the drive from Biarritz to Bourrouillan, DS Wilde still spoke not a word. Thornton was driving with Greg sitting in the front passenger seat and Wilde in the back, no longer reading, just staring straight ahead. Greg turned round to him.

'Are you always this quiet?' he said.

'I don't like small talk, sir,' replied the recalcitrant policeman.

'Shall we discuss something profound, then?'

'No.'

The two hour journey to Denis' house seemed interminable to Greg. Thornton was passive, staring at the road ahead. The little conversation they did have was, as DS Wilde had observed, nothing but small talk. Greg had nothing to do but worry as they sped through the avenues of beech trees. He worried about seeing Han and Ilse; he worried about Denis; he worried about Anton and whether he really was a member of a racist group and how that would alter the way he spoke to him. Most of all he worried about Jenny. DI Thornton had put doubt in his mind. He was still convinced the woman he was about to see was Jenny Gulliver. She had to be. He didn't know what a German terrorist was supposed to look like but no-one would cast Jenny Gulliver in that role. Besides, they'd been living with each other for months and it had been everything Greg had dreamed of – beyond his dreams, in fact.

The car pulled up in Denis' drive and Jenny came running out to meet Greg, hugging him, tears in her eyes. DI Thornton watched them closely as he drove off towards Nogaro.

'Who was that?' asked Jenny.

'I met some chaps from Chelmsford who are staying a little way away, they said they'd give me a lift from the airport so I rang Denis and put him off picking me up. Thought it was easier.'

'Really? That was lucky,' she said with a hint of suspicion in her voice.

Denis was standing by the front door wearing shorts that were just a little too short and a little too tight. Greg waved and wandered over to him, Jenny clinging to his arm.

'Alright?' asked Denis, coldly.

'Fine, thanks.' replied Greg.

Denis went inside.

'Everything OK, Greg?' asked Jenny.

'Yes, I think he wanted to pick me up at the airport. Anyway, how are you? Why didn't you answer your phone?'

'I lost it. There was such confusion after the explosion. They're saying it's a bomb, you know.'

'Yes, I heard. Couldn't you have phoned me on Denis' phone, or Anton's?'

'I only arrived here this morning and Denis said you were on your way. I was so pleased. I didn't think it was worth phoning you.'

'Oh, thanks.'

'Greg, I'm really sorry. I've been in a bit of a state, to be honest. You could have been killed and it would be all my fault. Anton's been so good to me. All that kerfuffle at Calais, it just reminded me of being back in Germany again.' Tears were starting to flow.

'Why did it remind you of Germany?' Greg's feelings for Jenny were different somehow. Had Thornton corrupted him? He felt suspicious of everything she was saying.

'I don't know; the stress I suppose,' she said through the sobs. She put her arms round him and pulled him close to her. 'I feel better now you're here.' She kissed his lips. 'Shall we go to bed?'

'It's a bit early. I think we should talk to Denis first and maybe have some dinner?'

He went through to the kitchen where Denis was fussing over a large cooking pot. Greg put his arm round his old friend. 'Thanks, Denis,' he said.

'I don't know what's going on, Greg,' he said, crushing some spices a little too violently with a mortar and pestle, 'and I'm not sure I really want to.' He turned to face Greg. 'I just hope you're not in trouble.'

'Of course not! You know me.'

'Yes I do, Greg, that's what worries me. Why did you invite Han here?'

'Shh!' Greg put his finger to his lips and looked out of the window. Jenny and Anton were sitting by the pool. 'Do you believe that girl out there is Jenny Gulliver?'

Denis looked at Greg. 'You told me she was. Are you having doubts now?'

'I don't think so. It's just that nobody who's met her since she came back had actually met her before.'

'But Han Koolhaven had?'

'Yes.'

'And what's brought this change of mind?'

Greg couldn't tell Denis. He couldn't suggest that his husband might be a terrorist or that he was under suspicion by the police of being involved in leaving a bomb in the camp in Calais. 'I thought it would be nice to see Han and Ilse, that's all.'

Denis grunted and went back to his cooking.

Jenny and Anton were swimming in the pool. She was wearing a small bikini and, Greg had to admit, looked very alluring. What he wanted, more than anything, was for Han to recognise her as Jenny Gulliver, prove Thornton wrong, and go back to the life they were happily living a week before.

The sound of crunching gravel heralded the arrival of Han and Ilse. Greg rushed out to meet them. 'Han, Good to see you,' he said. He gave Ilse a kiss on the cheek. 'And you, of course, Ilse. You're looking great. I can't believe it's so long since I saw you both.'

'It's our fault,' said Ilse. 'We've been so busy but we should have made time to see our friends.'

'We're following your latest series, Greg. It's very good. What's that Trudie Carling like?' Ilse gave Han a playful punch.

'She's fine,' said Greg. 'Look...um...I have a friend here with me but I don't want to introduce you by name, if that's alright? It's a bit complicated.'

Han looked at Ilse. 'How intriguing.'

Greg led them into Denis' kitchen, who flapped and told them his kitchen was such a mess, they shouldn't have come in here, before wiping his hands, kissing Ilse and shaking Han's hand. Greg was looking through the window. Jenny and Anton were deep in discussion. They were sitting at the side of the pool, their feet in the water. Jenny had draped a sarong around her to shield her from the hot sun, whilst Anton was just deepening the shade of his already tanned body. Han joined Greg by the window and looked at the two figures by the pool.

'Which is the mysterious one, as if I didn't know?' He nudged Greg's arm.

'Yes, it's the female. Do you know her?' Greg held his breath.

Han peered through the glass. 'Don't recognise her, should I?'

Greg rapped on the window pane. Jenny looked up and beckoned him to join them. He led the Dutch contingent through the patio doors and down by the pool.

'Hello,' said Jenny. 'I didn't know we had company.'

Greg indicated Han and Ilse. 'They're friends of ours who are holidaying nearby, so Denis said they should come over for dinner. Isn't that great?' He looked up at Han, hoping he would back him up.

'He didn't tell me. Anton Dubois, by the way, Denis' husband.' He held out his hand.

'Nice to meet you,' Ilse kissed his cheeks.

'And this is Virginia,' said Han. He was finding it awkward not to introduce Han and Ilse properly.

'Nice to meet you,' said Han, kissing her. 'Greg kept you quiet.' He smiled, feeling terribly uncomfortable and confused.

'He's been very busy,' she said.

'Are you an actress?' asked Ilse.

'No, well, not anymore.'

Greg grabbed hold of Han. 'Give us a hand with some drinks, mate,' he said pulling him back up to the house.

'She seems nice, Greg.' he said as they strolled up by the pool.

'Do you not recognise her?'

Han looked back at the group of people. 'Should I?'

They had reached what used to be a garage but now housed several crates of wines and spirits. 'Do you remember Jenny Gulliver?'

Han looked incredulously at his friend. 'Are you joking? How could I forget her?'

'Do you think Virginia looks a bit like her?'

Han stepped outside and looked across the pool at Ginny. 'Not really,' he said coming back into the cool of the garage. 'Why?'

Greg sat down on some beer crates stacked by the wall. He didn't want to answer. Han had said what he feared he would. He didn't recognise her. Ever since DI Thornton had put the idea in his head that Virginia Hoffman was not Jenny Gulliver, he'd started viewing her differently. He had so wanted Han to confirm what he wanted to believe but, in truth, was not surprised he hadn't. Ginny hadn't recognised Han either. Those two people had never met before.

'What's going on, Greg?' Han towered over him. Greg looked up, his eyes were red and watery.

'I don't know, Han,' he replied.

Han sat next to him on the beer crates and Greg told him the story of Jenny turning up in Maldon; how she knew so much about him; how she'd convinced him she was Jenny Gulliver back from the dead.

'Didn't you check her story?'

Greg shook his head. 'I suppose I wanted to believe her.'

'So what's made you change your mind? I could be wrong, you know.'

'You're not wrong, Han. That is not Jenny Gulliver out there. You'd have known. She'd have known you. Anyway, there's more. Did you hear about that explosion in Calais?'

'It was all over the news, yes. Something about immigrants, wasn't it?'

'Refugees, yes.' Greg explained as much as he thought DI Thornton would let him about events leading up to the explosion. Han sat open-mouthed.

'So did you...you know...deliver the bomb?'

'No. I don't think. Not knowingly, anyway. I thought I was taking in a food parcel.'

'Who else knows?'

'Well, apart from Jenny – Ginny, I can't call her Jenny now – Anton presumably.'

'Denis?'

'I don't think so. I don't think he knows about his husband's extra-curricular activities.'

'And I thought I was coming over for a relaxing weekend. Thanks, mate.'

Greg took hold of Han's arm. 'I'm sorry. I couldn't tell you. You're the only person I know who'd seen Jenny when she was...' Greg paused, reality hitting him, 'When she was alive. I so wanted that person to be her Han. I still miss Jenny so much.' His eyes were weeping again.

'What do we do now?' said Han. 'She's going to want to know who I am. Do I pretend to be someone else?'

Greg sniffed in a deep breath. 'She didn't recognise you; Jenny would have done. Introduce yourself, I want to see how she reacts.'

Anton poked his head round the door. 'Come on, we're dying of thirst out here.'

Greg stood up quickly. 'Sorry, Anton,' he said. 'We've been catching up.' He grabbed a couple of bottles of wine and Han picked up some glasses as Anton led them back to the party.

'I've been chatting to Ilse,' said Virginia. Greg's heart sank. What had Ilse said? 'You didn't tell me you'd helped set up their bar in Holland. We should go and visit.' She took his hand and laid her head against his leg. Greg felt revulsion spread through him. This girl he'd thought he'd been in love with for months, now held nothing for him but disgust.

'You'd be welcome anytime, Virginia. Our ignorant friend didn't introduce us, did he? Han Koolhaven.'

'Hi,' said Virginia. Suddenly her face changed. Was it a look of panic? 'Nice to meet you.' She glared at Greg. 'Please excuse me. I must go to the loo.' She stood up and walked rapidly towards the house.

'I'd go after her, if I were you,' whispered Han in Greg's ear. He excused himself and followed his soon to be ex-girlfriend. He went up to their bedroom to discover Virginia hurriedly packing a bag.

'What are you doing?' Greg stood by the door.

She turned to him, her face red and angry. 'Why the fuck didn't you tell me!' she yelled.

'I don't know. Thought it would be a surprise.'

'Too fucking right it's a surprise. What are you trying to do?' She looked scared. Greg hadn't seen her like this before.

'You didn't recognise him, did you?' he said.

'Of course I didn't, he's changed. He used to have long hair.'

'He knew you,' Greg lied.

Virginia stopped packing. 'Did he?' she said.

'Yep.'

'What did he say?'

Greg was starting to panic. He couldn't let her leave; he had to find some way of convincing her to stay. What would Thornton say if he just let her go? 'He said, you reminded him of Jenny.' Greg's eyes filled as he mentioned her name.

'What did you say?'

'I sort of told him about what happened to you. That's why we were so long. I didn't know what else to do.'

Virginia Hoffman looked at him, not sure whether to believe him or not. She needed to talk to Anton; let him know who Han was and Jenny's connection to him. 'I don't really want to sit and have dinner with him, Greg. Can't you say I've been taken ill, or something?' She came towards him and stroked his arm. 'I suppose I knew this day would come when my past caught up with me. I think I should just leave, Greg. It's not fair on you putting up with this pretence.'

'What pretence?'

'Pretending I'm not Jenny Gulliver because I'm not.'

Greg's pulse soared.

'Not anymore. Jenny Gulliver died in Germany when I changed my name. I can't just go back to being her.'

Greg held her close. It felt very uncomfortable. He had no tender feeling towards her now.

'Perhaps we should just tell the truth. Han won't give you away and Denis and Anton know the facts anyway, don't they? Come down and eat with us, please. Don't run away from me.' He looked at her half-packed bag on the bed.

Virginia Hoffman pulled Greg's face to hers and kissed him passionately. 'Do you trust me?' she asked.

Greg summoned up all his acting ability and answered in the affirmative.

'Do you love me,' she said. She was looking deep into his eyes. He returned her passionate kiss.

'Let's go downstairs,' he said.

'Greg, I don't want to talk about what's happened to me in the past. All that's over and done with now. And, if you can, please call me Ginny tonight.'

Greg felt relieved. He didn't want to call her Jenny. She wasn't Jenny. He didn't really want to talk to her at all but he knew he had to. He had to keep playing his part until Thornton did whatever he had to do to get an arrest. He waited while she dressed and then, taking a tight hold of her hand, led her down to where Denis was preparing to serve the meal.

*

The evening was strained, even though no-one mentioned Ginny's story – her past. Han didn't even acknowledge that he'd worked with Jenny. Denis kept looking at Greg and frowning. He obviously felt awkward, not knowing how to react. Ilsa and Anton were the only ones who seemed oblivious to the actual situation the others were in and the two of them were the life and soul of the party, the other four joining in with some effort.

Greg made sure that Ginny could spend no time alone with Anton. He didn't want her to let him know about Han. He knew she must be suspicious. If she wasn't Jenny Gulliver – as Greg was now sure she wasn't – and if she was working out of some right-wing organisation, she must know that both she and Anton were in danger. Greg didn't want him warned.

They adjourned to the poolside for coffee and more drinks. It was a warm evening, the moon high and stars spread across the open sky like fairy lights. It should have been idyllic but to Greg it was just miserable.

Anton agreed to help Denis make the coffee, Greg hoping Denis would not confide in his husband, and Greg left Ginny briefly with Han and Ilse while he went off to the toilet. Inside the house, Greg checked on Denis and Anton. They were busy preparing the coffee, Anton still jovial and Denis fussing over which cups to use. Greg stood in the living room, took out his phone and punched in the number DI Thornton had given him.

*

Virginia Hoffman was agitated. Han noticed she kept looking over towards the kitchen. The conversation had become stilted, in spite of Ilse's valiant attempt to engage her. Suddenly Virginia made a decision and stood up.

'Must go to the loo again, time of the month,' she said brazenly. She picked up her bag and hurried towards the house. Arriving at the glass patio doors, she caught sight of Greg talking animatedly into his phone. She turned left and went round the barn walking rapidly towards the road. She wasn't sure where she was going; she just knew she had to get out - and now. It was getting dark, despite the full moon, and she was disoriented. She took out her phone and tried to find some sort of satellite navigation but there was no signal away from the house. She turned right and started down the road in the direction, she hoped, of Nogaro. There were two large wine silos by the side of the road and the sight of them relaxed her slightly. She knew they passed these silos on the way to Nogaro – she was on the right road. The farmer's car was parked, as usual, between the two silos and it crossed her mind to steal it. It was unlikely to be locked; no-one bothered in this low-crime rural location and she knew how to hot-wire a car as old as this one. As she stepped towards it, something made her pause. Something wasn't right. This wasn't the usual car she'd seen there before. She stood for a moment looking at it. The driver's door opened abruptly and a dark figure stepped out.

'Fraulein Hoffman?' the figure inquired.

Virginia didn't wait to find out who it was that knew her name or what they wanted but turned and ran. The dark figure followed. She ran straight into the maize field on the other side of the road. The maize was high, about six feet tall, and she ran, battling against the stalks. She could hear someone following her and she zig-zagged, turning right, then left, going deep into the vegetation. Pausing for breath, she listened. She couldn't hear her pursuer. Where was he? She stayed still, listening but heard nothing other than the breeze rattling the cobs of corn above her head. She sat amongst the stalks, breathing deeply, trying to lower her heart-rate.

Outside the maize fields, the moon threw shadows from the silos across the road. Detective Inspector Thornton was joined by a breathless contingent of Greg, Han and Anton who had raced from the house as soon as Virginia's disappearance had been noticed.

'Monsieur Dubois.' It was statement rather than a greeting or question from Thornton.

'Hallo, Thornton,' replied Anton.

Greg stared at them 'Do you two know each other?' he said.

'I'll explain later, if the Inspector will let me,' said Anton.

Two of the local gendarmerie were standing at the edge of the field, powerful torches turned on the maize.

'You'd better go and find DS Wilde,' instructed Thornton. 'He'll be lost in there by now.'

The French officers walked stealthily into the field.

'What's going on?' Greg asked the DI. 'How come you're here and not in Nogaro?'

'Trust is something I do not find easy, Mr Driscoll, fortunately, in this case. If I'd left this to you, Virginia Hoffman would be far away by now. It was pretty obvious she would leave at the first suspicion of her cover being blown, so Wilde and I sat here in our car, waiting for you to let us know she'd gone.'

'And where is she now?' The voice came from behind Greg.

'Han Koolhaven, I presume,' Thornton held out his hand to Han before turning back to answer Greg. 'She's in that field of corn.

'Oh, great. You let her go,' said Greg.

'She won't get far, According to the local bobbies, there's an impenetrable hedge on the other side of the field. If the wild boars don't get her, she'll have to come out onto this road.'

Greg doubted the confidence of this Inspector. Ginny was too smart to walk into the hands of the law, he knew that. He was about to tell the DI what he thought when a shot rang out from the field, followed by two more and some shrieking sounds.

'What the...' Thornton rushed to the edge of the crop and yelled, 'what's going on?'

A rustling noise was approaching rapidly, the shrieking getting louder. The maize rippled and shook and a second later a large animal with curled horns charged towards them, blood spurting from its rear. The four men threw themselves to the ground as the boar burst out of the field and on towards them, shrieking and roaring. Another shot rang out and the beast fell. A gendarme, gun drawn, exited the corn, held the gun inches from the boar, fired again and kicked the animal's side. Blood and bits of brain splattered across the road.

'Where's the girl?' asked Thornton, picking himself up and trying to regain some composure.

The gendarme gave a Gallic shrug and, holstering his weapon went back into the field.

'She'll try to get to Nogaro and warn the others, said Anton. 'Perhaps I should get down there first.'

Thornton was thinking about his response when DS Wilde emerged. He had kernels of corn in his hair and his trousers were torn. He stood by the road looking forlorn.

'Wilde,' commanded his superior. 'Take Monsieur Dubois into Nogaro and come back here.'

Wilde trudged towards the car followed by Anton.

'Are you letting him go?' said Greg.

Wilde drove off towards Nogaro.

'Mr Driscoll, there are some things I've neglected to tell you, with good reason, but now is not the time. I think you and Mr Koolhaven should repair to the house and I will meet you there when DS Wilde returns. Coffee would go down well, if you could arrange that, please.'

'What about Virginia? What about Anton? You can't expect me to just...'

'Do as you're told, Driscoll, or I might be forced to do what my superiors suggested and take you into custody.'

Han put his hand on Greg's shoulder. 'Come on, Greg. Best do as we're told.'

Greg shook the hand from him and stormed up to Thornton. The two gendarmes came out of the field and stood next to the Inspector, their guns in their hands. Greg stopped, spun on his heels and headed back up to Denis' house, Han following, racing to catch up.

***

CHAPTER THIRTEEN

Denis was pacing up and down outside the front door whilst Ilse was doing her best to reassure him that everything was OK – even though she grave doubts about that herself. Her previous experience of meeting Greg Driscoll had resulted in people losing their lives. She fervently hoped this was not going to be the case again.

As Greg and Han approached, Denis ran towards them. He looked down the road. 'Where's Anton?' he demanded, his voice pitched high with fear.

'Nogaro,' muttered Greg as he pushed past his ex-agent and Ilse. He walked over to where Denis kept his good whisky and poured himself a very large measure.

'What's going on, Han?' Ilse was finding it hard to disguise her anger.

Han Koolhaven shrugged his shoulders and followed to where Greg stood pouring himself a second glass of Scotch. Denis come over and snatched the bottle from his hand. 'No more until you tell me what's happened to Anton!' he screamed.

'Do you know what Anton does?' Greg stared at Denis.

'What do you mean?'

'Do you know what he does with his little group of friends in Nogaro?'

'I think they play chess or something,' Denis replied.

Greg sat on a kitchen stool, his head in his hands. 'Is that a joke?' he said.

'No, it's not, Greg. What's going on here?' Denis put the bottle back on the table. Greg grabbed it and managed to pour another glassful before Denis wrested the bottle back.

'Your husband,' snapped Greg. 'Your husband plays chess alright, only he plays it with people's lives. He likes to blow up innocent men, women and children just because he doesn't like where they come from.'

Denis swung the bottle in his hand and would have caught Greg round the head had Han not intervened and grasped his arm. The bottle flew across the room, smashing against the wall, malt whisky cascading over the kitchen floor. Greg was standing now, fists clenched, glaring at his old friend.

'Sit down, Greg!' Han took command. 'I don't know what's going on here but fighting is not going to solve anything.'

Greg threw some whisky down his throat and perched back onto the stool. Denis was shaking. Ilse took his arm and led him to a chair by the wall where a wood-burning stove had been lit.

*

'I don't believe it!' Denis was standing, arms folded, listening to DI Thornton's explanation.

'I'm afraid it's true, Mr Young. Monsieur Dubois has been a great help to us over the last eighteen months.'

'Why didn't he tell me?' Denis was whining.

'He couldn't tell anyone. It was too sensitive.'

'Where does Greg fit into all this, though, Inspector?' Han sipped the coffee Ilse had made for everyone.

'That was Virginia Hoffman's idea, evidently. She'd been looking for a patsy in the UK and remembered a story Anton had unwittingly told about one of Mr Young's clients who'd been caught up in a scam before. She researched our friend Mr Driscoll, deciding he was an ideal candidate. He was on TV; he would get a lot of publicity for their campaign without realising what he was doing.' Thornton looked over at Greg who had taken himself off to the patio where he was looking pensively into the swimming pool. 'There's a chain of right-wing groups linking up all over Europe who want to stop all immigration. They don't care who gets killed in the meantime. Their idea is, if they blow up enough foreigners, they'll stop coming and stay in their own countries.'

'Even though the refugee's country is being torn apart by war?' said Ilse. 'It's just a question of which is worse and personally I think I'd risk it here rather than some of those places.'

'I still don't believe Anton would be mixed up in something like that.' Denis was standing by the window looking at Greg.

'The French police recruited your partner when he reported an incident he'd witnessed in a bar down in Nogaro. A group of young men had been verbally abusive to a young Moroccan chap who'd been drinking quietly on his own. They'd chased him out of the bar and beaten him in the street. Monsieur Dubois, sensibly, didn't intervene until they'd gone. He then went to check on the boy, who rejected his assistance and ran away. Your partner went to the local commissariat to report it. Two weeks later they had encouraged him to infiltrate the young men in the bar. They belonged to a group calling themselves "France pour le Francais", an organisation dedicated to kicking out foreigners. He played his part well, apparently, and soon became one of their main spokesmen, liaising with other groups across Europe, which is where he first met Virginia Hoffman. Of course, he was keeping the police informed whenever possible. News came up that there was a possibility of an attack on the camp being set up in Calais and that it might stem from somewhere in the UK, which is where I come in. Unfortunately we didn't get the details of the planned attack until too late. Monsieur Dubois didn't know about it until it had happened. It seems Fraulein Hoffman went off on her own on this one.'

'Dragging Greg along with her and getting him to do her dirty work,' said Han. 'Do you think he knew what he was doing?'

DI Thornton paused before answering. 'I don't believe he did, no.'

'But you knew he was getting involved, however unwittingly. Why didn't you warn him?' Denis was still looking through the window at Greg, who hadn't moved. He was just standing looking into the pool still. Denis turned to Thornton. 'He could have been killed.'

DI Thornton's phone rang and he left the room to answer it.

'Sit down, Denis. I'll get some more coffee,' said Ilse comfortingly. She touched his arm. A tear formed in his eye and Ilse reached up and hugged him round the neck. 'Try not to worry.' she said.

Han took down a bottle of Armagnac from the shelf. 'I think something stronger than coffee may be needed here,' he said.

Ilse looked across at Greg. 'We should get him in.'

Denis unlocked himself from Ilse's embrace. 'I'll go.' He opened the patio door and went to where Greg was contemplating the leaves floating on the surface.

Han poured Ilse a brandy. She smiled at him. 'Do me a favour, Han,' she said. 'If Greg Driscoll ever gets in touch again, find out what he really wants before agreeing to meet up with him.'

Han laughed quietly. 'He does seem to have trouble following him around, doesn't he?'

'What do you think we should do?' Ilse was watching the two men by the pool. They were talking.

Han didn't answer Ilse. He knew she wanted to go home and not get involved but Han's natural instinct was to help. 'Let's see what happens,' was all he said.

Ilse sighed and put her untouched brandy on the table. 'You knew that woman wasn't who Greg said she was, didn't you?' Han nodded. 'Is that why we are here, really, so you could confirm she wasn't this Gulliver woman?' Han nodded again. 'Why didn't you tell me?'

Han took Ilse by the shoulders and kissed the top of her head. 'I didn't know, Ilse. Greg asked me if I recognised her when we went to get the wine before the meal. She was nothing like the Jenny Gulliver I knew.'

'So why did Greg...?'

'He wanted to believe it was her, Ilse.'

The patio door opened and Denis led Greg back into the house. He picked up Ilse's Armagnac and took a swig.

'I suppose you all think I'm stupid as well as gullible,' he said.

'No, Greg. I think you've been duped by a very clever and evil woman,' said Han.

'She's not that clever, is she? She's been caught.' Greg accepted Han's offer of a refill to Ilse's glass.

'I can't believe Anton kept all this secret from me,' moaned Denis. 'I wonder what else he's not told me.'

The awkward silence that followed Denis' statement was interrupted by Thornton storming angrily into the room. 'They've let her go,' he said.

'What do you mean?' asked Greg.

'The bird has flown. Somehow she managed to get through the supposedly impenetrable maize field and is away somewhere. Monsieur Dubois is in Nogaro now with a couple of the Fascists. He's trying to find out where she's gone.'

'Will they know?' said Han.

'Probably not. This group is not very well organised. It seems they were taken by surprise.'

'Is Anton in danger, Inspector,' Denis spoke very quietly.

'He will have all the protection possible, Mr Young.'

'Meaning what?'

'Meaning he'll have all the protection possible. I just hope they haven't discovered that he's working for us. That really would put him in jeopardy.'

'Then stop him working for you.' Denis' voice was raised now. He was starting to shake again.

'I'm afraid that's not possible at the moment but depending on what happens here, I doubt he'll be involved for much longer.'

Denis did not feel at all comforted.

'DS Wilde is coming to pick me up to take me to Nogaro so as to watch the house they're meeting in. I'd like you all to remain here until I contact you.' DI Thornton was punching a number into his phone.

'How long will we have to stay here?' asked Ilse. 'We have a business to run in the Netherlands.'

'I'll get back to you as soon as I can, madam.' He left the room.

Han, Ilse, Greg and Denis sat at the kitchen table in silence, each harbouring their own thoughts.

'I suppose you're all going to blame me,' said Greg, re-filling his glass.

'Well, it's no-one else's fault, is it? You brought that woman here,' muttered Denis.

'I think you'll find Anton sent her to me first, so if anyone's to blame...'

'Don't you blame Anton,' Denis was waving his finger in Greg's direction.

Ilse coughed nervously. It looked like a schoolground spat to her. 'I think you two should calm down. It's no-one's fault, is it? No-one knew what was going on.'

'Anton did,' replied Greg.

'Leave it, Greg!' Han was on his feet, towering over the table.

'I don't know what to do.' Denis was almost in tears.

'Find another bottle,' suggested Greg brusquely.

'Drinking won't solve anything.'

The four of them sat for a long time, not speaking. Greg had been drinking heavily. Dawn was breaking over the lake, the sky crimson red as if angry with the whole situation. Ilse was leaning on the table, her head in her arms, Greg's head kept drooping onto his breast, his breathing heavy. Denis had moved from the table and was back in the armchair next to the stove. Only Han remained alert.

*

It was eight o'clock in the morning when Thornton reappeared. Denis had been pacing for over an hour. Greg was still asleep, head on the table. Ilse had made coffee again and Han was sitting where he had been all night.

The Inspector had entered without knocking. Denis ran up to him. 'Where's Anton?' he demanded.

Thornton turned round to reveal a very tired-looking Anton DuBois. Denis strode over to him, slapped his face and then hugged and kissed him. The two of them held each other and cried openly.

'Has she been found?' asked Han, not getting up.

'Not yet,' replied Thornton. 'She will be. We think we know where she's gone. All the border controls have her details. She won't get far.' Ilse handed him a coffee. 'Thank you,' he said, forcing a smile. Ilse didn't speak and sat next to Han, who took her hand.

Greg lifted his head and scowled in Anton's direction. 'Come back, then,' he muttered.

Anton extricated himself from Denis' grip and crossed to the table, wiping his eyes on his sleeve. 'I'm sorry, Greg. I couldn't tell you. Ginny went ahead with the Calais job without letting us know. The plan was to stop it before anything happened but we just didn't expect her to do it without telling us. She had her own people there. She fucked up, Greg.' He moved towards where Greg was sitting.

'Don't come near me, if you know what's good for you,' he said.

Anton stopped and looked at Han who shrugged his shoulders and offered no comfort. He wasn't prepared to take Anton's side. Anton felt ostracised. He was bitter. He hadn't wanted to get involved in this. All he'd tried to do was help a poor boy who was being beaten up – something he knew all about; he'd had his own share of homophobic abuse in his time. He shouldn't have agreed to help and yet, somehow he felt a thrill at playing the spy. He'd found he was good at it. No-one had suspected him. He hadn't realised that it meant losing friends because of it.

He never liked the woman calling herself Virginia Hoffman. The whole grooming of Greg was horrible and cruel but he hadn't been allowed to stop it. He'd considered confiding in Denis – after all, Greg was his friend – but it had been made clear to him that if he told anyone anything, he would lose all protection. He'd seen how the authorities were prepared to sacrifice people to gain their ends; look at those poor refugees in Calais. Anton felt dirty, despicable, demeaned.

Thornton was on the phone again. He'd moved through to the lounge but they could hear his voice in the kitchen, loud and angry.

'Just pick her up,' he was shouting. 'And don't shoot her!'

He came through to the kitchen. 'They know where she is. You were right, Monsieur Dubois. Somehow she found her way to Estang. The gendarmerie are there and Wilde is currently trying to stop them playing out some big Hollywood ending.' He looked at Denis. 'I need a lift,' he demanded.

'I'll take you,' said Anton.

'You can't!' Denis stood in front of him. 'It's not safe for you.'

'I'm alright to drive.' Han stood up. Ilse shook her head but to no avail. He let go of her hand.

'I'm coming with you.' Greg leapt off his seat and followed them out to Han's car.

***

CHAPTER FOURTEEN

Virginia Hoffman was sitting in the back room of a half-derelict house in the centre of Estang. The house was set back from the road and only the most inquisitive would notice the small camping gas lantern providing the light in the darkened room. There were three men huddled round the light with Virginia.

The house had been bought in its derelict state by one of the men, an Englishman called Colin, who was in the process of renovating the property. He was a builder by profession and was feeling the strain on his self-employed business – a strain he blamed solely on immigration. He had bought the building with a view to letting it out in the hope it would provide a boost to his income and he'd employed some local men to help with the restoration. Two of them, Leo and Valentin, now sat with Virginia Hoffman round the small light.

It had not taken long for them to realise their opinions about immigration were in complete harmony with Colin's, and within a month, Colin had joined the organisation they belonged to which was dedicated to kicking out the foreigners. No-one seemed to mind that Colin himself was a foreigner!

Virginia was cursing; mostly she was angry with herself. She'd let her guard down. Someone must have tipped the police off. Who was it? Greg Driscoll? She thought not: she hoped not. Anton? Surely not. He'd encouraged her idea of pretending to be Jenny Gulliver and duping Greg, hadn't he? Wasn't he the one who'd driven her across the country for meetings with the splinter groups? No, it couldn't have been Anton. Did Greg really think that Jenny Gulliver would want to meet up with the Dutch director again, after all the provisos she'd put in place. Why hadn't he told her? If he was intending to surprise her, he'd certainly succeeded in that. Someone had informed the police; they were waiting for her as if they knew her movements. Someone at Denis' house that night must have told them. Han Koolhaven? Or his little girlfriend. Virginia had taken an instant dislike to her. The Dutch and the Germans hadn't got on since the Second World War and nothing had changed even though they all supposedly belonged to this club called the European Union. She kicked out at a piece of rubble lying by her feet, sending it across the room.

'What are we going to do now?' asked Colin.

Virginia looked at him. What was she doing here with these amateurs? Why had she left Germany and got involved with these small-minded groups? She'd envisaged an International Organisation; a movement where all people were fighting for their own country. She'd wanted to show them how to do it. It was a mistake. She needed to get back to Germany and leave the French and the British to sort their own problems out. They were incompetent. They were not trained to be efficient like the German race.

'I need to return to Germany for a while,' she said.

'And how are you going to do that?' asked Velentin. 'Do you think they will not be looking for you at the borders?'

Virginia sighed. 'Of course they'll be looking for Virginia Hoffman, but it won't be Virginia Hoffman who crosses back into Germany, will it?'

'Anton arranging a false passport?' asked Leo.

'Anton?' Colin was irritably scraping his boot through the dust on the floor, creating clouds by his ankles. 'Can we trust Anton?'

Virginia Hoffman didn't know. She wanted to but she just didn't know. She couldn't take the risk.

There was a commotion at the front of the house and a fourth man ran into the back room.

'Arretez! Il y a des hommes qui arrivent,' he said quietly.

In a well-practised manoeuvre, Virginia threw herself into a small annexe, which would one day be a bathroom

238

and hid herself under an upturned bathtub covered with tarpaulins. The other men picked up their tools from the floor and started sanding and fixing skirting boards to the bare plastered walls. An ordinary day working on the renovation.

DI Thornton, Greg and Han stepped over the rubble bags and into the room.

'Bonjour,' said Thornton without any attempt at disguising his English accent.

'You can speak English,' said Colin, not looking up from his squatting position by the wall.

'We are looking for a German woman,' said Thornton.

'Aren't we all?' said Colin with a leer.

Thornton crossed to Colin and showed him a picture of Virginia on his phone. Colin looked up and shrugged. 'Bit old for me,' he said.

'She's known as Virginia Hoffman or possibly Gerta Roth. She also pretends to be an English woman called Jenny Gulliver.'

Colin stood up stretching out his back. He took the detective's phone and looked at the picture again. 'Never seen her,' he said.

Thornton showed the picture to Leo and Valentin, who both shrugged Gallically.

'Why are you after her?' said Colin. 'Who are you?'

'I'm a police officer from the UK. This woman is wanted for several illegal activities across Europe.'

'Oh dear,' said Colin. 'Well, as I said, I haven't seen her. Mind you, I hardly ever get out of here. Lot of work to do here, as you can see.' He bent down to carry on with fixing the skirting board.

Greg and Han were standing by a gap that was once a doorway. They were looking round the room. It didn't look like a safe house for terrorists but then neither of them had ever seen a safe house for terrorists, outside of a cinema. There was detritus all over the place. Greg stepped over some tools left on the floor and clambered towards the bathroom annexe.

'Be careful,' yelled Colin. It's not safe over there; I'd rather you kept away.'

'Is this your place, sir?' Thornton asked Colin.

'Yes it is. I'm renovating it.'

'Could I take your name?'

'Why?'

'Just a formality. You know what bureaucracy's like.' He took out a notebook and licked his pencil.

Colin smiled. 'Jeremy Thorpe,' he informed the Detective Inspector.

'Like the politician?' queried Thornton.

'I wouldn't know any politicians.' Colin was eyeing Greg as he stood looking into the annexe. 'Can you move away, please,' he said. 'It really is not safe over there. I don't want to be done for harming a member of the British bobbies.'

'I'm just looking around,' replied Greg. 'Is that a problem?'

'Not if you want to kill yourself. There's live electricity very close to your foot.'

Greg looked down. There was a bare wire by his feet. Whether it was live or not, he couldn't tell. He wandered carefully back to Han.

Thornton took a card from his wallet and handed it to Colin. 'Give me a call if you happen to come across this woman, Mr Thorpe.'

'Is there a reward?'

'Not at present, sir. Thanks for your help.' He started to clamber back over the rubble bags. Greg put a hand on his arm. 'Outside,' Thornton ordered.

Greg was agitated. He didn't want to leave. He knew Virginia was there. Han took him by the shoulders and led him through the front of the house.

'She's in there,' he hissed at Thornton as they hit the daylight in the street.

Thornton hurried him away. 'I know,' he said, as soon as they were out of sight. The fourth man, who was pretending to rub down the paintwork on the outside of the house, was watching them as they strolled away.

They went into a cafe round the corner from the building. Han ordered coffees while Thornton took out his iPad and started scrolling.

'Why did you leave? She's in that little room at the back. I saw her bag. It was one I'd bought her.' Greg felt a pang of guilt. He'd lavished quite a few presents on this terrorist. Thornton carried on scrolling. Greg sat quietly as the waitress brought the coffees to the table. As soon as she left, he nudged Thornton. 'Did you hear me?'

'I did, Mr Driscoll.'

'I agree with Greg, here,' Han interrupted. 'Why are we not watching the house? Why aren't you arresting these men?'

'Well, firstly,' said Thornton looking up from his tablet. 'I don't have the jurisdiction; secondly, the only misdemeanour any of them have committed is the English guy calling himself Jeremy Thorpe when his name is Colin Miller.' He held up his iPad and showed a picture of a group of young men waving flags with swastikas on them. In the middle of the picture was the man who'd called himself Jeremy Thorpe. 'He's a member of a far-right group based in the north of England. Being a member of that organisation is not actually a crime for some reason. If I had my way, any extreme group that incites hatred would be illegal but the great European Government that we kow-tow to, seem to think that's against basic human rights.'

'But if he's harbouring a known terrorist, surely that's breaking the law,' said Greg.

'Would that be the same known terrorist that was living with you in Maldon?' Thornton raised his eyebrows.

*

Inside the house, the three men put down their tools again. Colin Miller went to the annexe and lifted the tarps. 'You can come out now.' There was no reply or any sign of movement from underneath the bathtub. He bent down and looked; there was no sign of Virginia Hoffman. 'She's gone!' he shouted to the others.

'Good,' said Valentin. 'Let her go.'

Colin stood, silently thinking. He wasn't sorry to see the back of the German woman himself – he'd never really trusted Germans. They were selfish and arrogant in his opinion. The only trouble was, what sort of mess could she land them all in? Perhaps he needed to return to his homeland for a while, too.

'We haven't done anything against the law, as yet,' said Leo, as if reading Colin's thoughts. 'The Calais job was just her and her friends up north – nothing to do with us. They can't bring us into that.'

Colin had his doubts about that. 'Well, you'd better get on with what I pay you for, then,' he said, picking up his tools.

*

'Why are we just sitting here?' asked Greg for the umpteenth time. They were now on their second cup of coffee. Thornton had spent the whole time scrolling on his iPad, giving no information to the other two. A couple of older men had strolled into the cafe and were now quietly playing chess in a corner. Greg looked at them suspiciously, wondering if they were part of the same lot Anton had told Denis he mixed with. Maybe they'd been sent by the Jeremy Thorpe character to spy on them.

Thornton's mobile buzzed on the table. He picked it up and looked at it. 'Shit!' he said and went back to his iPad. The old men looked up from the board and tutted.

'What was that?' asked Greg reaching for the Inspector's phone.

Thornton slammed his hand on top of Greg's. 'It seems she's gone off again,' he informed Greg.

'Gone off? Where? How?'

Thornton calmly drained his coffee cup and paid the bill at the bar. Greg and Han followed him outside. Once in the sunlight, Thornton grabbed Greg and nearly lifted him off his feet. 'Can you just learn to keep your gob shut?' he said through gritted teeth.

'What did I say?'

'You cannot discuss anything that's going on here in public or in private. Do you not understand?'

'What did I say?' he reiterated.

Thornton put Greg down. 'Just try not to speak at all, if you can possibly manage that.'

Greg noticed one of the chess players looking at them through the window of the cafe. DI Thornton had gone back to Han's car and was sitting in the driver's seat talking on his phone.

'Come on, Greg,' said Han. 'I think we should go back to Denis' house. Ilse's not at all happy about all this. It's not fair on her.'

Han made Thornton shift across to the passenger side and placed himself behind the wheel. 'I need to get back to Ilse,' he said.

'Sure,' replied Thornton.

Han set off back to Bourrouillan'

*

Virginia Hoffman had slipped out of the back of the house. She'd heard Greg's voice: it had sent a shiver down her spine. She felt a longing: she wanted to hold him but knew that would never happen again. Regret was something she rarely tolerated but she knew she'd been bad to Greg. What was it about him? He'd been so trusting, so believing. It would be more than appropriate if he really was the one who had given her away. She ought to despise him. There were many things she detested in men like him - she'd always thought them weak - and yet why did she feel this hunger inside? Maybe she was getting soft.

She was out in the fields again, behind Estang. She had to get back home, start again, be with her own kind, the sort she knew she could trust.

There was a main road about a mile away. If she could get there she might be able to hitch a lift to a safer place. She put her bag on her back and started to wind her way through the fields.

*

'The French police, in their wisdom, decided to crash into the house and search for Fraulein Hoffman, who, by now had flown the nest. They arrested the four men we spoke to but had to let them go as there was no proof that they had committed a crime. They charged Colin Miller with irregularities on health and safety grounds but I don't suppose he'll be here long enough to answer them. The blame for all this is now falling on me, for some reason. So much for co-operation across the EU.'

DI Thornton was sitting at Denis' kitchen table. He'd been called away by DS Wilde, who'd turned up to take him straight back to Estang, where he'd witnessed the debacle the local gendarmerie were causing. It was now evening and there had been no sign of Virginia Hoffman.

Greg had spent the afternoon in his room going through the things Virginia had left behind in her rush to get away. He was still trying to find some proof, he supposed. He didn't know whether he was trying to prove she was the German terrorist Virginia Hoffman or whether he still had a slight hope that she really was Jenny - his Jenny. All he succeeded in doing was depressing himself. It slowly dawned on him what he'd been going through over the last couple of days – or the last few months, really. He had genuinely believed that Jenny had come back to him. It all looked so ridiculous now. He'd felt exhilarated, happier than he'd been for years. Jenny was his first love and, even though he knew he'd been in love with Helen Wilson, the Town Clerk, he realised that it had been little compared to his love for Jenny. He'd longed for her for over twenty years and suddenly there she was.

And now? Now his whole world had shattered again. Jenny <u>was</u> dead. He'd accepted that before and he'd grieved, in his way. Now he had to grieve all over again and he didn't know if he'd be able to cope.

Deep in her holdall, under the clothes she'd hurriedly thrown in the day before, Greg found a note. He'd attached it to the shoulder bag when he'd given it to her. It was a small card with a heart on it. Inside it read *"I love you Jenny Gulliver and I will NEVER let you go again!"* But he had to; he had to let her go all over again. Tears welled in his eyes and he didn't try to stem the flow. He'd been surprised that Virginia had even kept the card. He'd bought the bag months before. Maybe it was all part of her deception.

DI Thornton's return from Estang had shaken Greg out of what he told himself was just self-pity. He'd washed his face and come downstairs to see if Virginia Hoffman had been found.

'What happens now, then?' asked Anton.

'Well, she won't get past the border, hopefully,' said Thornton. 'And we have that list of most of her confederates that you gave us. They'll all be watched to see if she goes to any of them. Not much else we can do, really.'

'So you just let her go?' said Denis. 'Do you know how easy it is to cross into another country in Europe? There are no borders anymore.'

'Yes, I am aware of that, Mr Young. But I'm also aware of a thing called Europol, set up to support police forces across the European Union. If she tries to get into

Germany, which is what I suspect, the German police will find her.'

'You sound very confident, Thornton,' said Greg.

'Do I? Then I must be a good actor.'

***

CHAPTER FIFTEEN

Mary Stewart was in a bad mood. It was always the same when she paid a visit to her parents. She was forty years old and they still tried to treat her like a child. They'd argued, as always, about things that were no longer important; things that were long dead, as far as she was concerned.

It wasn't that they'd been abusive parents or anything. Ostensibly, she'd had a good middle-class upbringing. A good school – even though she hadn't been a good student – and a nice home in a Scottish village outside Glasgow. But they had had a very strict view of what was right and what was wrong. They weren't overly religious; they didn't read the bible every night, though they were regular churchgoers and did insist on grace being said before every meal. Mary refused to go to church and stubbornly made it clear that saying grace was a waste of time, as she went through her rebellious teenage years. She'd found living at home oppressive. There was no television in her parents' house; it was considered a bad influence and a distraction from real life. Real life? Her parents didn't have a clue about real life. Anything they didn't approve of – and there were a lot of things they didn't approve of – just didn't exist, as far as they were concerned.

She'd left home at the age of eighteen – run off, really. Run off and married someone her parents disapproved of. She'd often wondered if that was the only reason she'd gone off with Christophe – because they didn't approve. She didn't think so at the time. He was energising, exciting - not the sort of person she'd met in her parents little Scottish world. Christophe was a student, for a start, which meant he had to be a reprobate at least. He didn't go to church and above all of this, he was foreign! Swiss! Why would their daughter want to get involved with anyone who wasn't Scottish? If he'd been English it would have been bad enough but Switzerland was the other side of the world; their world anyway.

She'd left one night – eloped, she supposed, though she'd never say as much. Christophe had finished university and was heading back to a job in his homeland, when he'd asked her to join him. She hadn't thought twice and had upped and left.

Her parents had refused to even speak to her for more than two years. She'd tried. She'd phoned them but they'd just hung up on her. Eventually, just as she'd accepted the fact that there would be no more contact ever again, the letter had arrived. It had been a long letter, full of bitter recrimination, full of blame and it hadn't been until the very end of the long epistle, written by her mother, that the crux of the matter had revealed itself. Her father had had a stroke. Whether the letter had intended to or not, it piled guilt on Mary's head. She blamed herself. Christophe had actually been pleased, even gleeful, that his old adversary was now incapacitated. He'd tried to stop Mary from flying back to Glasgow. Retaining her independence, she'd told him she was going back, whether he liked it or not. For the first time she felt needed. Between the lines of admonition, she'd detected a need in her mother – a plea for help. Their whole 'nice' world was starting to fall apart. Her father was longer able to work and her mother had never actually 'gone out to work' – her work had been bringing up Mary (fail) and keeping a good, clean, middle-class house (pass). Mary pitied the two of them. She herself would certainly have been seen, by them, as a failure as a wife. She and Christophe couldn't have children – another disappointment to her father, who, even though he refused to accept Christophe as his son-in-law, considered that Mary's marriage was purely a means of perpetuating the family tree. As for being a housewife, well, Mary had never considered that was her responsibility.

She'd procured a job not long after moving to Switzerland, teaching English as a foreign language, to young people hoping to make it big in the increasingly important financial services London was providing. It was a well-paid job and she'd relished the fact that her pupils already had more qualifications than their teacher.

Mary's father, in typical stubborn fashion, had refused to give in to the disabilities caused by his stroke. He'd learned to speak again, albeit through a twisted mouth, which her mother found abhorrent.

It was Mary's idea that they should move to somewhere warmer than Glasgow. Maybe she wanted them nearer to her. Maybe she realised that if she was going to be of any comfort and succour as they grew older, she couldn't keep trekking back to Scotland. She wasn't sure whether she'd believed that they'd needed her or whether she'd needed them, but everything about her upbringing kept saying to her 'they're family'.

She'd found a small complex outside Zurich and, convincing Christophe that he would never have to visit, had signed a lease on a flat with on-site carers who were more than happy to look after her disabled father.

She was about to fly to Scotland to deliver the news personally, when she received another letter; speaking on the phone was still rare.

"I'm sure you will be feeling very smug," it read. *"We have thought about what you said on your last visit and have bought a small villa in the South of France. We have sold the house for good money and are now retired. This*

place is very nice, a bit too Catholic, but there are several Scottish people who live in the vicinity – they call themselves ex-pats – and they have made us feel very welcome."

There was an address but no phone number.

'It's bloody miles away and difficult to get to,' she'd said to Christophe. 'That wasn't the point. They might as well have stayed in Scotland.'

'The further away the better, as far as I'm concerned,' her husband had replied.

In some ways it had been better, her parents not being on her doorstep, she mused as she drove in Christophe's dark blue Peugeot 2008 SUV company car along the D931. She was on her way to Manciet, where she would pick up the N124 to Toulouse and on towards Switzerland.

It was a twelve hour drive from her parents' place at Aire-Sur-L'Adour. She had travelled the journey many times now and knew the return was mostly Autobahn after Manciet. Christophe said he couldn't understand why she didn't fly most of the way and then hire a car. She hadn't been able to explain to him that the drive was needed to calm her down after seeing her parents. She liked driving and somehow it helped her relax. She usually stayed overnight so she didn't have to drive both ways in a day but that hadn't been an option this time.

She'd thought this visit had been going better than usual until after dinner. She'd given her mother an embrace - not reciprocated - as she picked up her bag, containing just a change of clothes and a toothbrush and headed for the spare room.

'Your father doesn't want you here anymore.' Her mother had stood with her arms folded in the doorway.

'What?'

'It's too much for him.' Her mother had opened the front door but Mary had stood her ground.

'What on earth do you mean?'

Her mother had held her head high and just said, 'He thinks it's for the best.'

'Does he? And what do you think, mother?' Mary had shouted at her. There was no answer. Her mother stood there staring at her, showing no emotion.

'Mother?' Mary had pleaded.

'You chose to leave this family many years ago, my girl. Don't think you can come waltzing back into our lives now. It was your choice.' Mary picked up her bag and strode towards her car. She didn't look back as Mary's mother closed the door on her daughter for the last time.

Mary had driven off at speed, leaving skid-marks in front of her parents' villa.

Twenty minutes later she was still fuming as she raced along the road. Driving was not relaxing her. It had crossed her mind to turn back; have it out with them. She banged her hands on the steering wheel in a futile attempt to stop her eyes from watering.

Whether it was the tears, tiredness or her lack of concentration, she couldn't say, as she suddenly became aware of the figure of a woman standing in the twilight right in front of her in the middle of the road. She slammed on the brake and tried to swerve. She felt the bang on the front of the car as she skidded to a halt, a few yards further down the road. She stayed frozen at the wheel. She'd hit the woman, she knew that; she'd felt, as well as heard, the impact. Something inside her wanted to just drive on. There was no-one else around, no-one would have seen the accident, no-one would know. She looked tentatively over her shoulder, expecting to see a bloody mess. Instead, there on the verge, the woman was staggering around, obviously shaken but definitely not dead. Mary opened the car door and walked, shakily back up the road.

Virginia Hoffman had a lump appearing on her right knee. She was cross with herself; she thought she'd timed it to perfection. Certainly she'd swung her bag at the right time to create the impact on the front of the car but somehow the front wing had caught her knee as she leapt away from the oncoming vehicle. It was sore but not broken or anything serious, just bloody painful. She started to stagger again as she saw the driver approaching. 'A woman. That's good,' she thought. 'No flirting would be needed.' She wasn't in the mood for flirting.

'Est-ce que vous etes blessee?' asked the driver carefully.

'Hopital,' whimpered Virginia in a feeble voice.

'Je n'ai pas te voir,' apologised Mary.

'Are you English?' Virginia was irritated. The driver was irritating her, speaking slowly in poor French.

'Scottish,' replied Mary.

Virginia hobbled towards her. 'Can you take me somewhere?'

'To the hospital? Of course. I think the car's OK.'

'That's good.' Virginia knew the car would have little more damage than a dent in its front. She'd done this sort of thing before.

Mary supported Virginia to the car and helped her into the passenger seat. 'I'm not sure where the nearest hospital is,' she said. 'I expect there must be one in Manciet, about fifteen minutes away. Will you be alright? I could call an ambulance.'

'No, I'll be fine,' said Virginia.

'I suppose I should report the accident,' Mary was getting her phone from her bag.

'No need. There's no harm done.'

'I'm so sorry.' Mary started to cry. Deep sobs. It was as much from her parents' rejection of her as the collision.

Virginia put her hand on her leg. 'It's OK. Really.'

Under the dashboard, by the gear lever, Virginia spotted a tray which contained some coins and a packet of mints. Also in this tray was a red booklet with a white cross on the front which she recognised immediately as a Swiss passport. Virginia smiled and studied Mary. She had dark hair, cut short like a boy. She was wearing a flowery dress that made her look dowdy. A quick appraisal of her figure showed she was, more or less, similar in shape and weight to Virginia. She patted Mary's leg again. 'Don't worry, everything will be OK.'

Mary turned the key in the ignition. The car fired into life and she set off, driving carefully towards Manciet.

'Where are you going?' asked Virginia. 'I mean, after Manciet. Where's your final destination?'

'I live in Switzerland, just outside Zurich. I've been to see my family.' A lump came to Mary's throat as she mentioned her parents.

'Are you going through Grenoble?'

'I go past it, why?'

'It's where I'm staying at the moment.'

'Grenoble? That's a long way from here.' Mary was getting suspicious. 'I think you need to go to the hospital first.'

'No. I'm fine. Just a bang on the knee. If I can get to Grenoble, I can see my own doctor in the morning. I'd much prefer that.' Virginia smiled at the woman. 'I'm sure it wasn't your fault but you were driving very fast for that road. I only just escaped being killed.'

A shiver of guilt ran over Mary. She knew this person in her passenger seat was telling the truth. 'I'm really sorry. I was a bit distracted. I've had a big row with my mother,' she said swallowing back more tears.

'Hey, it's OK. I was a bit distracted myself. I've been to see my boyfriend – well, ex-boyfriend now. That's why I'd like to get home rather than be where he could find me. He's not a very nice person and I've upset him. I shouldn't have done that.'

'Are you in danger?'

'I think I could be if he finds me.' Virginia smiled at Mary who tried to smile back. There was no warmth in either of their expressions.

'Ok.' Mary's voice was barely a whisper.

There was silence in the car for a while. Mary was conscious of the fact that the reason that this woman was in her car was due to her bad driving and now she was driving her halfway across France. She was driving more carefully than was necessary. Normally she would be going a lot faster. Virginia was sitting quietly, working on her plan.

Several hours passed with little conversation. Virginia appeared to be asleep. Mary's head was starting to nod as well and she needed to fill up with petrol. They were past Montpelier but still several miles from Grenoble.

'There's a services just up ahead. Do you fancy a coffee?' she said.

Virginia opened her eyes. 'You bet. I was just about falling asleep there. Do they have a Leclerc at the services, do you know? I need to pick up a few things.'

Mary looked at her passenger. Was she serious? 'I think there is but we're not that far from Grenoble, really.'

'It won't take me long.'

Mary pulled into the services and parked. There was a large Leclerc hypermarket in a complex that included several bars and food outlets.

'I'll be in that bar, there,' Mary pointed to a place with plate-glass windows, overlooking a landscaped area next to the motorway.

'OK.'

Mary watched Virginia head for the hypermarket. 'Do you want coffee?' she yelled to the woman's back. She was limping, her knee obviously giving her a great deal of pain. Guilt swept over Mary again. 'Or something stronger?'

'Coffee. Black will be fine,' Virginia called over her shoulder as she entered the Leclerc.

Mary went into the bar. She needed something stronger than coffee but didn't dare. She was in enough trouble as it was without risking drinking and driving. A morose sense of foreboding surrounded her. She didn't know this woman she was giving a lift to. She really shouldn't have taken her this far. She should have left her at the hospital in Manciet. However, if she had done that, she'd, no doubt, have had to report the accident to the gendarmerie, entailing a longer stay in France. She just wanted to get home as soon as possible. She knew Christophe would show little sympathy over her parents' disowning of her – he'd also be cross about the dent in the front of the car – but at least she'd feel safe and that was one thing she didn't feel at this moment. She ordered two coffees and went to sit by a window, watching the cars along the highway.

*

The girl at the checkout scanned the items the woman had bought and put them into a plastic carrier bag. She took no notice of the woman or the items that she'd purchased. The girl was near the end of her shift and was looking forward to a promised late-night out with the girls. She took the cash and moved onto the next customer.

*

Mary waved to Virginia as she stood at the entrance to the bar. She held a plastic carrier bag in her hand as she shuffled over to the table and sat down.

'Are you OK?' Mary indicated Virginia's leg.

'Yep. I picked up some paracetamol.' She took a blister pack out of the bag, pressed two into her hand, threw them into her mouth and washed them down with some coffee. 'Right as rain,' she said, smiling.

Mary had finished her coffee and wanted to get on the road again. She would have to detour to go into Grenoble, which would add even more time to her journey and she was tired and emotional. The coffee had not revived her at all. 'I really need to get going,' she told her companion.

Virginia drained her cup. 'Ready when you are.'

'I still need to get fuel,' said Mary as they walked slowly back to the car.

'No problem. I suppose I should give you some petrol money.'.

'I don't think that will be necessary.' Mary wanted nothing more to do with this woman. She just wanted to drop her off somewhere and get home. She felt uncomfortable as Virginia followed her out of the car at the pumps and stood just a little too close to her. 'You should stay in the car,' she said. 'Your leg looks pretty bad to me.'

'It's OK,' was all the answer she received. She put her bank card into the self-service machine and, covering the keys with her left hand, punched in her PIN.

'Do you know,' Virginia was leaning over Mary's shoulder. 'Most people actually use the year of their birth as their PIN, so they can remember it. There must be thousands of people born in the same year with the same PIN. You'd be surprised how seldom people change their PIN, even though it's really simple to do. My friend works in a bank.' She smiled at Mary as she placed the spout into the fuel tank of the car. Mary made a mental note to change her PIN as soon as she got home. Had this woman been watching her as she entered her PIN? How did she know her PIN was the date of her birth? The sooner she got to Grenoble and got rid of her the better – and she'd make sure she kept her card safely in her pocket.

The automatic cut-out on the pump kicked in as the tank reached its capacity and the two returned to their seats and set off.

'Whereabouts in Grenoble?' asked Mary. 'I'll have to come off the main road here.'

'I'll tell you. It's not far from the main road. I'm on the outskirts of the town.'

They were still about three-quarters of an hour from the turn-off for Grenoble and Virginia, evidently invigorated by the caffeine, chatted continuously as they drove. Mary was concentrating on her driving and trying not to be irritated by her. It was dark now and re-routing to Grenoble meant travelling along country roads with no streetlights, something she was not at all keen on. The road they turned off onto was well-lit, however, as it went through a small town but after that the street lights finished, shrouding the surrounding fields with gloom. The well-signed roads gave way to rough narrow lanes. Mary was worried whether she would be able to find her way back to the main highway.

'I forgot to pee,' said Virginia suddenly.

'You're nearly home, aren't you?' Mary didn't want to stop.

'I won't be able to wait that long; coffee goes right through me. Just pull off there.' She pointed to a small track that looked like it led through a small copse to a farm.

'You can't pee in the open!' Mary's nice Scottish background came to the fore.

'Just pull over, quick!' Virginia was wriggling in her seat. Mary certainly didn't want her to wet herself in Christophe's car. She had enough explaining to do as it was, so she acquiesced and turned into a dark recess between the trees.

'It's my time of the month, as well!' Virginia leaned over to where she'd thrown her carrier bag but couldn't reach it, so she left the front seat and went into the back of the car and started sorting through the contents of her plastic bag.

'Please hurry,' said Mary. 'My husband is expecting me and I'm already late.'

'I'm sure he'll wait!' Virginia's voice seemed changed. She didn't sound like the 'English Rose' she had earlier. Her tone was more guttural. Mary looked in the rear-view mirror. There was a look in Virginia's eyes that frightened her. She decided that, as soon as this woman got out of her car to pee, she'd drive off and leave her. If she reported her to the police she'd just have to deal with the implications. She should never have taken this stranger with her.

'I'll just text him to let him know,' said Mary, digging in her bag for her phone. She was shivering, although it was a mild night. Something wasn't right.

Suddenly a blinding light shot through her brain, followed by the most searing pain she'd ever felt, followed by nothing. She slumped forward onto the steering wheel.

Virginia Hoffman calmly exited the rear of the car, opened the driver's door, unhitched the seat-belt and let Mary's body fall out onto the floor. The road was set a few feet higher than the surrounding area where the trees grew and Virginia kicked the woman's corpse until it rolled down the incline. The head smashed against a tree and lay there, half-hidden in the long grass, like a doll some child had ejected from a passing car.

Half an hour later a plastic carrier bag landed in the undergrowth several yards away from the body. The car started up and drove back towards the motorway.

*

The dark blue Peugeot stopped at the border crossing.

'Hello Mary. How were you parents?' The customs officer did no more than flash the passport under the green light that read the chip and handed it back.

'Aye, good.' replied the driver.

'Say hello to Christophe.'

'Aye, will do that.' The car drove off into Switzerland.

Christophe's father, in his little customs hut, thought it strange that Mary had said her parents were good. He knew the problem she had with them – Christophe had told him enough times. He also thought it odd that she'd said 'Aye', like that. In all the years he'd known his daughter-in-law, he'd hardly ever heard her say 'Aye'. He shrugged his shoulders and took the passports from the family in the next car.

The driver of the Peugeot felt uncomfortable. She hadn't expected to be recognised. Maybe she should ditch the car. That would make crossing into German more difficult, though. She drove on.

***

CHAPTER SIXTEEN

'It might be a good idea for you to disappear for a while, Monsieur Dubois.'

DI Thornton was again sitting in the kitchen at Denis and Anton's house. He was waiting to return to the UK – not in disgrace, exactly - but he knew that the French Authorities viewed his actions as little more than incompetent interference. Part of him was inclined to agree.

'And where am I supposed to go?' replied Anton.

'Personally I don't care but I doubt you'll be particularly welcome amongst your compatriots here anymore. Word will have got out.'

'Do you mean he's in danger?' Denis put his arms round his husband's neck. He was scared – they were both scared.

'Work it out for yourselves,' said Thornton.

'You can stay at mine for a bit,' suggested Greg.

'I'm not leaving my home.' Anton's bravado only gave Denis more distress.

'I'm just saying I wouldn't stay here, if I were you.' Thornton finished his coffee and stood up. 'I'm sorry you got involved in this. It's not something I would have sanctioned - putting a civilian in this sort of peril.'

Greg snorted. 'Didn't seem to bother you in my case,' he muttered.

'With you, Mr Driscoll, I was trying to keep you from being arrested and thrown in a cell for terrorist activities involving several fatalities! Although I may have failed in that – there is still a possibility that you could be charged.'

'But he didn't do anything!' Denis was now feeling protective towards both of his friends.

'Apart from leave a bomb in a camp full of defenceless men, women and children, you mean?'

'But he didn't know that's what he was doing.'

'Leave it, Denis.' Greg could see the vulnerability of his position. He walked to the window and looked out over the sloping lawn that led down to the lake. One thing he agreed with the Inspector about was Anton's safety. The nearest neighbours were over half a mile away, it would be the easiest thing in the world to get rid of someone round here. He turned round to Denis and Anton. 'I think you should both come and stay with me for a while.'

'That just makes it look like I'm involved,' argued Anton.

DI Thornton raised his eyebrows and went to the door. 'Come and see me when you're back home, Driscoll,' he said and went out to meet DS Wilde, who had drawn up in the driveway.

At first it looked like it was a car accident – apart from the fact there was no car – and the body was only wearing underwear. The woman's head had smashed against the tree causing massive damage to the brain. The French police did a quick search for tyre marks only to discover there had been numerous vehicles passing along this track over the last few days. It led up to the farmhouse, owned by the man who'd found the body whilst walking his dog and who was now standing being quizzed by an officer.

He explained that it was his dog that had discovered the corpse. He appeared pretty shook up, something the gendarme found strange. He must have seen his fair share of animals being slaughtered. He couldn't see the difference, unless he knew the woman, which he claimed he didn't.

A shout came from the undergrowth. One of the officers fought his way through the long grass holding up a plastic carrier bag in his gloved hand.

The officer in charge viewed the contents. It appeared to be half-filled with human hair, a sort of bronze colour – dyed, by the looks of it. Underneath he discovered brand new hair trimmers, some scissors and an empty can of coloured hair spray. Also at the bottom of the bag, sticking through the plastic, was a bradawl. He removed the woodworking tool and examined it. The sharp pointed spike was tinged in red and had something that looked like small pieces of body matter attached to it. Slipping it into a clear evidence bag he called over the pathologist who was bending over the body and told her to look for a small stab would.

It took only a matter of minutes for her to ascertain that a mark on the back of the woman's neck was a puncture wound inflicted by a thin sharp instrument – such as a bradawl – and was most probably the cause of death of this unfortunate woman, lying in the grass by the pathologist's feet.

The Inspector sighed and walked back to his car to phone in his report. It looked as though he was going to miss his dinner date with his wife again.

*

'I still think you should both come and stay with me.' Greg had packed his bag and was savouring a farewell Armagnac in the kitchen. Denis had frowned and pressed his lips together when he'd asked for the brandy.

'It's only ten o'clock in the morning, Greg,' he'd protested.

'I've decided I'm a nervous flyer,' smirked Greg. He had a flight booked for two in the afternoon from Biarritz. Denis had taken some persuading to drive him over to the airport. He didn't want to leave Anton alone following DI Thornton's warning.

'I'll be perfectly alright, Denis. Stop fussing, please.'

'But you know what Thornton said yesterday.' Denis was still flapping, pretending to do some washing-up that had already been done.

'I know what he said, Denis. I also know that you hardly slept a wink all last night. We can't live our lives in fear. You were jumping at every noise.'

Denis polished a glass vigorously with a cloth. 'I don't understand why you won't come to Biarritz with us,' he said, putting the glass back into the washing-up bowl, shiggling it about in the soapy water before starting to polish it again. 'We could have something to eat there, maybe even stay the night somewhere nice – have a break, you know.'

Anton took the glass from Denis and put it on the draining board. He gave him a kiss and brought his husband back to the table. 'I'll be fine, Den, honest. Anyway, Ramona's coming to clean in an hour so I won't be on my own and you'll be back before I even notice you've gone.'

'Oh God! I'd forgotten Ramona was coming. I'd better tidy up.'

Anton took Denis by the shoulders and forced him to remain seated. 'We pay Ramona to clean, Denis. There's no point in doing it before she gets here.'

'Perhaps I should wait till she gets here before we go,' said Denis looking at Greg.

'No, Den. Greg will miss his flight. You two get along now, I don't want you to have to speed along that motorway.'

Greg picked up his bag. 'Invitation's still open if you change your mind. I have a spare room, you know.'

'Maybe in a week or two we could come for a short holiday.' Anton hugged his partner.

'Do you mean that?' asked Denis.

'Yes. A break would be good but I refuse to run away right now. There's things I have to do first.'

Denis looked at him suspiciously

'It's alright, Den. Nothing to do with fascists!'

Greg was standing at the door, holding his bag and feeling awkward. He wanted to go so he could get a beer or two at the airport before the flight but he could see Denis was still reluctant to leave. He was hugging Anton and stroking the back of his head.

'You'd better go, Den,' whispered Anton. 'Greg will miss his plane.'

Greg smiled and shrugged his shoulders. Denis moved away, still holding Anton's hand. 'Are you sure you won't come with us?' he pleaded.

'No. I'll see you soon. I'll give your love to Ramona.'

Denis sighed and led Greg to his car. Anton stood at the door and waved them off. He was feeling anxious. He'd convinced himself that if anyone was going to come and find him, they were unlikely to do it broad daylight. Nevertheless, he checked the patio doors were locked, as well as the front and kitchen doors, before going upstairs to his computer. Although tracing his ancestry had started off as a cover for his activities with 'France pour le Francais', he had become fascinated to find out more. He'd never felt he had roots. Most of his early life had been spent in the UK. He'd never really known his extended family. His father had been dead for some time and his mother was back in England suffering with dementia. There had been little contact for years, Anton having handed over the care of his mother to the local authorities. She didn't know who he was anymore, anyway, and Anton had assuaged his guilt at abandoning her by convincing himself that she was better off without him. He'd come to feel that Denis was all the family he had, but after signing up to an internet search site, he was discovering that he did have relations, still alive, across France - people he'd never met or even known about.

He wanted to change all that. He would go and visit his mother when they went over to Greg's and try to make amends and apologise – even if she didn't know what he was talking about.

He switched on the computer and brought up the site, which had all his father's side of his history saved, and settled down to start delving into his distaff line.

The banging on the front door sent his heart rate soaring. He wasn't expecting anyone. A few moments thought helped him to realise that it was probably Ramona. But Ramona had keys: why would she knock on the door? Maybe he'd double-locked it. He stood up and looked out of the window but from where he was, he couldn't see the front entrance from where the hammering was emanating. Slowly he edged down the stairs, listening. The banging had stopped. He went cautiously to the door. There was a spyhole built into the wood, through which he peered. He couldn't make anyone out, the fish-eye lens didn't give a clear view anyway. He waited, not quite knowing what to do, part of him wishing he was on the road with Denis and Greg after all.

A rapping on the windows of the patio doors nearly stopped his heart. He turned and could see a figure standing peering into the room.

'Monsieur Dubois?' The figure was knocking gently on the window-pane.

'Who is it?' Anton tried to stop his voice sounding shaky.

'Hello, I am Ramona's nephew, Raul. She not well. I come clean.'

Anton crossed the room and peered out. The figure was a tall, lean young man with long dark hair flowing over his shoulders. He was smiling and waving his hands that were enclosed in bright pink rubber gloves.

Anton relaxed slightly and opened the door an inch, keeping it braced with his foot, in case the youth tried to force his way in. He didn't. He just stood smiling his charming smile. Anton smiled back. He was charmed. The boy was wearing blue denim jeans and a t-shirt – the sort that used to be called 'grandad vests' when Anton was his age. The short was unbuttoned, exposing the young dark skin of the youth's upper chest. Over his shoulder was hung a tapestry shoulder bag.

'What's the matter with Ramona?' asked Anton.

'She fall. She hurt leg.' The boy had a Spanish accent, like his aunt Ramona. 'She send me, I come clean, now?' he added, still grinning and waving his gloved hands as if to prove he was willing to do the scrubbing.

Anton opened the door. 'Yes, you can come and clean now.'

The boy walked into the room and looked around.

'Would you like coffee?' ventured Anton.

'No. I here to work.' He waved his pink gloves again. Anton pondered on whether this boy had ever cleaned in his life, but went to the cupboard to show him where Ramona kept the various sprays and dusters she used to maintain the unpolluted atmosphere Denis liked to live in.

He felt the hand of the youth caress his back and work its way to his chest. He was frozen momentarily. He'd always been completely faithful to Denis – he hadn't even looked at another man, he wasn't the promiscuous sort – but this boy was captivating. He held the boy's hand and closed his eyes.

There were various jars of bottled fruit from their garden, soaking in sprits of one sort or another lined up on shelves above him. It sent a heady aroma of alcohol and polish through the cupboard.

Something cold touched the back of his neck and he wondered what it could be. It was the last thing he ever wondered as the bullet exploded, sending his brain splattering over the inside of the cupboard. The bullet, having passed through Anton's skull, smashed into a jar of sloe gin on the shelf, spraying dark liquid, which mixed with the contents of Anton's head as it slipped down the walls.

The youth let Anton's body slide to the floor. His gloves were a deep red colour and he licked them clean. He wasn't sure whether it was blood or the unidentified liquid in the jar, but he savoured the taste, nonetheless.

Leaving the patio door open he went to the front of the house, mounted the bicycle he'd left leaning against the wall, and set off down the road.

A car passed him as he cycled down the hill away from the house. The Spanish woman driving looked at him without recognition – his hair was covering his face – and turned into Denis and Anton's house.

*

Denis had been anxious throughout the journey to Biarritz. There had been a lot of traffic and he'd had to sit in a line of non-moving vehicles, held up by various roadworks, and it had taken a lot longer to reach the Autobahn than usual.

'I'm going to be late at this rate,' grumbled Greg.

'You've plenty of time; you'll just have to forego your pre-flight piss-up!' said Denis, tight lipped.

'Oh I'm terribly sorry,' Greg replied. 'Did you forget I'm an alcoholic?'

'Don't be ridiculous, Greg. You know I gave up trying to reform you years ago. You'll just have to get a drink on the plane if you're late. It's not my fault.' Denis slammed on the brakes to avoid the car that had stopped suddenly in front of them. 'For fuck's sake,' he screamed.

'Calm down, Denis. What's the matter with you?'

Denis looked at Greg, puzzled. 'I'm worried about Anton! What do you think's the matter with me? Why couldn't he just come with us?'

'He'll be fine. Your cleaning woman will be there by now.'

'I don't think a Spanish charwoman would be much use against a terrorist!' The traffic moved forward again and they turned onto the motorway.

'It'll be alright, Denis. Try not to get paranoid.'

Denis shot an 'if looks could kill' glance at Greg and picked up speed. Greg knew he had good reason to be worried – he knew this group could be ruthless – Virginia had shown him that at Calais. Risking anything untoward against Anton now seemed unlikely, though. They must know he'd be under surveillance from the police. Even so, Greg could understand his friend's concern. He sighed and looked at his watch. At least, if they kept this speed up he would still have time for a pre-flight aperitif.

He said 'cheerio' to Denis at the drop-off point outside the small airport, reassured him again that he was sure Anton would be waiting for him at home, and headed for the bar.

His phone rang before he'd even ordered a beer.

'Anton's not answering his phone!' Denis sounded scared.

'There's probably no signal, Denis. Where are you?'

'In the airport car park.'

'There you go. I expect they block signals in case they interfere with flight control.' Greg signalled that he wanted a beer to the young girl behind the bar.

'How come I'm talking to you, then?' Denis' voice was raised.

The girl poured Greg a draught lager. 'I'm sure there's nothing wrong, Denis. He's probably by the pool or something; left his phone indoors.'

Denis wasn't convinced. He had a premonition that something was very wrong. He put the car into gear and headed rapidly in the direction of his home.

*

Ramona's screams could have been heard in Nogaro had anyone been listening. She'd opened the door and put her bag on the kitchen table, as she had done many times before. There was a pungent aroma of alcohol pervading the atmosphere and she tutted, expecting to have to clear up another of the post-party messes that had been occurring with increasing frequency since their actor friend had arrived to stay with his girlfriend. Romana didn't approve of him or her. She'd come to terms with cleaning for the two gay men – they were paying her, after all, and she was quite happy to pretend they were just friends – but when it came to men and women sleeping together out of wedlock, she experienced a conflict with her Catholic upbringing. It was wrong. She always crossed herself before going in to clean their room.

There was no sign of anyone. She poked her head out of the open patio door and called both their names but without reply and she went over to the cleaning cupboard to start her work. The smell of alcohol was stronger in this location. As she opened the cupboard door, what remained of Anton's head fell against her legs, blood and brains still wet and gleaming in the sunlight that streamed through the patio door.

*

Denis' stomach turned over as he drove up the hill. Three police cars and an ambulance were filling the driveway outside his house. He skidded to a halt and ran from his car, leaping over the grass verge and through his beloved herb garden to the open front door. He was greeted by a number of people in white overalls standing round a black zipped-up body bag. A shivering Spanish charwoman was sitting on the sofa sobbing uncontrollably.

***

CHAPTER SEVENTEEN

One thing Greg Driscoll had learned from Virginia Hoffman was how to put music onto his phone. There was an app she'd installed which meant he could link up to his computer and download his music to his mobile. He was grateful, as it meant he could stick his headphones in his ears whilst he flew across the channel, which helped him ignore the young child he found himself sitting next to on the plane - not that he blamed the child for being irritable. The poor kid's mother and father were evidently making the most of the end of their holiday by drinking quantities of the overpriced alcohol served by the airline and totally ignoring their offspring.

He arrived at Stansted and went through to the terminal. He thought, briefly, about having a quick pint at one off the bars but a glimpse through the large plate-glass windows reminded him of his fellow passengers and he thought better of it. He'd get back to The King's Head and have a few there. His conscience pricked him for a second. Was he becoming a snob now he was a TV star? A couple of people had recognised him on the plane. No! He convinced himself that he just preferred The King's Head to airport bars.

He went over to the taxi rank and managed to persuade one of them to take him as far as Maldon – at an extortionate rate. He stuck his headphones in again, in case the driver wanted to talk to him about Trudie Carling. On the journey, the music he was playing stopped suddenly. He looked at the screen. It was blank. He shook the phone but there was still no music and nothing on the screen. 'Bugger,' he said under his breath. 'At least the phone decided to pack up when I'm nearly home and not in France,' he thought. He could see the cab driver looking at him in his rear-view mirror, so he kept his headphones in and smiled. He really didn't want to chat.

Gareth was behind the bar as Greg wandered in from the taxi. He still had his small case with him – he hadn't bothered to drop it across the road to his house as he was just going to have a quick pint and then go home to unpack.

'Ah, Gareth, you know about phones, don't you?' he said as the landlord pulled his pint of Kronenbourg.

'Yeah, you talk to people on them.'

'Well, mine's buggered.' He handed his phone over to him. He knew Gareth had fixed a few of the locals' mobiles in the past.

Gareth took the phone and pressed the power switch. 'No battery, mate. When did you last charge it?'

'I don't know. Yesterday sometime, I think. Shouldn't have run out by now, surely.'

'Depends on how much you've used it.'

'I haven't made a call all day.'

'Used any apps?' Gareth was plugging Greg's phone into a power point.

'No. Well, I listened to some music on the flight. That doesn't use up the battery, though, does it?'

Gareth gave him a pitying look and went off to serve a customer in the other bar. Greg went to sit at the long table. His favoured seat by the small window was occupied by a young couple. Not only were they being very loud but they had a large dog they appeared to think was their child. It was sitting on the seat, slobbering, whilst they noisily cooed and cuddled the animal, telling everyone in the whole of Maldon, what a good boy their little monkey was. It amused Greg that the beast was neither little nor a monkey and he considered giving them that useful information but thought better of it. The King's Head advertised itself as a 'dog friendly' pub and Greg had noticed an increase in the number of four-legged friends dragged in while their owners enjoyed a drink or two. Other pubs in the slowly gentrifying area were beginning to ban animals, using their more food-based fare as a reason. Greg appreciated the fact that the King's Head had kept up the tradition of allowing dogs but, as with the many children who frequented alcoholic establishments these days, he was becoming increasingly intolerant of them and their, supposedly, responsible adults who should have been looking after them. People seemed to behave in pubs as though they were still in their own living rooms, totally ignoring the fact that other people may not be interested in their offspring – be they children or dogs. He castigated himself for being so grumpy, wishing his phone was working so he could put his headphones in his ears and shut them all out. He really was starting to worry about his attitude towards his fellow human beings these days.

His mind wandered back to the camp at Calais. Had that bomb really been in his rucksack? Was he responsible for those refugees being killed? He looked over at the young couple with the dog and smiled at them.

'I hope he's not annoying you,' she said, stroking her pet.

'No,' Greg lied and laughed. 'He's a lovely boy!'

'He is,' said the girl. 'Who's a good boy, then?' She threw a dog biscuit across the bar. The beast scrambled off the seat and skidded over the floor, his tongue lapping up the morsel, leaving a trail of saliva.

Wendy bounced into the bar and nearly fell headlong over the dog, which ran whimpering back to the safety of its surrogate parents. She looked daggers at them as they cuddled and cooed some more. Wendy waved an imaginary glass in Greg's direction indicating that she was prepared to buy him a pint. He nodded.

'Hello stranger,' she said, bringing the drinks over. 'Ginny not with you?'

Greg took a deep breath. 'Ah!' he said.

'Ah?'

'It turns out that Ginny wasn't actually who I thought she was.' He didn't dare look at Wendy.

However, instead of gloating and saying 'I told you so', as Greg had expected, she came round the table and sat next to Greg on the long bench. 'I'm sorry,' she said.

Greg spent the next hour telling Wendy as much as he thought he was able to about Virginia Hoffman and the various right-wing organisations she was involved with. He told her that she'd had some connection to the bomb in Calais but didn't tell her that the bomb had probably been planted in the food parcel from Maldon that Wendy had been so instrumental in organising. Her expression had changed from incredulity to worry as Virginia's story unfolded.

'And what about Denis and his friend?' She still couldn't bring herself to call Anton his husband.

'Denis had no involvement with any of the groups - and Anton,' Greg paused, not sure what to say. 'Well, he was sort of working with the French police. I'm sure they'll be looked after, if necessary.'

Wendy held his hand and pecked his cheek. 'Poor Greg,' she said.

'Oh, I'm alright.' He smiled and went to the bar for more refills.

'You've got a lot of missed calls, mate,' said Gareth as he poured the drinks.

'What do you mean?'

'On your phone. It's half-charged and you've got a load of missed calls showing. Were you supposed to be somewhere else?'

Greg wracked his brains. 'No,' he replied. 'Can I have a look?'

'It's your phone.' Gareth took Greg's money and went to fetch the mobile.

'Are you OK?' said Wendy as he put her glass of wine in front of her.

'Yeah, Gareth says I've loads of missed calls on my phone. I can't think who'd be ringing me. I'm not working at the moment.'

'Probably that call from Hollywood you've been expecting for thirty years.' Wendy grinned at him. 'Or the press; you haven't been in the papers for a while.'

Greg gave her a playful punch. 'Could be my agent I suppose, with that Hollywood job!' He wagged his finger at her. 'You never know, young lady. You never know.'

'I wouldn't get too excited, if I were you,' she said, sipping her wine.

'You do a great deal for my ego, you know that?'

Gareth crossed to the table with Greg's phone. 'I took it off flight mode, by the way. That's probably why you didn't get the calls while you still had some battery.'

'Thanks.' Greg looked at the screen and placed his finger on the calls icon that had a figure 8 by it indicated how many missed calls he had received. All eight calls were from Denis' phone. A sickening feeling came into Greg's stomach. There were three voice mails indicated and Greg punched in the number to retrieve them.

The first voicemail Greg couldn't interpret. Denis must have been upset. There was what sounded like wailing going on in the background. All he could make out was, 'It's Anton! It's Anton!' Why was Anton ringing him on Denis' phone? Had something happened to Denis? The second message was more succinct. 'Where the fuck are you, Greg? Greg? Answer your fucking phone!' It was

289

Denis, evidently clearly upset. He rarely swore like that. The third message just said, 'Phone me as soon as you're home.' There was a long pause during which Greg could hear Denis sobbing, followed by, 'Anton's dead!'

Greg ran from the pub across the road to his house. The green light was flashing on his answerphone. He didn't need to listen to the messages to know who they would be from. He picked up the phone and punched in Denis' number in France.

'Denis, I'm so sorry. What on earth has happened?' gasped Greg as the phone was picked up in Bourrouillan.

'Someone shot him in the head,' came the matter-of-fact reply. 'They won't let me see him.' Denis sounded like he was in a dream.

'I'll come back over,' said Greg.

'No! No, don't, Greg. There's nothing you can do here.' Tears rolled uncontrollably down Denis' cheeks. He wondered if they would ever stop. He took out his handkerchief and blew his nose. 'I knew, Greg. I knew this would happen. I should have been here.'

Guilt hit Greg. It was because Denis had been taking him to the airport that he hadn't been there. 'But if you had, Denis...'

'...I'd have been killed as well?' Denis sobbed again. 'I think I'd have preferred that to what I'm going through now.'

Greg didn't know what to say. 'Is someone with you?' he said eventually.

Denis sighed. 'Only half the French police force and a wailing Spanish charwoman.' He looked round his living room. The body bag had been taken away and the overalled forensic people were spreading powder, taking samples and photographing the cleaning cupboard where Anton had spent his last moments. A uniformed officer was trying to take a statement from Ramona. It was taking a long time. In between wailing she was speaking in Spanish and they'd had to fetch an interpreter.

'I told you we should have waited for Ramona to arrive before setting off for the airport, Greg but, oh no, you wanted to get a drink or two in before you flew, didn't you? I hope you enjoyed them, Greg.'

Greg didn't answer. He knew Denis was venting his anger – his grief – looking for some reason for Anton's murder. Greg suspected he knew the reason. Denis was right, they should have insisted on Anton coming with them. He should have urged them to come and stay with him in Maldon. To get away from any danger. A thought flashed into Greg's mind. Was he safe? Was Maldon any safer than Bourrouillan? Virginia would have told them where he lived, wouldn't she?

'Do they know what happened, Denis?'

Denis answered quietly. 'No.' Denis knew it was something to do with that group in Nogaro and that awful woman Greg had brought into their lives. How could he have been so naive? They both knew that Jenny Gulliver had died twenty years ago. Why had Greg been so stupid?

'What can I do, Denis,' he heard Greg say. 'You know, to help?'

'Keep away, I'd suggest.'

'Denis, I want to help. I think I should come over.'

'No!' Denis shouted down the phone.

'Denis,' Greg pleaded.

'I have to go, Greg. I'll be in touch.' Denis disconnected leaving Greg feeling wretched, still holding the lifeless phone in his hand.

'Where'd Greg go to?' Gareth leaned over the bar to speak to Wendy who was sitting alone. It was very quiet in the pub, Wendy being the only occupant of the 'Members' bar'.

'Dunno,' she replied. 'Looked at his phone and ran off. Probably was Hollywood wanting to get hold of him, after all.'

'Must have been something important, he left his pint.'

'I know, I thought he'd be back by now. He's left his case as well.' Wendy indicated Greg's luggage still under the table. He'd been gone for over half an hour and Wendy was getting bored waiting for him to return. I'll drop it over to him. I ought to be getting off, anyway.'

'Well, if Greg's got the call from Hollywood, I'm sure he'll be back to celebrate soon.' Gareth picked up Greg's pint and threw it down the sink.

Wendy picked his case and headed for the door. She crossed the road and hammered on Greg's door. 'Come on, Mr Movie Star. Let us in on the news.'

Greg pulled himself up from the sofa, blew his nose and wiped his eyes before going slowly over to let his post-lady into his house.

'What is it, then? Are you off to the U, S of A?' Wendy looked at Greg's face. 'Oh my God! What's happened?' She put Greg's case down and closed the door.

Greg was sitting back on the sofa. Wendy came across to sit next to him. She didn't speak, waiting to see if Greg wanted to divulge. He looked at her and smiled while his eyes dripped tears.

'Anton's been murdered,' he said quietly.

'Oh God! Poor Denis.' Wendy gave Greg a hug and disappeared to the kitchen to make coffee for him and a sweet tea for herself. It was starting to get dark outside as though a storm were approaching. 'Appropriate,' she thought. She brought the mugs through to the living room. 'Your outside light's on,' she said.

The two of them sat in silence for the best part of an hour.

***

CHAPTER EIGHTEEN

Greg Driscoll spent the next two weeks in almost solitary confinement. He went to the King's Head once but only stayed for a pint. He'd stocked up on scotch and cigarettes from the supermarket and was living off a whisky, nicotine and microwave meal diet. He hadn't answered the door to Wendy any morning, even though she was still rapping the knocker daily. He was in a state of depression. He wanted no contact with the outside world – he hated the outside world – it had taken away everything he loved and needed. Even Denis wasn't ringing and somehow he couldn't summon up the courage to ring him. He'd switched his mobile phone off and sat watching terrible daytime shows - shows he couldn't understand why they'd been made; unless they were for other people who didn't want to use their brains; didn't want to think.

He was lying on the sofa, wondering why anyone would want to mortgage their lives to buy a big house in the country, when the phone rang. As usual, he let the answerphone pick up for him.

'Answer the fucking phone, Greg Driscoll, or I will come over and knock your bloody door down!'

Greg sighed and carried on watching his programme.

'*If your arse in not in the pub in twenty minutes.*'
continued Wendy. '*I will break your door down. Do you think you're the only one with troubles in the world, you selfish git? I'm on my way to the King's now. Don't make me get the heavy mob in!*'

Greg ignored her and flicked through the channels for the tenth time in the last half an hour. His eye caught a scene he recognised and he stopped flicking. It was an old episode of 'Gone for a Song' being repeated. He watched it for a while; criticising every word he'd said, every move; every nuance. He wondered why he'd ever wanted to be an actor.

The door shook in the lintel as Wendy heaved her great weight against it. 'Open up, Greg. Come on. I'm not going away.'

Another thumping followed. 'Come on, Greg.' It was Gareth. He could break the door down if he wanted to.

Greg pulled himself up from the sofa and opened the door.

Wendy stormed in, waving her hands about. 'It stinks in here!' She went towards the overflowing ashtray and whisked it off to the kitchen.

Gareth stood in the doorway. 'You look a right mess, mate,' he said. He looked towards the television. 'Watching your past glories won't help, you know.'

'Won't it?' Greg was back on the sofa. 'What will, then? Sitting across the road with everyone thinking I'm stupid? Thinking I caused the death of my oldest friend's husband? Thinking I screw women so I can get myself in the paper? Will that help?'

'No. But no-one thinks that.'

Greg sneered at him.

'The thing is; my takings are down since you stopped coming in and I thought you might like to help me out.' Gareth grinned.

'Go and have a shower,' said Wendy, coming back into the room. 'I'll clean up the mess in here while you're cleaning up the mess on you.' Greg sat still. 'Come on, Driscoll. Give us a hand Gareth.'

The two of them physically picked him up and carried him upstairs. When Wendy started to remove his clothes, he finally agreed to go and have a shower but insisted he was not going to the pub.

Half an hour later he was sitting at the small table by the window in the 'Members' bar'.

*

It had been four o'clock in the afternoon when he'd been pressganged into re-joining life in the 'Members' and now, as he re-entered his front room it was half-past five. He reluctantly had to admit that his friends had been right to drag him out of his solitude – he was feeling better than he had for weeks. The pub had been quiet, they were the only ones in the bar, Gareth had fed him a proper meal and he'd managed a couple of pints of Kronenbourg. They'd only let him go home because he'd promised to return later that evening. He'd made up his mind – with a bit of helpful persuasion from Wendy and Gareth – to ring Denis in France. However, as he stood with the phone in his hand, his nerve was faltering.

Greg was still holding the phone when it rang loudly, almost making him drop the handset.

'Hello, Denis?' he answered into the receiver.

'No, DI Thornton,' came the reply. 'I assume you heard about Monsieur Dubois, then?'

Greg sat on the sofa. 'Of course I have.'

'Nasty business. I told him he wasn't safe.' Thornton seemed removed from the emotion of the situation.

Greg sat still, not wanting to ask the next question. 'Why are you ringing me? Am I in danger?'

The pause was long enough to worry Greg.

'I wouldn't have thought so, really, Mr Driscoll, but vigilance would be advisable. Have you been over to France?'

'No, Denis didn't want me there.'

'Probably sensible. There's nothing you can do there.'

That's what Denis had said. Greg felt useless and unneeded. The dark cloud was starting to hover above his head. He was hurting again, surely he could do something? He took a deep breath. 'Do you know what happened?' he asked the DI.

'Apparently someone put a gun to the back of his head and pulled the trigger.'

'Oh shit! Denis said he's not allowed to see him – even to identify the body.'

'Not surprised, there'd be no face to identify.'

Greg shivered. 'So is there a chance the body might not be Anton?'

'No, it's definitely him, I'm afraid. There are many other ways to identify corpses these days.' There was another pause. 'I was wondering,' continued the Inspector, 'whether you would agree to having a chat with me. Off the record, so to speak.'

'Why?'

'There's a few things I'd like to find out. I'm no longer on this case but I'm still intrigued.'

'I don't know what I can tell you. I didn't know anything about it until...well, until you involved me.'

'I suggest you were already involved, Mr Driscoll.'

'Not knowingly.'

'I don't think that's a defence that would stand up in court and you have not been exonerated.'

'But...'

'...but nothing, I'm afraid. The French will want to nab someone for the Calais bombing and, if they manage to link this as well? You're lucky it was only a few migrants that were inconvenienced last time. This is a French passport holder who's been killed.'

Greg sighed. 'If it was me that planted that bomb, maybe I should be nabbed.'

Thornton didn't comment. 'I'm not doing anything this evening. If you're free I could come over to Maldon and we could have a drink. I'll be over at nine. Is that pub opposite you OK?'

*

DI Thornton strolled into The King's Head just before nine o'clock. He went into the larger bar at the back which overlooked the river and sat watching the boats bobbing on their mooring drinking a pint of the local bitter. He'd never really seen the attraction of places like Maldon before – he'd always been a city man. He'd thought Chelmsford was quiet when he'd first been posted there but Maldon? That was like going back in time to some village from the 1950's. However, as he sat there wondering if Driscoll would actually turn up and talk to him or not, he had to admit that the vista from the window was relaxing. The stress he'd been under since being thrown off the French case the day before started to feel like it was ebbing away with the tide. Maybe he was getting old and ready for retirement. He looked round the bar. It seemed as though at least half of the punters were retired. There was a lull about the place, tranquil, indolent even. He wondered if it ever got lively.

'Are you looking for Greg?' The girl behind the bar called across the room. It was Tallie, leaning on the pumps, looking bored.

'Driscoll?' he replied. Tallie nodded. 'Yes I am.'

'Other bar,' she said and went to serve some more beer to one of the customers who'd been boring her for the last two hours.

Thornton took the remains of his pint and went through to the front bar. Greg was sitting alone at the small table by the window. There was no-one else in the 'Members'' and Thornton wondered how on earth pubs like this continued to stay open. 'Can I get you a drink?' he asked Greg.

'No, I'm fine, thanks, I have one.' Greg didn't look up.

Thornton sat opposite him. It was an uncomfortable seat – a bench that was too close to the wall behind for him to relax. He perched on the edge. 'Thanks for seeing me,' he said. Greg didn't answer. 'Tell me about Virginia Hoffman again,' he continued.

'I don't want to talk about her.'

Thornton sighed and continued. 'Like I said on the phone, I'm intrigued. Did you have no suspicions about her at all?'

'No.' Greg swigged back his pint.

Thornton could see a difficult evening ahead. He polished off the rest of his pint and pointed to Greg's glass. 'Lager?'

'Kronenbourg.'

He went to the bar. Greg looked at this policeman and wondered again why he was here. He didn't believe he just 'wanted a chat off the record'.

'Have you found her yet?' he asked as Thornton put a pint of Kronenbourg in front of him.

'No. We think she's gone back to Germany.'

'You think? What happened to Europol?'

Thornton stretched out his back and tried to shift to a more comfortable position. 'Mr Driscoll, can I trust you?'

Greg shrugged his shoulders. Thornton looked at the table. Maybe this had been a bad idea. He wanted to find out how much Driscoll knew about this Hoffman woman. They'd spent quite a long time living with each other. She must have let something slip. Since he'd been removed from the case, he'd started to become obsessed with her. He could feel it happening. It was a flaw in his character, he'd been told early in his career; he didn't think so. If he wanted to get to the truth, living and breathing the case was the only way he knew. And suggesting he'd screwed up in France, only made him more determined than ever. He wanted to find this woman – to stop her. He looked up at Greg. 'She'll have a new identity,' he informed him.

'Whose life is she trying to ruin this time?' Greg took a gulp from his pint.

'I don't know, yet.'

'Do you expect her to contact me? Is this a warning?'

'No. I think she's gone. Lost in bureaucracy. Nobody seems that bothered and that's what irritates me, Mr Driscoll. I want to know why.'

Greg took a long drink. 'Do you have a first name, Inspector?'

'Gerald.'

'In that case, Gerald, please call me Greg if you want my trust.'

'Alright, Greg.' Thornton sipped his pint. 'There was a woman found murdered near Grenoble in France. She'd been travelling back to Switzerland but never made it. Her body was found in some wasteland.'

'Who was she?'

'A woman of Scottish descent called Mary Stewart.'

'So what's the relevance?'

'According to the French police there isn't any but that's because they haven't bothered, or have been told not, to look.'

'Meaning?'

'Next to the body, a plastic carrier bag was found. In the bag was the murder weapon – a woodworking tool – a brand new hair trimmer; some scissors; a dark-coloured hair spray and a packet of paracetamol. Also in the bag was a quantity of human hair – auburn in colour, though probably dyed. There was a lot of it. Someone with auburn coloured hair had cut it all off and sprayed what was left a dark brown colour.'

Greg knew what he meant. 'Virginia?'

'I think so. I tried to connect the pieces before I was removed but I was denied the opportunity.'

'Well, presumably the French police and Europol will know who they're looking for now. I hope they get her.'

'They won't.'

'You sound very certain about that.'

'I am.' Thornton took another drink. 'Do you remember that I told you Hoffman had various aliases?'

'Yes, you said she was called Gerta something.'

'Gerta Roth, yes, and I suggested that was probably not her birth name, either.'

Greg shrugged. He didn't want to know any more about this woman who'd pretended to be Jenny Gulliver.

Thornton took an iPad from his bag, brought up a photograph and showed it to Greg. A man in a shiny suit was standing on some steps outside an important-looking building with several people standing behind him.

Greg looked up at Thornton. 'Should I know this person?' he queried.

'Probably not. Do you recognise anyone else?'

Greg studied the picture. Apart from the shiny suit, there were three other men and a young woman in view. No-one he knew came to mind. He handed the tablet back. 'No-one,' he said.

Thornton flicked the screen. 'This is a close-up of the woman standing at the back.' He showed it to Greg. 'Could that be the woman you knew as Virginia Hoffman or Jenny Gulliver?'

Greg looked again. 'She's a lot younger. I don't know. Could be. Why?'

'Did she have any distinguishing marks, Greg?'

'Like what?'

'A tattoo, maybe?'

Greg laughed. He hated tattoos. 'No, definitely not, Gerald.'

'Perhaps a scar? On her neck?'

Greg looked at the photo again. Virginia did have a scar on her neck, he remembered but the photo wasn't defined enough to see this girl's neck. 'She did have a small scar,' he said.

Thornton flicked the screen again and showed Greg a close-up. There, where her neck met the collar-bone, was a small tattoo. It was a black swastika. 'The removal of a tattoo like this would leave a scar, Greg. Was Virginia's scar where this tattoo is showing?'

Greg nodded slowly. He recalled the mark on her neck. It looked like a skin graft where such a tattoo could have been removed. He'd never asked her about it, assuming it was a legacy from her supposed abduction and imprisonment.

'The man in the photo is called Helmut Mayer. He is in the German Bundestag, allegedly a member of the Social Democratic Party. However, before his elevation to Government, he was heavily associated with the National Democratic Party, an unelectable, far-right, ultranationalist political party. Neo-Nazis dedicated to ridding Germany of all immigrants.' He pointed to the photograph. 'This was taken at a rally some ten years ago.'

'So? I can't say I'm surprised that Virginia Hoffman is in attendance, in that case, are you?'

'Not at all. Especially as Helmut Mayer is her father.'

Greg looked up at the Inspector.

'It's my belief,' continued Thornton, 'that Helmut Mayer is protecting his daughter. I think that's why neither the German police nor Europol have bothered looking for her.'

'So she'll just disappear, then. Good riddance, I say.' Greg supped his lager.

'Yes, I suppose so. Until she tries to blow up some more immigrants.' Thornton indicated Greg empty glass. 'Another Kronenbourg?'

Greg nodded. What was Thornton trying to do? Why was he giving him this information which, surely, should have been classified? He wanted nothing more to do with this woman.

Thornton brought Greg his drink and sat down again. 'I want to find her,' he said.

'Why?'

'I don't like her. I don't like what she stands for. I want to stop her.'

'I thought you were off the case.'

'I am, Greg, which annoys me. I've given the right people this information and they are ignoring it. They told me that Helmut Mayer doesn't have a daughter.'

'Have you thought that you might be wrong, then, Gerald?'

Thornton took a sip of beer. 'I'm not wrong, Greg. I have a contact in Germany who says everybody knows about Mayer's daughter and her activities.'

'So why the denial?'

'I'm not sure. I want to know if there's anyone higher up determined to stop me getting to this woman.'

'What? You mean in our Government?'

Thornton shrugged his shoulders. 'Someone is protecting her and it's not just her father on his own. Helmut Mayer owns a company that just happens to hold the franchise to one of our main railway lines. He is also is a major shareholder in a firm that provides IT support to our own Government's computers. I suspect that upsetting him could cause a great deal of disruption and embarrassment.'

'Why are you telling me all this?' Greg was perplexed.

'I want your help, Greg.'

'I don't see what I can do.'

'I want you to help me find her.'

Greg laughed again. 'I suppose you know how big a country Germany is? What do you want me to do, go a-wandering with my knapsack on my back yelling 'Virginia, where are you?''

'Just a thought.' Thornton gulped the end of his pint. 'When do you start on the new series?'

Greg was thrown for a second by the abrupt change of subject. 'Er...early next year.'

'Trudie Carling in it again?'

'I expect so.'

'Well, good luck with that.' Thornton stood up. 'I'll be in touch,' he said and left Greg nursing his confusion.

'Copper?' Gareth was standing next to the table.

'How'd you guess?' said Greg.

'You in trouble again?'

'Do you know, Gareth, I haven't got a clue.'

Greg went out to the terrace for a cigarette. The night was very dark now, cloudy, no moon or stars shining. He looked across at the old station. There were lights on in what were now offices in the refurbished building. 'I'm so, so sorry, Jenny,' he murmured, a tear forming in his eye. He put his cigarette out in the ashtray and went home.

***

CHAPTER NINETEEN

The outdoor light in Greg's back yard was shining brightly through the window again as Greg entered his living room. He went straight to the back door and opened it. 'Hello?' he called. There was no reply. He looked up at the security light and banged his hand against it. It carried on shining as brightly as before. The back gate was open again and he walked down the path to slip the bolt back across. He thought he saw a movement from the corner of his eye and he turned in time to see a cat scramble up the fence into the neighbour's garden. Their security light flashed on. Greg smiled and reminded himself to get some pepper spray – or whatever it was that kept cats out of one's garden.

His 'chat' with DI Thornton had made him anxious. He didn't need this on top of Denis's tragic news. Poor Denis. Greg really wanted to go over and try to give him some comfort. Denis had done it enough times for Greg but he didn't want him and Greg had still not picked up the phone. He'd ring him tomorrow; he may have changed his mind by then.

He went into the kitchen, re-locking the back door, and switched on the kettle. Swilling a mug under the tap, he threw a spoonful of instant coffee in whilst he waited for the water to boil. He lit a cigarette and looked out of the window. The outside light extinguished itself and the yard was plunged into darkness again. He poured his coffee, added some milk and went towards the living room.

'Hello, Greg.'

He almost dropped his mug as he turned to see the source of the voice. There, standing at the bottom of the stairs was a young woman, smiling at him.

'Katy! What are you doing here?'

She took a step towards him. 'I wanted to see you again. It's been too long, Greg,' she said.

'How did you get in?'

'Through the back door, silly.' She giggled.

Greg tried to remain calm. He knew Kate Freeman had been incarcerated in a secure hospital, following her conviction for killing her father. There was a moment of extreme awkwardness as neither of them quite knew what to say. Kate Freeman had been building up the courage to speak to Greg for months. She'd stalked him. She'd hung around in his back garden but when he appeared she found she didn't have the bottle to speak to him. She'd observed him going to and from The King's Head but never found the nerve to just walk in and say 'hi'. Now, on impulse, she'd walked into his house as he went to close the gate. The problem was she hadn't thought what to do next.

Greg broke the atmosphere at last. 'Well, look at you,' he said feigning pleasure at her appearance. 'Sit down, Katy. Would you like a coffee?'

'I'm not allowed coffee,' she said, settling herself on the sofa. 'Or tea,' she added.

'Nor alcohol, then, I assume.' Greg desperately needed alcohol right now.

Kate giggled. 'Are you trying to get me drunk?'

'No!' said Greg quickly. He smiled at the young woman.

'Sit with me, Greg, please.' She patted the seat of the sofa next to her. 'We've a lot to catch up on.'

'Er...now's really not a good time, Katy.'

'Why?'

Kate Freeman was the last person Greg wanted to discuss Anton's murder with. He didn't want to bring back memories of her father's murder. That man had abused her physically and sexually for years until she'd finally snapped and stuck a kitchen knife in his chest – thirteen times – until he was dead. She'd then implicated Greg by saying she'd done it for him as her father tried to stop the affair they were having – a situation that was completely untrue; they had never been in a relationship other than in Kate's mind.

Greg had to think quickly. There was no way he could sit all cosy on the sofa next to her. He didn't know what her mental state was. She'd been in a secure hospital for years. Was she better now? Could she ever be better? What would she do if he told her to go?

'Katy,' he said, 'I have to go over to see Gareth at The King's Head and they're about to close.' He stood by the front door willing her to leave.

'That's OK,' she said, not moving from the sofa. 'I can wait here for you.'

'No, Katy.' Greg was panicking. If he left her here, there would be no telling what he might come back to. 'I'd like you to come with me.'

'But I'm not allowed alcohol, remember. Unless you are trying to get me drunk.' She pouted at him. It was not pretty.

'I'll buy you a water.'

Kate started laughing. It scared Greg; it wasn't a fun laugh, it was almost maniacal. 'You are silly,' she said. 'You don't buy water, it comes out of the tap.' She laughed again.

'I'd still like you to come with me.' Greg was getting desperate. The pub was about to close and he had to get Kate out of his house. What he'd do then, he didn't know.

Kate gave an over-dramatic sigh and stood up. 'Alright then, but I don't want to be long.'

'Yes, just a quick one while I talk to Gareth. Don't you have a coat or anything?' He noticed she was just wearing a baggy t-shirt and shorts. It was quite cold outside.

'I've got you to keep me warm.' She put her arms round his neck and laid her head on his shoulder. Greg felt physically sick. He opened the door and led her across the road.

Gareth was still behind the bar. Most of the stools had been place upon the tables, ready for the cleaner the next morning. He raised his eyebrows as he saw Greg come in with Kate clinging to his neck. 'We're about to close,' he said, looking at his watch.

Greg shook his head, trying to convey that he needed Gareth's help. 'Kronenbourg and a tap water, please, Gareth.' Greg was pleading with his eyes. Gareth looked at the unlikely pair and went to pour the drinks.

'Who's he?' said Kate loudly.

'That's Gareth, he's the landlord,' replied Greg.

'No he's not! Where's John?'

'John left about six years ago,' said Gareth handing over lager and the glass of water.

'Let's sit down.' Kate pulled Greg to the same table he's vacated barely an hour before. She pushed Greg onto the bench and slid herself along, resting far too close to him for any comfort.

Gareth followed them over. 'Aren't you going to introduce me, then, Greg?'

'Of course. This is Katy, Gareth, an old acquaintance of mine who's turned up unexpectedly.'

'Hello Katy,' Gareth held out his hand.

'It's Kate to you!' she screamed. 'Only Greg can call me Katy now.'

Gareth recoiled. Who was this latest woman Greg had got himself involved with?

'So where are you living now, Katy?' Greg spoke loudly enough for Gareth to hear.

'They found me a house, but I don't like it.'

'That was good of them. Where is it?'

Kate turned to Gareth who was standing a little way from the table. 'Why are you here?' she said. 'I'm talking to Greg.'

Gareth looked at Greg and pulled a face that suggested Greg had finally 'lost it' with this one and started back to the bar.

'Gareth's alright, Katy. You don't have to go, Gareth.' Greg was pleading again.

'I don't want him here!' Kate was shouting again. Gareth, deciding not to throw her out just yet, retreated to safety.

'So where is this house, Katy?' Greg was still speaking loudly. 'Are there other people there?'

'Of course there are. They won't let you come in, though. They won't let me have a boyfriend back to stay.'

'Who are they, Katy? Are they like carers?'

Kate gave him a friendly slap. 'You're being silly again. They're all just friends.'

'And where is it?'

'Witham.'

'Witham? That's miles away.' It was about six miles away but a long way for her to get home.

Katy took a small sip of water. 'It's a very grand house. It has a name instead of a number.'

'Wow!' said Greg. 'What's the name, then?'

'Philip Morris House,' she said proudly. 'But I'm not going back there now.'

Greg looked over at the bar but couldn't see Gareth. There was no-one else in the pub. Greg forced down the remains of his pint. 'I need another quick one,' he said.

'No!' screamed Kate again. 'A quick ONE was what you said!'

Gareth appeared in front of the bar. 'It's closing time,' he said. He noticed Greg's terrified expression and knew it wasn't because he was not going to get any more alcohol.

316

'Katy lives at Philip Morris House, Gareth. She says she doesn't want to go back there tonight.' Greg hoped that Gareth would know Philip Morris House. It had to be some sort of halfway house to help people get back into the community after they'd been seriously ill, like Kate Freeman. Please, Gareth, his eyes pleaded. 'Do you think I could get another pint?'

'I'm very cross with you, Greg,' castigated Kate. 'You're going to have to stop this drinking. I won't put up with it, you know.'

'Last one, eh?' Greg looked over at the bar. Gareth had poured him a pint but left it on the bar. He was nowhere to be seen.

Kate leaned over and started to stroke Greg's thigh. He tried to remove her hand but she was strong and determined. He couldn't shift her. She put her head next to his cheek and started to lick him. Greg laughed nervously. 'You're tickling me,' he said.

Kate pulled away. 'I've seen you on the telly,' she said curtly.

'Oh,' said Greg, glad of the sudden change in her. 'I hope you enjoyed it.'

'I didn't,' she replied not looking at him. 'I'm not jealous but I don't want to see you with that Trudie Carling ever again. That will have to stop!'

'I can't stop it, Katy. It's my job.'

She turned to him, her face very close to his. 'It's not your job to enjoy it. I won't have it!' Her voice was rising again.

Gareth was standing by the front door. The pub was closed and all the lights were off in the other bar. Gareth had just left the light over their table on in the 'members''. It created an eerie scene. Greg prayed that Gareth wouldn't make them leave. He wanted to get his pint from the bar but Kate had him trapped on the bench.

'I could do with the loo,' he said in an effort to get away from her.

'You'll have to wait till we're back,' she said refusing to be manipulated into moving.

'Katy, you're not coming back with me, tonight. You have to get back to Witham. I'll get Gareth to call you a cab.' Greg had had enough and thought between him and Gareth they'd be able to handle Kate's reaction, whatever that was going to be.

She stared at Greg, totally expressionless. She slowly edged along the bench away from him and looked at her barely touched glass of water. She picked it up and took another small sip. Without warning, she threw the rest of water over Greg Driscoll, raised her arm and threw it at the wall in front of them. There was a framed print hanging

318

there and as the empty vessel met the front of it, an explosion of glass like the pellets of a shotgun shot across the table to where Greg and Kate were sitting. Greg ducked and covered his face. Kate sat still as the shards ripped into her face and arms. Blood spurted from the torn flesh. She sat, not moving, just bleeding. Suddenly, a piercing scream emanated from her throat. Her mouth was open wide, her head shaking from side to side, centimetres from Greg's face, spraying little flecks of blood. Gareth flew to the table and grabbed Kate round the shoulders pulling her up and away from the bench.

There was a polite knock at the door. 'It's open,' shouted Gareth.

A large man in a suit came in followed by a rather fierce-looking woman.

'Hello, Kate,' said the man calmly. 'We wondered where you were.'

'Get out!' screamed Kate. 'Get out! I'm with Greg. I don't need you.'

The woman stepped forward in a no-nonsense way. 'Come on, Freeman. Time to go home.'

Kate stopped screaming and looked at the woman, suddenly terrified. She started shaking all over. She was still bleeding, despite Gareth doing his best to stem the flow with blue paper.

The man took over from Gareth. He had a medical case with him and he took out a roll of gauze and calmly mopped her up. 'It's OK, sir. We'll deal with this now.'

Kate looked at Greg, her eyes filled with tears. Suddenly she pointed at him. 'He tried to kill me!' she yelled. 'He tried to kill me like he killed Pops!' The man picked her up and carried her outside, like she was a child.

'Which one of you rang us?' said the matronly woman.

'I did,' replied Gareth.

'And who are you?' She turned to Greg and pointed at him.

'My name's Greg. I knew Kate before...well, before.'

The woman turned on him. 'And why are you encouraging her to break her curfew? This is not the first time. She's mentioned you before. We try so hard to rehabilitate these girls back into society and people like you just screw things up for us and we get the blame.'

'I didn't encourage her,' Greg shouted back. 'She broke into my house.'

The woman turned on her sensible heels and left.

Greg sank back on the bench feeling exhausted. 'Can I still have that pint, Gareth?'

'No you can't.' Greg looked up. 'But you can have a very large brandy and you can tell me what the hell all that was about. Oh, and I'll get you a cloth to clear that mess up.'

*

It was two in the morning by the time Greg dragged himself across the road to his house. Between the two of them they'd managed to empty half a bottle of the pub's brandy and Greg could feel it swilling about with the lager he'd already had earlier in the evening.

He had told Gareth the whole story of Kate Freeman; about her father; how she'd stabbed him and then Greg being accused of raping her and murdering her 'Pops'. Gareth said he'd heard about it when he'd first come here but Greg's part hadn't been mentioned. It was just a local story, gossip mostly, he'd thought and old news now. He'd warned Greg to stay away from her and to let Philip Morris House know if she turned up again.

Greg put his key in his door and let it swing open. He stumbled and had to hold onto the door jamb. 'Must be getting old,' he thought to himself. Maybe he couldn't handle the sort of quantity he used to manage any more. His head was starting to throb. He fell onto the sofa and was instantly asleep.

Wendy hammering on his front door added to the thumping that was still going on in his head. He dragged himself up from the sofa and flicked the latch. The pale morning sunlight seared into his eyes and he went back inside, followed by his post lady. She took one look at Greg and went through to the kitchen. 'You'll be wanting your coffee black, then, looking at the state of you.'

'Morning Wendy,' he groaned. 'What time is it?'

'Eight-thirty,' she yelled from his kitchen. The kettle sounded like a steam-hammer going off in his brain and he went upstairs to the bathroom. He threw some water on his face and looked in the mirror at the old man staring back at him. His eyes were bloodshot, his hair sticking out all over the place. Was that a bald patch appearing? He threw some more water at the ancient greybeard and towelled his hair dry, before taking a deep breath and going downstairs.

Wendy was sitting at the kitchen table, two mugs in front of her next to a couple of brown envelopes. 'Probably junk mail,' she said indicating the letters.

Greg put them straight in the bin. 'That's all you deliver these days,' he grumbled.

'Most people communicate by email or text nowadays. The golden age of letter writing is dead and gone.'

'You'll be redundant before long.' He went to the fridge and poured some milk into his black coffee.

'Heard anymore from Denis?' Wendy asked.

Greg had all but forgotten about Denis and Anton. A sickly sensation roamed about his stomach as he thought of his poor old agent grieving over his murdered partner. 'No,' he replied. 'I'll give him a ring later.'

'And how was your rendezvous last night?'

'How do you know about that?' It never ceased to amaze Greg how quickly news travelled in Maldon, usually through the channels of the Royal Mail, it seemed.

'You were supposed to come and meet me, remember? I came in and saw you with some bloke who looked like a bobby. Didn't you see me?'

Greg shook his head.

'I thought not. I didn't stay anyway. How much did you have to drink with that policeman last night?'

Greg smiled. 'I thought you meant...' Perhaps he had overdone the alcohol consumption – The meeting with DI Thornton had shifted to the back of his mind. He shivered involuntarily as the memories flooded back.

'How many did you have?' persisted Wendy.

'Three or four pints, I suppose.' he didn't mention the brandy.

'I meant rendezvous. You seem to imply there was more than one.'

'Ah!'

'Ah?'

'You might not believe this, Wendy, but when I got back from the meeting with Thornton, the bobby – which, by the way, was something and nothing – Kate Freeman was standing in my living room.'

'What! I hope you had her arrested!' Wendy slammed her mug down on the table spilling tea onto the Formica top.

Greg calmly fetched some kitchen roll and handed it to her. 'What would I have her arrested for?'

'Trespass; harassment; gaol breaking; she's a criminal.' Wendy mopped up the spilt tea, reminding Greg of the cleaning up of Kate's blood that he and Gareth had spent a fair amount of time doing the previous night.

'She's ill, Wendy. She'd not a criminal. She's still quite sick.'

'What was she doing here? Why isn't she locked up?' Wendy looked as though she was trying to scrub the pattern off the table-top.

Greg took the soggy kitchen roll off her and threw it in the bin. 'She lives at a halfway house in Witham. She was allowed out during the day, it seems, but had an evening curfew.'

'So, I repeat, what was she doing here? It was gone nine o'clock when I saw you so it must have been well past her curfew.'

'Yes it was, Wendy. And I don't think she'll be allowed out again for a while. They came and took her away. They were very rough with her, I thought.'

'Well, they shouldn't have let her out in the first place, if you ask me.'

'I didn't.'

'What?'

'Ask you. Anyway, it's all sorted now.' Greg hoped that was somewhere near the truth. 'I felt sorry for her.'

'You're too bloody soft, you are. That's why you end up getting yourself in the shit all the time. Talking of which, I'd go and have a bath, if I were you, you stink like a brewery.' She stood up and hitched her bag onto her back.

'You're not me,' retorted Greg. 'Go and deliver the rest of your junk mail.'

Wendy was at the front door. She shook her head. 'Three or four pints,' she muttered. 'I don't think so.' She wandered off up the hill.

Greg finished his coffee. He sniffed his clothes. Wendy was right, he did smell of alcohol. He didn't remember spilling anything last night. He recalled Kate glass of water being thrown at him before she smashed it against the picture. He took off his shirt and trousers and chucked them on the pile of other dirty clothes in front of the washing machine and went upstairs in his boxers.

Grabbing his dressing-gown from his bedroom he went through to the bathroom and spun the hot tap. He thought briefly about just having his usual shower but Wendy had put the appealing idea in his head of a long relaxing soak in the tub. He had no plans for today other than to try and forget yesterday – all of it.

He slipped down into the hot water and felt the tension float away from his muscles. His head had stopped throbbing and his earlier vow of 'never drinking again', was also drifting away as he planned a lunch-time pint in the King's. He needed to apologise to Gareth for Kate's behaviour, after all.

The phone rang in the living room. He let the answerphone pick up.

"Greg, it's Gerald Thornton. I've been giving some thought to what we were discussing last night and I think I've come up with something. Can you give me a ring?" He left his mobile number.

Greg lay still in the bath, listening. The water was no longer hot enough to alleviate the constriction creeping back into his body. What plan did Thornton have? If it involved Greg going to Germany he could think again. Greg put his head under the water and stayed under as long as he could. It was something he'd done as a child when his mother and her boyfriend were having a drunken row and stressing him out. It was his way of hiding from the world; from reality. When his lungs were about to burst, he thrust his head up into the air and breathed out. Taking in a new lungful, he levered himself out of the bath and grabbed his towel. His headache had returned, he noticed.

Scrambled eggs on toast are always a good brunch and a dampener for the hangover until it was time for the dog to bite again. He went through to the kitchen, ignoring the answerphone's insistent flashing green light – he'd heard the message and wanted nothing to do with it. His mobile was on the floor by the sofa, where he'd thrown it the previous evening, and he went and picked it up, looked at the screen, noting there were no missed calls or messages and put it on the kitchen table. He cracked some eggs into a pan and stuck some sliced white bread in the toaster. He remembered he ought to phone Denis but thought he had better wait till he'd eaten. He was putting it off, actually. He didn't know what to say. How many times can you tell someone how sorry you are their partner got killed? That wasn't what Denis needed – he needed support and Greg was supposed to be his friend. What was he thinking? He sat at the kitchen table and punched in Denis' number into his mobile phone.

***

CHAPTER TWENTY

DI Thornton was at home. He'd been forced to take leave by his chief. Apparently the powers that be thought he was not dealing with the stress he'd been under following the debacle in France. He had a month on full pay to chill out and he would then be assessed as to whether he was fit enough to return to work or not.

Thornton had not taken it well. He'd argued with the chief, pointing out that the incompetence of the French police force and the lack of co-operation had been the cause of the mission's failure. His insistence that he could still catch the Hoffman/Mayer woman and scotch the plans of the far-right groups were just ridiculed, leaving him with a choice of taking leave or facing a disciplinary hearing.

Maybe the chief was right. He knew he was becoming obsessed with Birgit Mayer. He recognised the signs. It was the reason his wife had left him ten years ago. He could hear her words. They echoed in his head daily. *"You're like a dog with a rabbit, aren't you?"* she'd said, *"you just can't let things go!"* Their marriage had lasted barely five years. She'd been right; he was obsessive when it came to his work: That's why he was a good copper, why he'd risen through the ranks quicker than anyone else. Policing had all changed now, though. They didn't want people who used their initiative; people who carried on until they got their man – or woman. They had computers now that were far cleverer than he could ever be.

But he had a plan. He just needed to persuade Greg Driscoll to go along with it.

*

Denis Young sat in a hotel in Biarritz. He couldn't stay in Bourrouillan any longer. He'd arranged for the house to be put on the market and removed himself to Biarritz whilst he perused his future. He'd had to contact Anton's mother and tell her the tragic news. Denis had never met Anton's family – they hadn't been at the wedding, they had disapproved. It had taken some time for Denis to trace the mother and eventually she was found to be in a home in Brighton. When he told her she had not believed him. She had insisted that Anton was there in her room with him and that she was looking at him at that very minute. Denis thought that maybe dementia could sometimes be a blessing. The British police had tried to deliver the news in the end but met with little more success. Denis considered it was probably best for her not to know the truth.

All this time Greg hadn't phoned him. He hadn't spoken to him since the day after Anton's death. Denis hadn't wanted to speak to anyone and he'd said as much but, somewhere inside, he thought that at least Greg would have shown some support. Denis had rung Greg once during the past two weeks but only got his answerphone and, as Greg hadn't phoned back, he rather petulantly didn't try again.

So, he was pleasantly surprised when Greg's number showed up on his mobile. It took some time for Greg to get round to asking for advice from his old friend. He'd gone through the condolences again but Denis told him he still didn't really want to talk about Anton; it was too painful. When Greg told him what Thornton had said about Virginia, Denis' emotions exploded.

'He wants me to help him find her.'

'You're mad! She killed Anton and now she'll kill you. You're so stupid, Greg. I don't know how you could ever believe that cow was Jenny Gulliver! Stay away from her.'

Greg wanted to say that Denis had believed she was Jenny but realised it was only because he'd convinced him. Denis had been sceptical.

'If you even think of going over to Germany to find her, Greg Driscoll, I will never speak to you again, probably because you'll be as dead as Anton!' He disconnected and threw his phone across the room.

*

Anton's funeral was a quiet affair. His remains had finally been released by the Gendarmerie and Denis had flown back to the UK knowing that what was left of his life-long partner was currently in a box in the hold of the same aeroplane. He'd arranged for the funeral directors to meet the plane at Gatwick airport and transport the body to Brighton where the funeral was to be held. Anton's mother, in a brief moment of cognisance, had insisted he came home to her, but she'd since forgotten that, still convinced that the framed photograph of Anton in her room was actually him.

Denis had checked himself into a local hotel. There was no-one coming to the funeral. He doubted that Anton's mother would even make it. She wouldn't understand anyway. There had been no contact from Greg and Denis had not told him the date of the funeral, something he was regretting now, as he sat in front of a dressing table in his hotel room, tying his black tie round his neck. Even that Detective Inspector was unable to come; he was off sick apparently due to stress. Denis wished he could take a month off from his stress but he couldn't; it was always there. It was sitting in a box waiting to be burned in the morning. But it still wouldn't go away after that, he knew. He didn't think it would ever go away.

He was convinced that he'd be the only person at the crematorium in the morning but maybe that was for the best. He'd never known any of Anton's previous friends and the only people he was sure his husband knew in France were currently in custody – not that he wanted any of them there.

He sat on his bed feeling more alone than he'd ever felt in his life. He'd tried to ring Greg but had only got his voicemail. He regretted his outburst to him and prayed that his friend hadn't actually gone to Germany to find that awful woman. If he had...it didn't bear thinking about. Not now.

There were two other people at the crematorium. The mother didn't make it. These were people who seemed to get pleasure going to other people's funerals – sort of professional mourners, he assumed. Anton hadn't been at all religious and the service – if that's what it was called – was taken by a registrar. He kept it brief, thankfully, and Denis shed a tear as the box disappeared behind the red velvet curtains. A suitably theatrical end he supposed. The final curtain call.

He wandered back alone to his hotel, raised a gin and tonic at the bar and returned to his room to contemplate what to do with his life.

One person who had been in touch was an old client, an ex-actress called Barbara Wiseman. She had left London some years ago to 'make it' in Hollywood. Needless to say it had never happened and she now scraped a living as portrait painter – actually a painter of people's pampered pets. She was divorced and lived alone in a suburb of Downtown Los Angeles, far from the glamour she'd dreamed of when she'd left old England's shore for the bright lights.

Barbara had an old friend in Helen Clarke. It was Helen who'd told her of Denis' tragedy and she'd immediately invited him to come and stay for a while. Denis knew he couldn't stay living in France and, as Greg had disappeared from the face of the earth since they'd last spoken on the phone, there was no-one else he wanted to spend time with in London. He needed to be far away from Bourrouillan, Brighton and London right now. The United States was certainly that.

Anton's remains had been scattered on Brighton beach – a ceremony that, much to Denis' annoyance, had been high-jacked by the local gay community. Someone Anton had known from his days as an actor had read about the funeral in the paper and persuaded Denis to allow Anton's final act on earth to be witnessed by all his friends in Brighton. Denis wanted to point out that he didn't think Anton had had any friends in Brighton - and just because they were a gay couple it didn't mean they were 'friends' with every gay person in the world. However, he didn't have the fight left in him anymore and he watched sadly as the groups of crying men helped to wave Anton off on the wind before having a wild party on the beach. Denis didn't stay for the wake.

Two weeks later, Denis Young was in America though apparently it still wasn't sufficiently far from Bourrouillan. He'd left the selling of the house to his solicitors, hoping that he would have to have nothing more to do with it. It turned out that selling a property in France was not as straightforward as he'd remembered when he was buying one. E-mails from his solicitor were a daily occurrence.

Barbara Wiseman had been married to a minor Hollywood producer who had promised her castles in the air but had delivered nothing more than a small tenement, very much on the ground. He'd not stayed long – he'd had more castles to build for other gullible would-be starlets – but she'd kept the tenement and her green card which allowed her to stay in the States and try to earn a living.

Denis had still been contemplating what to do with the rest of his life. Helen had told him she'd welcome him back to the agency but he couldn't see himself working for her; it would be too difficult for him to accept that it was no longer his own business. Besides the whole theatrical business had changed since he was last involved in it. He didn't need the money, so he'd politely refused Helen's offer and accepted Barbara's invitation to get away to the other side of the world.

*

Greg was the only person in the 'Members'' as he sipped his pint, looking out of the small window at a barge just pulling away from the quay. It was unusual for the barges to be out on pleasure cruises this late in the year but as it was full of people dressed in their best clothes, he assumed it was obviously a wedding reception of some sort. He looked at the crowd with some envy as they stood raising their glasses of champagne to the newlyweds. They were enjoying life – having fun. He wondered if he would ever feel like that again. There was no fun in Greg's life at the moment. Even sitting here with his pint wasn't that enjoyable. He wondered about Denis and what he was up to; where he was. He'd heard nothing from him for weeks. It wasn't like they'd been in daily contact since he'd moved to France but it was all different now. Denis had had Anton with him and Greg had had Virginia or whatever she was calling herself these days. Now they were both alone and Greg wanted to see his old friend – be like they used to be. He supposed though that nothing would ever be like it used to be anymore.

There was a voice in his head that kept saying *'phone him'*. He picked up his mobile and looked at it. There was no signal. 'I'll phone him when I get home,' he told himself and went over to the bar. As he stood, waiting for Soozie to stop talking to the customers in the other bar, his phone bleeped. The vagaries of the mobile telephone system never ceased to amaze Greg. How come there was no signal ten yards away at his table and yet he was now receiving messages?

The message wasn't from one of his contacts as it only showed up as a number on his screen; not a name. He opened the message as Soozie came over and pulled him another pint of Kronenbourg, without asking. He thanked her and paid.

'Cheer up. Might never happen,' she said handing him his change.

Greg didn't answer. He just stood transfixed by the words in his phone.

'I know where she is. I'll meet you in the King's Head at four o'clock. Gerald.'

Greg looked at his watch. It was ten to four. A cold shiver ran through him as he sat back in his seat and waited.

*

'There's a woman been sighted in a place called Potsdam about thirty-five miles from Berlin.' Thornton was sitting opposite Greg at the small table. His contact in Berlin had seen the Mayer woman. He hadn't been able to tell the chief – he'd already been told that there was no more budget for this. It was the problem of the French now, he'd been told: He didn't care. He'd use his own budget and his own time and he would get this woman who bugged him and, if necessary, her corrupt father and bring them to justice, if it was the last thing he did.

He had his iPad out again. He flicked the screen and brought up a picture of a woman with short, mousy-coloured hair.

'That could be anyone' said Greg but he knew who it was.

'It could be Mary Stewart or the woman who took her identity after murdering her.' He moved two fingers on the screen, causing the image to enlarge. It showed a scar on the woman's neck, just by her collar-bone. 'I want you to contact her.'

Greg nearly choked on his beer. 'You are joking, of course!'

'Not really.'

'She'd kill me. I was the one who nearly got her caught.'

'You'd have protection.'

'Like Anton, you mean?'

Thornton sat quietly. He needed Greg to help him. He needed to find this woman and bring her to justice. He still wasn't back at work; his paid leave seemed to have become indefinite. There was no hearing, no assessment, no inquiry. He'd just been told not to come back for the time being. He'd spent the last month in regular contact with his man in Berlin.

The man's name was Curtis Zimmermann. It wasn't his real name, he'd been given it when he'd joined the secret service and been sent to Germany. He was a pawn in the vast organisation that was MI6. His job was to listen and report back to his Head of Department – a person he'd never met – in code. He had procured a job at Deutsche Telekom, working in their offices in Berlin, communications being his speciality, but he'd started his career in the Metropolitan Police Force in London and had worked closely with Gerald Thornton. Thornton, in fact, had been instrumental in recommending him to the Service and helping him to achieve his youthful ambition to become a spy. He soon discovered that working for MI6 was nowhere near the same as being James Bond!

He'd been surprised when Thornton had renewed his acquaintance and asked him to help with a private project he was working on. His own department at MI6 was following a similar line, keeping watch on Helmut Mayer. They didn't think his daughter Birgit was anything more than an irritation but they did acknowledge her existence. Thornton's insistence that she was more important than they believed intrigued him. Thornton had always been very astute and if he was right, and Curtis Zimmermann helped to expose her, maybe they would see his worth and give him the promotion he longed for.

'I'm going for a cigarette.' Greg stood up and went out to the terrace. November was bringing with it the cold winter winds and he wished he'd brought his coat out with him as, once again, he cursed the lawmakers that made him stand outside to smoke.

The barge of wedding guests was away in the distance now. He could see the large red-brown sails disappearing across the estuary. They reminded him of Jenny, her pre-Raphaelite hair blowing in the wind. He turned and looked at the old station and sighed. He took a deep breath, feeling the cold air fill his lungs. It made him cough. He looked at the end of his cigarette, took another from his pack and lit it from the glowing end of the first one, before stubbing it out in the ashtray.

His phone bleeped again – obviously he was in another hot-spot. 'You'd think he could come out here if he wants to talk to me,' he thought, assuming it was Thornton wondering why he was taking so long to smoke a cigarette. He took his phone from his pocket and opened the message.

"I miss you xxx" it read.

Greg looked at the top of the screen. This wasn't from the same number as Thornton had used last time and it wasn't one of his contacts. He didn't know who it was who was missing him. Denis? No. He was one of his contacts. Kate Freeman came into his mind. She used to have his number but he'd changed phone since then. He brought up the keyboard on the screen and typed *"Who is this?"*

The answer came back in seconds. Greg's legs turned to jelly as he read the one word answer.

*

Denis Young was sitting at a bar in downtown LA. Barbara had gone to some feminist artist's meeting. She'd invited him to join her but he'd politely declined and had wandered along to the watering hole for the evening. He'd spent a few evenings in this bar over the last few weeks – he couldn't say it was his favourite bar in the world but he liked the fact that they usually showed a World News channel on their televisions as opposed to American football or baseball games. It was late, past eleven o'clock and he watched as several redneck types argued over a game of pool.

He was sitting on a high stool downing gin and tonics. He wasn't drunk but he knew that just a couple more would make his walk home a little more difficult. Still, he ordered another one "to help him sleep". He had a little laugh to himself remembering how he'd berated Greg Driscoll over the years for trying to blot out the world with alcohol. He was starting to understand how Greg felt.

The television was showing a studio debate on the recent German elections. A female presenter, who looked to Denis as though she'd be more suited to one of the many beauty pageants they still held in this country, was discussing whether another four years with Angela Merkel as Chancellor would be a good or a bad thing for the United States. Denis didn't care; he'd never been to Germany and would, most probably, never visit the States again.

'We've got a guy playing music in here next week.' The bartender was leaning across the bar. He was a musclebound man who evidently spent his spare time pumping iron in the gym. Denis wasn't sure if he was being chatted up or not. It had been a long time since he'd been looking for any sort of relationship with anyone other than Anton. A shiver of guilt shot down his spine as he thought of his dead husband.

'Oh, that sounds good.' He tried to be polite.

'I think you'll like him,' said the bartender, presumably talking about the musician. 'Plays a mean guitar.'

'I'll try and get in to check him out,' replied Denis.

The bartender winked at him. 'I'd get in early, if I were you. He's very popular.'

Denis smiled and took a swig from his glass. 'I'll see what I can do.'

He left the remains of his gin and wandered back to Barbara's. She was waiting for him.

'I cooked eggs for you,' she said.

'Oh, sorry. I didn't think you'd be back yet,' apologised Denis.

'It's nearly midnight. I was about to send a posse out.'

'You fuss too much, Barbara. I was just in a bar downtown. Actually they've got a guy playing guitar in there next week. Do you want to come? I think I owe you a night out.' He wanted Barbara to come as protection against the bartender, apart from anything else.

'To a downtown bar? You know how to spoil a girl, don't you!' She smiled. 'I'd love to,' she added.

*

Greg walked through to the 'members' bar. The pub had become busier; a young woman with a baby strapped into a buggy that was nearly as big as a car, filled the corridor in the back bar. He turned into the 'members'. Another large buggy was blocking the doorway. A woman, holding a baby in her arms, tutted and pulled the buggy away with her foot, giving Greg a sneer as he shuffled by the obstruction. Where had they suddenly all come from? He remembered the days fondly, when children weren't allowed in pubs. Thornton had bought Greg a pint of Kronenbourg without asking and was patiently waiting at the table.

'I've had a strange message,' said Greg as he re-joined him.

'Can I see?' he said, holding out his hand.

Greg passed him his phone and he read the three messages on the open page.

'It's a German number from a pay-as-you-go phone,' he stated.

'How do you know?'

'It's my job, Greg. What are you going to do?'

Greg downed the remains of his pint and picked up the one Thornton had bought him. 'I'm not going to Germany.'

The DI sipped his ale and looked over at the woman with the baby. 'I wouldn't like to bring a baby into this world,' he said. Without altering his line of vision he continued, 'It could be a way of catching her and stopping her and her friends killing anyone else. Help to make a better world for young things like that baby over there.'

'I'm not prepared to be a martyr just on the off-chance you might not fuck up this time.'

The baby let out a shriek and the mother stroked its back.

Thornton looked at Greg and raised his eyebrows.

'No, Gerald. How do I know these messages are from Virginia or whatever her name is these days?'

'Who else do you know in Germany that might have your personal phone number and call herself Ginny?' He pointed to the name which was the one word on the last message.

He had a point. Greg didn't know anyone else in Germany. But why was she getting in touch with him? Surely she knew that he was the one who'd informed on her. After what had happened to Anton, he had no inclination to go anywhere near her or her so-called friends.

'We would give you complete protection,' said Thornton. 'You'd never be alone with her, unless, of course, you wanted to be.'

'I can't, Gerald. I'm just an actor. I'm not some sort of undercover operative or whatever you call them. Why can't you trace this number and find her yourself?'

'Can't trace a pay-as-you-go number.' Thornton looked over at the baby, who was whimpering. 'Poor kid,' he muttered.

***

CHAPTER TWENTY-ONE

Stansted airport at the beginning of December, at the comparatively early hour of eight in the morning, was not somewhere Greg Driscoll wanted to be. He was sitting next to DI Thornton. The weather outside was typically British – raining and bloody cold. He desperately wanted a cigarette but there was no area set aside for smokers anymore. How were people supposed to cope? What if you were about to go on a long-haul flight? You might not be able to smoke for nearly a whole day! He cursed under his breath.

Thornton looked up from his newspaper. 'It's good for you.' he observed.

'That's easy for you to say as a non-smoker.'

Thornton nodded. He knew how Greg felt. He'd been a smoker – something else he'd been forced to give up in an effort to save his marriage.

The call for their flight was announced and they picked up their bags and walked across to the gate. There was a moment when Greg nearly turned back and went home with Denis' warning - *'If you even think of going over to Germany to find her, Greg Driscoll, I will never speak to you again. Probably because you'll be as dead as Anton!'* - still ringing succinctly in his ears, but he couldn't turn round now. Thornton had done a good job on his psyche.

He was right. Someone had to try and stop these terrorist groups while they were still relatively small and insignificant, before they grew into a big movement. Birgit Mayer was only getting away with it because of her influential father. Thornton's plan was to expose Helmut Mayer through his daughter. Greg was not convinced he had the power to do that but he duly followed him through the gate and out to the aeroplane.

Four hours later he was sitting outside a cafe in Potsdam. It was a grubby place, alongside a river that looked polluted with scum floating on the top. The sun was shining here but he was still cold. He wrapped his coat round him in a vain effort to get warm. He didn't know why he had to sit outside in this weather but orders were orders and Thornton had emphatically told him he must sit at that table and wait. Birgit Mayer would turn up at some point, his informers had said. Greg was to attract her attention. Thornton was nowhere to be seen. A man in a cap was reading a newspaper at a table a few yards from where Greg was sitting. Apart from a couple of men in overalls standing inside at the bar, there was no-one else in the cafe. Greg was nursing a beer and feeling extremely uncomfortable and nervous.

He had been fitted with a small microphone and a battery pack, concealed in a leather shoulder bag, currently lying on top of the table, which would relay any conversation straight back to wherever Thornton was hiding himself. A minute earpiece was concealed in Greg's ear, through which the DI could guide him.

Greg had managed to make his beer last for half an hour and he looked around for the rather surly man who'd served him in order to ask for a refill. However he seemed to be involved in a discourse with the two workmen. Greg stood up and picked up his empty glass.

'Where are you going?' Thornton's voice rattled off his eardrum.

Greg looked around not sure how to answer. He leaned over the table and spoke in the direction of the shoulder bag, 'To get a beer,' he whispered, hoping the man in the cap didn't notice anything odd.

'Take the bag,' ordered Thornton.

Greg picked it up from the table and went to the bar where he stood politely waiting for the barman to finish some sort of altercation he was having with one of the men. Eventually he noticed Greg, grabbed his glass, refilled it and thrust back at him, all the while continuing to shout and gesticulate at the other customer.

Greg turned and started back to the door, just as three young men with shaven heads entered. They had tattoos on their necks and faces and were wearing sleeveless vests, under some sort of camouflage jackets and tatty jeans that finished six inches above their ankles, the latter being clad in shiny black mid-calf length leather army boots. The men at the bar stopped their conversation and looked at them. One of the skinheads shouted something in German and the barman pointed to a door behind the bar.

Greg stood still, feeling rather out-of-place in his comparatively neat Levis, shirt, V-necked jumper and faux-fur collared bomber jacket.

One of the skinheads caught sight of him and yelled something aggressively in German, pointing a grubby finger at him. Greg shrugged his shoulders in a way he hoped said he didn't understand German. It was evidently the wrong thing to do as the young tattooed man took a step in his direction, his right hand feeling for something in his back pocket. Greg wanted to run but fear paralysed him.

'Komm da weg!'

Greg knew the voice even though he couldn't understand what it said. It came from the doorway. The three skinheads stopped and looked at the woman with short black hair, cut like a boy, who stood with her hands on her hips just inside the cafe.

Greg remained rooted to the spot. The woman was wearing camouflage combat trousers, a green sleeveless vest, a jacket and boots similar to the boys. There was a newly-inked tattoo of a swastika on her neck. She was staring with disbelief at Greg Driscoll.

He attempted to speak but only croaked. He cleared his throat and tried again. 'Hello Ginny,' he said.

*

'What the fuck is he doing? Can you see him?' DI Thornton's voice sounded loudly in the ear of the man in the cap. He pulled up the collar of his jacket and spoke quietly.

'He's getting a beer. She's arrived.'

'Is he with her?'

The man looked through the window of the bar. 'Yes,' was all he said.

*

'What are you doing here?' Birgit Mayer whispered. She was aggressive and Greg was scared. He didn't know what to say or do. He wanted to run. The woman stepped closer to him and grabbed his arm. 'Come outside,' she hissed.

Greg let her lead him back to the table he'd just left. She looked at the man in the cap, who folded up his newspaper and stood up. He touched his cap as he walked past. 'Guten tag,' he said and wandered off down the road.

'What are you doing here?' she asked again.

'You sent me a text. You said you missed me.' Greg wanted to pick up his beer but was afraid his hand would shake.

Birgit sneered at him. 'You are so stupid!'

Greg, following the instructions in his ear, took out his phone and brought up the message page. 'There,' he said putting the phone on the table before he dropped it.

Birgit looked at the messages on the screen. 'I did not send these,' she scowled. She no longer sounded English. She didn't sound a bit like the woman who'd convinced Greg she was Jenny Gulliver. She now had a violent guttural quality to her voice. 'You should go,' she said.

'I've come a long way, Ginny. I wanted to see you so you could explain what happened. One minute you were in my arms and then you were running away from the police. What happened?' Greg thought it was one of the worst scripts he'd ever had to deliver but Thornton had insisted on what he should say.

'You know what happened, Greg. I know you know. You were there in the house in Estang. I heard you. Why are you here? It's not safe for you.' She put her hand over her new tattoo as if to shield it from Greg.

Tell her you know who her father is.' Thornton echoed in Greg's ear. *'And put the bag on the table, I can hardly hear anything.'*

'I miss the time we had together, Ginny,' said Greg ignoring the Detective Inspector. He reached out his hand to touch hers but she pulled it back away from the table. 'I mean it, Ginny. I don't care what you've done. I miss you.'

'Stick to what I told you. What the fuck are you doing?'

'Greg, don't do this.' Birgit was staring at Greg. He couldn't tell what she was thinking but there was something in her eyes he recognised: something kind, something softer. He held her stare until she looked away.

One of the tattooed youths came to the door and yelled something in German. Birgit yelled back, her eyes now spitting fire again. The youth slammed his hand against the door jamb and stomped off into the bar.

Birgit looked back at Greg. There was a tear sliding down her cheek and she wiped it away angrily. 'Don't do this, Greg,' she reiterated in a harsh whisper.

Greg picked up the shoulder bag and placed it back on the table. 'Shall I go?' he asked.

Birgit looked away. 'Yes,' she answered quietly. Greg stood up. Suddenly she looked up at him. 'No,' she said. 'Don't go.' She looked away again,

The two of them sat in silence. Thornton was yelling in Greg's ear but he found it easy to ignore him. He reached out his hand again and this time she let him take hold of her.

'You really ought to go, Greg. You don't know what's going on here.' Her voice was soft again, like Jenny's.

'I want to know, though. I want to understand.'

She looked at him, trying to read his mind. Was he telling the truth? She'd believed Anton DuBois - she didn't want Greg to end up like him. Her heart was fluttering as she stared into his eyes. She had to look away again. Why was he here? Why did she feel like this? She'd never let her heart rule her head. The real free Germany was far more important than how she felt about this stupid Englishman.

'You'll never understand, Greg. I'm sorry.' She withdrew her hand again.

'Try me,' said Greg. 'What is it you're trying to do?'

'I have to go,' said Birgit standing up.

'Please stay.' Greg stood up as well and took hold of Birgit. She squirmed and tried to get away but Greg put his arms round her and pulled her lips towards his. She turned her face and he kissed her cheek. Slowly she turned back to him and met his lips with hers. He felt her body relax and he held on tightly. She moved her head to his shoulder and hugged him.

'This is so wrong, Greg. Please go,' she sighed.

'No. I'm not going anywhere, Ginny.'

Birgit pulled herself away from him and took a card from her back pocket. 'Meet me there at eight o'clock,' she said and ran through the bar into the room at the back.

Greg looked at the card. It was a business card for a bar somewhere in Potsdam.

'Where the fuck has she gone?' Thornton's voice bellowed in Greg's head.

He reached up and dug the small receiver from his ear, walked over to the shoulder bag on the table and threw it inside. Leaving the bag on the table, next to some Euros for the beers, he went off along the riverbank.

The man in the cap passed him, went to the table Greg had just vacated, picked up the bag and the Euros and walked off in the other direction.

*

Birgit was distracted as she sat in the small room at the back of the bar. The three skinheads were arguing with each other. She didn't really believe that they had any interest in 'the cause'. All they wanted to do was beat people up. Immigrants were just an easy target for the youths. Beating up immigrants wasn't the answer – it only made them more determined. They needed to be evicted, sent back to their own countries, instead of letting them scrounge off hard-working German people.

She felt dubious about the planned demonstration the next day. It had all been her father's idea. He wanted control of the Bundestag. He wanted to be Chancellor so he could push through his policies. The policies were right of course - Germany for German people - but it scared Birgit. He was becoming a megalomaniac and she doubted whether his belief in 'the cause' was just a way to achieve his own advancement. It was a big day tomorrow. The rally outside the Bundeskanzleramt in Berlin was to take place as the members of parliament arrived to decide who would join the new coalition government. Following the elections, the Christian Democrats had increased their number of seats but still didn't hold a majority, so would have to join with one of the other parties to form a government. The whole situation was a mess. The SPD didn't want to work with Angela Merkel's party and Helmut Mayer was working hard to get his colleagues to understand that they could work from the inside much better than just as an opposition. They would try to stop any debate about the possibility of permitting even more supposed refugees into the country – irrespective of whether they were ISIS terrorists or not. Birgit and her associates had managed to call together a large number of people to demonstrate. Until the question of the coalition was resolved, Angela Merkel would remain as Chancellor.

Birgit knew it could possibly be her last act on this earth. It was her responsibility to detonate a bomb as the Chancellor arrived. She was aware it might be an act of martyrdom and would probably make her not much better than the terrorists she was trying to keep out - but she knew her motive was right. It also had nothing to do with religion. Her faith was in 'the cause'. She hated religion. She was an atheist and firmly believed that religion was the root of all evil - another reason she was prepared to die for 'the cause'. There would be no retribution; she'd be dead, gone, no more. She wouldn't have to stand in front of a throne and confess her sins, she wouldn't live in eternal flames and she wouldn't have twenty virgins waiting for her – not that she wanted twenty virgins anyway, she'd always thought that was an odd reward.

She was annoyed with herself. Was she having second thoughts? She'd been prepared for this for weeks but now...now bloody Greg Driscoll had turned up. Was her faith starting to falter just because he had shown her some affection? She looked at the three thugs she was supposed to be briefing for the big day. She knew they wouldn't take any notice. Her only hope was that they and their friends scrapping would distract the police, if not the Chancellor's own personal bodyguards. Maybe she didn't need to be caught.

She banged her fist hard on the table and tried to bring some order to the meeting.

*

'What the fuck were you doing?' DI Thornton was out of breath. He'd run from the truck he'd been in to catch up with Greg as he'd passed. Greg kept walking at a furious pace. He didn't know where he was going. He just wanted to get away. He felt dirty. He had no feelings towards Birgit. Using his charm to try and ignite any affection she may have had for him made him feel sick. He hadn't followed Thornton's orders. He'd gone off on his own and got caught up in the situation. He didn't know why. It had just happened. He wanted out: He wanted home: He wanted Jenny Gulliver to be alive and waiting for him. None of that was going to happen, though. He knew he'd have to meet Birgit Mayer at the bar at eight o'clock.

Thornton grabbed his shoulder. Greg flung round, his clenched fist ready to strike.

'Don't even think about,' snapped the DI, taking hold of Greg's arm and twisting it behind his back. 'What's going on?' he said in Greg's ear.

'Let me go!' Greg squirmed, his arm hurting.

Thornton ignored the request. 'Why are you defying me? I need to catch that girl and you've just let her go. You were supposed to find out her plans so she could be caught red-handed.'

'I'm meeting her tonight.' Greg felt the pressure against his arm relax slightly. 'At a bar somewhere,' he added.

Thornton took a step back and let Greg go, ready in case he was foolish enough to try another punch. Greg rolled his shoulder to ease the pain and turned to the policeman. Much as he wanted to, he resisted the urge to beat him to a pulp.

'Good,' said Thornton. 'We'll get you wired up again. Where's the bar?'

'You won't wire me up.' Greg was defiant. 'I'm not taking that risk again. I think I have her trust. I don't want to break that. I remember what happened to Anton.'

'You might have her trust but do I have yours?'

'What? You think I'm suddenly going to become a fascist and join her little party? I'd better get going, then. There must loads of tattooists who do a good swastika round here!'

'Where's the bar you're meeting her at?'

Greg handed Thornton the business card Birgit had given him.

'I'll be outside in the truck. I need you to find out when she's going to make her next move. There's something brewing - I know that I just don't know what or where.'

'Why do you think she'll tell me?'

Thornton just smiled. Charm had never been something he'd possessed in abundance. It was a shame; it could be a useful weapon for a detective.

***

CHAPTER TWENTY-TWO

Birgit Mayer sat on her bed wondering - wondering why she was here, in this squalid, dirty dwelling. It was a squat - a disused block of flats. It was disused for a reason. Rats had taken up residence long before she and her cohorts had moved in less than a month ago. At least she had a room of her own – they'd given her that respect as the oldest member of the group, as well as being one of only two females in the group. She had a bed of her own, if you could call it that. It was mattress on the floor – an old, soiled mattress – with a sleeping bag on top of it. There was a tatty chest of drawers with a mirror attached to it. Birgit was looking at the mirror at the moment. A large crack ran through its middle and the silvering had turned a dark brown colour round the edges but this didn't obscure the fact that she was looking at a forty-three year old supposedly adult woman who was staring back at her with sad eyes. She turned her head away and focused on the bare floorboards. A tear dripped down her nose and she swished it away as if it were a wasp.

This was Greg Driscoll's fault. A year ago, she hadn't even heard of this actor. Now, she couldn't erase him from her mind. What was he doing here? What was she doing here? A year ago she knew why she was following her father's manifesto. She agreed with him. Immigrants were coming into her country and slowly destroying it from the inside and no-one could see it happening; no-one was prepared to do anything about it. And yet now?

Her father was a wealthy man. He'd made a lot of money exploiting cheap labour. He'd taken over businesses – failing businesses admittedly – in other countries and turned them into successful companies, and she'd benefitted from his wealth. Her childhood had been all that many people could have wished for - a good education, exotic holidays, posh hotels - yet now, here she was in this filthy dump, waiting to go and commit a crime against another person who was also standing up for their principles. She had never felt so confused.

What had she wanted from her life? To leave something behind, she supposed. Not money. That would happen anyway. Besides there was no-one to leave it to. She had never wanted to marry nor have children. All her relationships had been ephemeral – short-lived and transient. As soon as any man had started to get serious she'd run. Why was that? Fear? Of what? Commitment? She didn't think so. She had been committed to her father's cause all of her adult life. Maybe that was the problem.

She'd run away from Greg Driscoll, though not out of choice this time She hadn't felt the need to run from him yet. She'd run from the authorities who were trying to stop her fulfilling her duty to her father. But, for the first time, someone had come running back - had found her; had wanted to re-kindle something. No-one had ever done that before.

And now she had arranged to meet him; to sit with him and talk. About what? If she told him her plans for the next day he'd try and stop her, wouldn't he? And she was afraid that she would let him. That couldn't happen. Not now. Not this close. She looked in the cracked mirror again, ran her hands through her shorn hair and left the room.

The woman behind the counter called the security guard as Birgit Mayer walked in. He stood watching her. She was aware of him. She was used to this but she knew she had a secret weapon. A platinum credit card with the name Mayer on it. She looked through the evening dresses. The short ones were no good, they would show the tattoos she'd had done on her ankles. It had to be a long one. She took a frock from the rack which prompted the security guard to approach. Without looking in his direction she put her hand in her pocket and held up the credit card. She then turned and showed her driving licence, with her photograph on it, as proof to this idiot that she was the daughter of a multi-millionaire politician and would not be messed with. The guard was confused. This woman, dressed like a teenager who didn't have two euros to rub together, was holding an exclusive credit card in his face. His first thought was that she'd obviously stolen it but the photo on the driving licence certainly looked like this person. The hair was cut differently but it was obviously her. He studied it closely and handed it back. Birgit re-racked the dress and went over to the assistant and demanded that she show her the best evening outfit they had in the shop. Birgit Mayer was enjoying herself. It was the sort of thing she used to do as a student – pretend to be poor before producing evidence that she was, in fact, one of the super-rich.

She looked at herself in the mirror and laughed. She hadn't worn clothes like this for over twenty years. Ordering the assistant to put her tatty combats in the expensive-looking branded carrier bag, she punched in the number for the credit card, and walked, in a most ladylike manner, to the door before turning, raising a finger and yelling, 'Fick dich' and exiting the shop.

*

Greg was in the bar at Potsdam promptly at eight o'clock. There was no sign of any woman in combat trousers and a vest, with a tattoo of a swastika on her neck. It wasn't that sort of bar. Greg guessed it was probably the poshest bar in town and it reminded him of his last date with Jenny Gulliver in London twenty-odd years ago. There was obviously some money in Potsdam, even though Greg had seen no evidence of it where he had been. He had wondered if they would let him in, in his Levis, shirt and bomber jacket but no-one appeared to be bothered. Even so, he felt completely under-dressed. He ordered an overpriced beer and sat in a corner where he could see the entrance. He didn't hold out a lot of hope that Birgit would actually arrive. She'd used a ploy to get rid of him and he'd bought it. He looked around. Maybe she'd sent him here as a joke to make him feel stupid. She'd said he was stupid. Maybe she was right. Or maybe he was sitting here waiting to be assassinated.

He'd almost finished his lager when he spotted her. She was wearing a long sleeveless dress with gloves that came up to her elbows and carrying a small Gucci handbag. Heavy make-up covered the tattoo on her neck. She wore stiletto heels and had an expensive-looking necklace pointing down to her semi-exposed cleavage. She looked like the proverbial million dollars.

'You could have warned me that I should dress for the occasion,' he said as he stood to greet her.

'I've seen your wardrobe, Greg. I didn't think there was much point.' She sat at the table while Greg fetched the drinks.

'I'm sorry to bring you here, I know you must feel uncomfortable, I just wanted somewhere where no-one would know me.'

'It's fine,' said Greg. 'Very nice place.' He hoped his sarcasm didn't show.

She clinked her glass with Greg's. 'Prost.'

'Cheers.'

They sat in silence for a while, neither of them quite knowing why they were there.

'You look beautiful,' said Greg at length.

'I feel bloody ridiculous,' she replied, her mouth turning into a smile.

'This is a bit weird.' Greg felt completely out of his depth, in more ways than one.

'Sorry.' Birgit looked down into her drink. There was an ice cube slowly breaking up and she watched as a piece detached itself and drifted to the other side of the glass, free from the restraints of the bigger cube. She was sure now that meeting up with Greg was a mistake. It had been selfish to involve Greg; selfish and extremely dangerous. But this could be the last night of her life. She wanted to enjoy it, to enjoy being with Greg Driscoll again as she had for those months in Maldon.

'Do we have to stay here?' Greg leaned over and spoke quietly in her ear.

'I have to be careful, Greg,' she answered. 'Do you have a hotel room?'

Greg nodded and smiled. He didn't want to go back to his room with this woman but he equally didn't want to stay here.

Birgit put her hand on his leg and swigged back her drink. 'Come on, then,' she said.

*

DI Thornton and Zimmermann still in his cap, sat in the back of the truck outside Greg's hotel.

'Should have wired him up with a mini-cam,' said the cap. 'Could make interesting viewing.'

Thornton looked at him with disdain. 'I'm sure you could find some porn not too far away, if you're desperate,' he said.

'So do we just sit here all night?' Zimmermann pushed his cap to the back of his head and scratched his bald patch.

Thornton sighed. He didn't want to sit here all night either. It was uncomfortable, apart from anything else and, even though it was stuffy in the back of the van, the night was getting cold. 'Do you have a better suggestion?' he asked his colleague.

'There's a bar over the road. That'll be open till three.'

Thornton looked at him. He was feeling despondent. Was he wasting his time – not to mention his money? He'd brought Driscoll over here and all he seemed to be doing was re-kindling his romance with the suspect. The bar was a tempting option. At least it would be warm and might have a bit of air. It was coming up to midnight and they had been here for three and half hours already. Driscoll had been given a phone that was untraceable and told to relay any information he found out. Thornton checked his own phone, as if by doing so it would spark into life as Greg got in touch. The screen remained blank.

Zimmermann was looking through the darkened window at the back of the truck. He had a direct view of the hotel's front door. It was a shabby place, a tall concrete block rising high into the Potsdam sky - the sort of hotel where you could rent rooms by the hour. Several women wearing too much make-up and very little else had come and gone whilst he'd watched: with men in suits following a few minutes later.

*

Greg Driscoll lay on his bed wondering what the hell he was doing. An empty bottle of Champagne sat upside down in a metal ice bucket. The carpet was strewn with discarded clothes. Birgit's passionate lovemaking had taken him by surprise. It was if they had never made love before.

367

She was aggressive then tender, screaming with pleasure then crying like a baby.

She sat on the edge of the bed, her back to Greg. He slipped out of the bed and came to sit next to her. She took his hand.

'I have to go, Greg,' she said, after a while.

He just nodded as she stood up and started to dress.

'There's something I'd like you to know, Greg,' she said, not looking at him.

'What?'

She turned, still in just her underwear, and sat next to him on the edge of the bed. 'You are very special, Greg.' She paused and looked away. 'But I can't see you again.'

'Why not?' He held onto her hand.

'My name's not Virginia.' She was staring at the mirror on the dressing table in front of them.

'I know,' replied Greg.

'I thought you might. Do you know who I am?'

'Bridget someone?'

Birgit laughed. A tear squeezed its way from under her eyelid. Greg reached up and wiped it away.

'My father is a very important man, Greg, and he wants me to do something that's not right.'

'What does he want you to do?'

She gripped his hand tighter. 'I can't tell you that, Greg.'

'If it's wrong, don't do it.' Greg put his hand on her chin and turned her face towards him. Another tear escaped and they both let it roll down her cheek and drip onto the bed.

'You can't understand,' she said, lifting her hand to stroke his hair. She brought her other hand up and held onto either side of his face. She leaned towards him, pushing him back onto the bed, caressing him, kissing him, tousling his hair. She looked deep into his eyes. 'Damn you, Greg Driscoll,' she whispered, tears cascading now. 'Why did you come here?' She stood up.

Greg grabbed her wrist, holding her back. 'Don't go,' he said. 'Don't do it.'

She tore her arm free and pulled her dress over her head, fitting her feet into her shoes. Grabbing her long gloves and her bag, she strode towards the door. 'Don't be in Berlin tomorrow,' she said and exited the room.

*

Zimmermann was still looking out of the truck's window. There was not a great deal of night-life going on. Even the working girls seemed to have done their business and gone somewhere else. The hotel door opened again and a woman in a long dress hurried away along the road. She was carrying a pair of long gloves in her left hand.

'I think we have some action,' he said.

Thornton looked out of the window. 'That's her. Why hasn't Driscoll phoned?'

'Probably shagged out,' replied Zimmermann.

'Follow her,' ordered Thornton.

'In the truck?'

'No, on foot. I'm staying here.' Thornton took his phone out and punched in the number for Greg's untraceable phone.

*

Birgit Mayer ran along the dark street. Her high heels were incapacitating her so she kicked them off and left them lying by the side of the road. She wouldn't need them again. Her head was spinning. What was she doing? Why had Greg Driscoll followed her here? She stopped running, leaning against a wall, catching her breath. A car drove past slowly and came to a halt. A large man in a greasy suit leaned over and yelled out of the open window.

Birgit glared at him with contempt. Part of her wanted to take up his offer of a paid encounter – after which she'd take great pleasure in slitting his throat. Instead she snarled, 'Mach es dir selber!' and spat in the direction of the car.

The greasy suit shouted something back that she didn't bother to listen to. She was racing down a side street between the buildings. The man was excited but as opened his car door to follow her, he spotted a man in a cap looking at him. He had a phone in his hand and was either calling the police or taking photographs of his car. He slammed the door shut and drove away at a pace.

*

'What did you expect me to do? Lock her in?' Greg was angry with Thornton.

'I told you to keep her with you. Where has she gone?'

'I haven't a clue.'

'I'm coming in. Don't you dare move!' Thornton disconnected, slammed the door of the truck and headed over to the hotel.

Greg sighed and dressed himself. He went to the bathroom and threw water onto his face. The man in the mirror smiled. He appeared younger than the last time Greg had looked at him.

He opened the door to Thornton. 'Is she coming back?' asked the detective.

Greg shook his head. 'She tells me I will never see her again.'

'Shit!' said Thornton barging his way into the room.

'Yes it is, really.' Greg closed the door. He stood reading the emergency instructions pinned to the back of it, wondering if he'd be able to make sense of them if he ever needed them. Thornton paced up and down by the window.

'Did she tell you anything?' he said.

Greg stopped reading and came to sit on the bed. 'She told me a lot of things, Gerald. She said I was special.'

'You know what I mean, Driscoll. I know she's planning something. You were supposed to find out when and where, not satisfy your own lust.'

'Pull her in and ask her yourself, then.'

Thornton looked out of the window into the Potsdam night. Even if he wanted to, he knew he had no jurisdiction to arrest her. He also knew that it would achieve nothing.

'She told me not to go to Berlin tomorrow.'

Thornton turned to Greg, 'Why?'

Greg shrugged his shoulders. Thornton's phone buzzed.

'She's in a squat off Am Speicher,' said Zimmermann. *'Shall I wait?'*

'What's happening in Berlin tomorrow?' Thornton yelled into his phone.

'Apart from the government trying to sort out the shit the elections have left them in, you mean?'

'What's happening?'

'They're voting on whether to accept the new coalition. Anyone who's anyone will be turning up to try and get themselves a top job in the new regime.'

'How stupid am I?'

Neither Greg nor Zimmermann answered.

'Where?' It was a stupid question.

'The Reichstag building in the Platz der Republik.'

Suddenly it all seemed so patently obvious to Thornton. The German Republic had recently held their elections. A new government was about to take its place as the Bundestag. They would choose their new Chancellor. First, though, they had to decide which parties would be in the coalition. The current Chancellor, Angela Merkel, was pro-active in encouraging refugees to settle in Germany, something that Birgit Mayer and her cronies would not be pleased about. This would be the ideal place to make a stand and raise their profile.

'Get back to the truck,' he told Zimmermann. 'And you, Driscoll, you're coming with me. Now!'

'Where to?'

'Berlin!'

***

CHAPTER TWENTY-THREE

An e-mail from Helen Clarke was disturbing Denis Young. She'd been trying to get hold of Greg Driscoll for some time. There were things to sort out with his contract for the next series of 'Once in a While', which was due to start rehearsing in the New Year. Greg had not been answering phone calls or e-mails and she was concerned. Denis had tried to contact him too but to no avail. Barbara told him not to upset himself and suggested that Greg was off on a bender somewhere and would be in touch when he sobered up. Barbara Wiseman did not have a very high opinion of Greg Driscoll. 'You needn't worry, Denis,' she tried to assure him.

Denis had one week left on his visa and was flying back to London in four days. He'd try to find his erstwhile friend and client then. For now he said he would try not to worry.

*

Greg Driscoll was worried. He was sitting cramped in the back of a truck with darkened windows next to a lot of electronic equipment. He'd had no sleep for thirty-six hours and was feeling listless. His head was throbbing.

DI Thornton and the man in the cap, whom it appeared was called Zimmermann, were also in the back of the vehicle. Zimmermann had a pair of headphones clamped over his cap and onto his ears. He was listening to something intently.

'They're coming out,' he said.

Thornton left the back of the truck and heaved himself into the driver's seat at the front. He was wearing jeans and a tatty shirt and sported a cap similar to Zimmermann's. He turned the key in the ignition and put the vehicle into gear.

Three buses were lined up in front of them and were currently filling up with, mostly, young men holding hand-made placards. Thornton couldn't understand the words scrawled across them apart from the word 'Merkel.' Some of them portrayed ill-drawn cartoons of the current Chancellor, who was expecting another four years in office.

The convoy of buses set off into the morning drizzle and Thornton tucked the truck into the traffic two cars further back. He'd seen Birgit Mayer and her friends join the second bus in the procession and was determined to keep them in sight.

Greg, in the back of the truck, was trying to stay awake. Zimmermann still had his headphones on his head and was listening in. He'd been out in the early hours as the buses had arrived and, whilst pretending to chat with the drivers, he had managed to leave listening devices on the buses. He was now eavesdropping on the conversations currently taking place. Whilst he knew Birgit Mayer was on one of the buses he was tuned into, he couldn't hear her. Any speech was drowned out by shouting and singing.

Birgit was not shouting or singing. She was dressed once more in her combat trousers and vest and was sitting by the window watching the traffic splashing through the puddles on the road to Berlin. The rally was to take place outside the Reichstag building. The police would try and keep them away from the cortege carrying the VIPs to the parliament building but she knew she'd be able to get near enough for what she had to do. The explosive device was in a canvas army shoulder bag. She also had her Glock 29 pistol tucked into the back of her trousers. The Glock 29 was a semi-automatic firearm that could shoot off up to ten rounds in a matter of seconds.

*

In spite of the weather, the lawns outside the Reichstag Building were covered with people. Most of them were there to see and cheer for their respective members of Parliament and it appeared a festive occasion. There were vans selling bratwurst and even a pop-up bar, Greg noticed. However, in the far corner, cordoned off by a phalanx of Polizei, there was a small group of shaven-headed young people shouting and holding their arms out in front of them at a forty-five degree angle. It would have been quite frightening if the group had been any bigger but they were being well controlled and Greg had to admit he'd seen scarier scenes at football matches. Once again, he thought that Thornton had miscalculated. He couldn't see any serious trouble happening here.

The two of them were mingling with the crowd. Thornton looked extremely uncomfortable in casual dress instead of his usual work clothes.

'You could have worn your suit, you know,' observed Greg. 'There's plenty of suited people here.' He looked around at the groups of individuals, sheltering under umbrellas - office workers, some organised school parties, young people and old. It seemed the whole diversity of Berlin had turned up.

Thornton didn't answer. He knew Greg was right. Undercover work was not something that suited the detective inspector. He was wearing the tiny earpiece and listening for some sort of report from Zimmermann.

Zimmermann had infiltrated the rowdy crowd on the other side of the police line and was looking for any sign of something about to happen. There was nothing going on other than some banter with the policemen and Zimmermann was pretty sure that nothing was about to occur. Thornton could be obsessive - he remembered this from when he'd worked with him in London - and he was very obsessed with this Mayer woman, even though he'd told Thornton that MI6 had looked into her and didn't see her as a real threat. Besides, the police presence was too strong for such a small group of youths.

The constant bellow of 'sieg heils' galled him. It was sick that these hooligans were emulating the Nazi regime. It disturbed him having to join in and pretend to be part of them but that was his job. No-one had questioned or suspected him as he'd attached himself to the crowd, some even slapped him on the back, pleased for anyone to swell their numbers. He couldn't see the Mayer girl amongst them. There were a few females, mostly younger than Mayer, but it was a mostly male dominated assembly. He turned and asked the skinhead next to him if he fancied a bratwurst but he looked at him as though he were mad and took a can of lager from his bag, opening it as if to explain that it contained the only food he needed. Zimmermann squeezed his way through the throng. He needed to report to Thornton and finding somewhere quiet and discreet enough was proving difficult.

A number of people were starting to accumulate on the steps outside the Reichstag. Greg assumed, correctly, that these were the newly-elected members of the German parliament, happy to show themselves off to their supporters. More 'sieg heils' resounded from the corner, hands and fingers pointing in the direction of the building. Large black cars came and went, dropping off their important passengers before getting away as soon as they could.

'There's Helmut Mayer.' Thornton pointed to a large man in a pale suit standing at the edge of the group. A woman in a sharp suit held an umbrella over the fat man. He had a smug look on his face and was the only one to acknowledge the neo-nazis in the corner.

Zimmermann came through on Thornton's earpiece.

'She's not here,' he said.

'She has to be, we saw her get off the bus.'

'The other yobbos are here but not her.'

Thornton looked around the people he was amongst. She could be anywhere in the conflux surrounding the parliament building. He'd never be able to spot her through the umbrellas if she was somewhere in the crowd.

'She must be there. Find her!' ordered Thornton.

Zimmermann bought his bratwurst. He was starving; he'd not eaten nor slept since the previous morning and he was wet, cold and thoroughly pissed off. He wandered around the back of the baying mob, eyes peeled for a woman in combats but she wasn't there. He caught sight of one of the skinheads who'd travelled with her on the bus and asked if he knew where she might be. He shrugged his shoulders and carried on shouting abuse at the politicians. Zimmermann noticed he had brass knuckledusters decorating each of his hands. He moved away, deeper into the melee.

A cheer went up around the crowd on the lawns as another black car with tinted windows drove up to the steps of the Reichstag. The horde of people pressed forward, sweeping Greg and Thornton with them. Greg found himself separated from Thornton and crushed against the metal barriers at the side of the driveway. The car drew to a halt outside the building and the chauffeur opened the rear door to allow Angel Merkel to step out into the weak December sunshine. She turned and waved. The 'seig heils' sounded louder and at a quicker tempo from behind the police cordon. She ignored them and started walking slowly up the steps to greet the waiting members, most of who were applauding. The clapping and cheering all but drowned out the noise from the neo-nazis.

Suddenly Greg spotted Birgit. She wasn't amongst the neo-nazis; she was less than twenty yards to his right, at the front of the crowd, only the metal barriers between her and the chancellor's car. She put her hand into her bag and took something out that she threw – not at the car but further down the drive. The explosion was little more than a flash – a firework. There was no loud blast but it was enough to distract the police for a moment. Angela Merkel was bundled back into the car. Birgit Mayer hurdled the barrier in front of her, her right hand digging into the back of trousers.

Greg yelled as she fought his way through the panicking people around him. Leaping over the barriers, he ran after her. 'No! Birgit, no! Don't do it!' he screamed.

She managed to fire off five rounds before the high-powered bullet hit her full in the centre of her chest, throwing her through the air into Greg who was by now close behind her. He caught hold of her and the two of them smashed into the tarmac.

'Did I get the Chancellor?' she whispered, turning her head to look at Greg.

A deep red pool was forming on her chest, her green vest soaking up the blood like a sponge. Greg looked away in the direction of the Reichstag. Angela Merkel's car was away down the drive. A group of people were standing over a body on the ground. It wasn't the Chancellor.

'Yes, you did,' lied Greg as he held Birgit's head. Police were standing around pointing their rifles at them and shouting in German. Greg held onto Birgit.

She tried to smile, her watery eyes drifting in and out of focus. 'Thanks,' she said, her voice choking on the dark blood emanating from her mouth.

'For what?'

'For lying. I wasn't aiming at her.' The watery eyes grew paler and her body jerked as she coughed up more blood and mucus. Greg felt the wet slime on his face but didn't move. Birgit Mayer's bodyweight suddenly increased as her muscles ceased to hold her and her heart stopped beating. Greg held onto the dead body as the police shouted at him in German. He stayed still, holding her close. It was the second time in his life he'd hugged a dying woman who'd called herself Jenny. The police moved in and pulled Greg away. He noticed one of the officers kick the side of Birgit, before calling over the paramedics. Greg was handcuffed and thrown roughly into the back of a police van.

*

Denis and Barbara walked into the downtown bar. It was early evening and, despite the bartender's prophesy, the bar was not very busy. It seemed the guy with the guitar was not quite as popular as he'd made out and he was not attracting much of an audience.

They ordered their drinks and Barbara said she was more than happy to sit at the bar rather than one of the grubby-looking tables. The bartender seemed disappointed that Denis was not only with a friend but that the friend was female. Maybe he'd misread the signs.

'It's all kicking off in Germany,' he said as poured two large gin and tonics.

Denis looked at the television screen – it was showing a baseball game. 'Why? What's happened?' he said without particular interest.

'Someone got shot,' he said, bringing a bowl of nuts over for his customers to savour.

'Really?' Denis turned to Barbara and lifted his glass. 'Cheers,' he said. 'Thanks for putting up with me. You were right. It was what I needed.'

'You're welcome anytime, Denis. It's nice to have some company that doesn't have four legs, to be honest.'

Denis looked at her quizzically.

'Pampered pets?' she said. They laughed.

There was a sudden furore by the pool table. The bartender yelled across to the two rednecks. They were complaining because the television had been changed to the World News channel – even though they hadn't been watching the baseball.

'It was some politician. Look.' The bartender was leaning over the bar, pointing towards the TV screen.

Denis sighed and turned to the screen. What he saw made him instantly nauseous. There, in front of his eyes, was Greg Driscoll holding the bleeding body of the woman he knew as Virginia Hoffman.

'Fucking hell!' he screamed. His glass slipped from his fingers and smashed on the floor.

*

It took DI Thornton and Curtis Zimmermann twenty four hours to get Greg released. He was to be deported. Thornton had had to tell his superiors what he'd been up to and had been told he would definitely be on a disciplinary charge as soon as he set foot back in the UK. The British Embassy in Berlin as well as MI6 had been called in to convince the German authorities that Greg Driscoll had nothing to do with Birgit Mayer's actions and that he'd been trying to stop her.

No-one in the Bundestag was particularly unhappy at the demise of one of their members. He'd never been welcome as a member; he'd been arrogant and overbearing. His views had been further to the right than even his own party had dared to be. He'd openly opposed the Chancellor and her policies which, as far as most of the members were concerned, had just wasted time in the Bundestag. They had all assumed that he'd arranged the small neo-nazi protest. What confused them was the fact that one of them had been the assassin. What confused them even more was that the assassin was his own daughter.

***

CHAPTER TWENTY-FOUR

Greg Driscoll was sitting next to Gerald Thornton on the plane back to Stansted. Neither of them had much to say to each other.

Greg's mind was filled with Birgit Mayer - the meeting at the bar by the river: the night in the hotel: the episode outside the Reichstag. Mostly his head kept replaying the image of her flying through the air into his arms, a large bullet-hole in her chest. He couldn't work out how he was supposed to feel. By rights he ought to despise her; she'd lied to him: pretended to be the one person who had obsessed him for the last twenty years. How had she known about Jenny? How had he she known how he would react? Was she just the epitome of evil? And yet, two nights previously she hadn't seemed evil. They'd made love – real love with passion and feeling. Was that all just an act? And what about the Reichstag? Had she always intended to kill her father? Or was her plan really to assassinate the Chancellor? Whichever, she must have known it would be her final act; that it would be a suicide job. Greg didn't know. He couldn't fathom it in his mind. He just wanted to switch off.

His time incarcerated in the cells in Berlin had not been pleasant but he'd been numb throughout the ordeal. He had been interrogated by some German policeman who spoke English with a guttural accent. He hadn't understood what they were asking him. He'd tried to explain that, although he had known Birgit Mayer for some time, he'd known nothing about her neo-nazi activities before that day. The interview had carried on late into the night, when they were interrupted and Greg was sent back to his cell. The German police were not happy to be overruled by the British authorities and, no matter how much Greg inquired, he was not told what was going on. In his solitary cell, he'd just about resigned himself to an extended stay in Berlin, courtesy of the German government, when he was, literally, thrown out of his cell into the custody of DI Thornton.

Thornton's mind was currently on his future – or lack of it – with the police force. The disciplinary charge would most probably take months and, in the meantime, he would remain on paid leave, doing nothing and vegetating. He'd always been a policeman and if that was going to be taken away from him he had no idea what else he could do. He knew other ex-officers who'd gone into some sort of private company providing security for various individuals and businesses but that wasn't for him. He didn't want to be a babysitter and, as he neared his fiftieth birthday, he had no intention of becoming a bouncer. He supposed he could make inquiries regarding private investigation but his confidence in his detective abilities was at an all-time low following the mess he'd made of this case. He should have left it alone – let the Europeans get on with it. Why had he become so obsessed with Birgit Mayer?

He thought back to the stories his father used to tell him about the war as a child - how he'd been one of the first to enter the liberated death camps in Poland: the utter despair he'd witnessed on the faces of the inmates who'd been so abused by the Nazi regime. He remembered his father crying as he relayed all the details to him. It was the only time he'd seen him cry. It scared him. His mother used to try and stop his father 'filling his head with such things' but Thornton had wanted to know. He'd wanted to ease his father's pain. When his father had developed dementia and was moved into a home, his mother had blamed Gerald for encouraging him to recount things that were better left forgotten. Now, his father could recollect very little else. Thornton had vowed then that if he ever had a chance to avenge the evil the Nazis had inflicted, not only on the masses but on the solitary man who was his father, he would. It had become yet another of his obsessions and it was why he wanted the Mayer girl and her cronies destroyed.

It was a bumpy landing. Greg looked at Thornton and, for the first time that day, they smiled.

'I'm sorry I got you involved in all this, Driscoll,' said the DI.

'I don't think it was you that got me involved, Gerald. I just hope it's all over now.'

'It will be,' promised Thornton. 'I think you've redeemed yourself, Greg. After all, it was the Mayer girl who took the bomb into Calais, wasn't it?'

Greg looked at him again. He knew it was Greg that took the bomb in and he knew he was now asking him to agree to blame Birgit. What choice did he have? It was her idea. She was dead now. He had to get on with his life. 'I suppose it must have been,' he replied.

'Just try and keep your head down for a while, Greg.'

He nodded. He'd like to do just that but he suspected that the 'Once in a While' team might want to spin some publicity out of this.

The plane stopped taxiing. They took their bags from the overhead lockers and queued to disembark.

*

Denis had caught the earliest flight he could back to London and was now sitting in his old office. He watched Helen Clarke trying to sort out a difficult client on the phone who was complaining about being out of work and blaming it on his agent's incompetence rather than his own

lack of talent or commitment. It reminded Denis of why he
didn't want to come back into this business.

Helen put the phone down and sighed. 'Are you sure
you wouldn't like to come back and run this place again,'
she said. He shook his head and smiled. 'I don't know how
you managed it for so long,' she added.

'Nor do I now.' There was a moment's silence as
Denis sipped the rather weak tea Helen had made him. 'Has
anyone actually gone to Greg's house since he went
missing?'

Helen frowned. 'He hasn't gone missing, Denis. He
was obviously in Germany, although why he couldn't
answer his calls, I really don't know.'

'What do you think he was doing over there?'

Helen shrugged her shoulders. Much as she valued
Greg financially as a client, she didn't actually like him
very much.

'I think I ought to go to Maldon,' said Denis. 'There's
a couple of B and B's I could check into. I've nowhere else
to go so I may as well pitch up there and wait to see if he
returns.'

Helen shook her head. 'You give him too much of
your time, Denis, if you ask me.'

'I know,' sighed Denis. He took a slurp of the tea and
wondered if Helen still kept the bottle of office brandy in

the desk drawer. If she did, she hadn't offered him any. He picked up his bag, kissed Helen on the cheek and started for the door.

'Try not to worry, Denis. He's not worth it.'

Denis was getting a bit sick of people telling him not to worry. He turned back to Helen to inform her that Greg Driscoll was probably her main client and was keeping her business financially sound at the moment but she had already turned her attention to her computer screen. He said nothing and went out of the door.

*

Greg opened the door of his cottage and picked up the few bits of junk mail Wendy had pushed through his letterbox. It felt as though he'd been away for months rather than three days. He went through to the kitchen and chucked the post in the bin. The answerphone was flashing and he pressed the play button as he passed by. There were eight messages, the voice told him. Three were from Denis, each getting more anxious, three from Helen Clarke, each getting more angry, and the final two were from journalists, each offering more money for an exclusive story.

Greg didn't really listen to the messages. He flipped the kettle on before he realised there was no milk. He contemplated going to borrow some from The King's Head but thought better of it. He thought he might as well just go over there and have a pint and something to eat to save him having to go out to the shop. He went upstairs and leapt into the shower, trying to scrub away the filth he felt was consuming him. He scoured the cheek where Birgit Mayer had bled on him but, however pristine his skin became, the memory would never be cleansed: he knew that. He dressed in clean clothes and started down to the living room. The rapping of the door knocker made him jump and he paused halfway down the stairs. It would be Wendy. She always seemed to know when he was at home. Maybe, if he waited, she would go away. He didn't want to talk to anyone at the moment. The door-knocking persisted and he resigned himself to the fact that, even if Wendy did go away, she'd only be in The King's Head, and he didn't want to have to avoid that place.

He went to the door, opened it and turned back into his living room. He was surprised not to hear Wendy's raucous voice blaring out from behind him. He turned and looked through the open door. Denis stood there motionless, tears rolling down his cheeks. Greg rushed over and hugged him, pulling him into the privacy of his house. Neither of them spoke for a long while. Denis sat on the sofa and composed himself. Greg remained standing.

'What were you doing, Greg?' Denis said eventually.

'Helping the British police force, apparently.'

'You could have been killed.'

Greg felt a quiver through his nerves. He actually hadn't considered the danger he'd been in before. Even as Birgit had taken the bullet in front of him and the Polizei had their guns trained on him, he never thought he might actually have been shot. It had all happened so fast.

'Have you eaten, Denis?' he asked. Denis shook his head. 'Come on, then.' Greg grabbed his jacket.

'Are we going to The King's Head, by any chance?' Denis slowly stood up.

'I thought we might.'

'Good, I think I need a drink!'

Greg clapped his arm round his old friend and led him across the road.

***

CHAPTER TWENTY-FIVE

Denis was to stay at Greg's cottage until after Christmas, whilst sorting out a flat to rent in London. He'd decided that was the best place for him now. He wouldn't be able to stand living out here, he was certain of that. He needed to have some life round him. He had money in the bank and there was still the house in Bourrouillan to sell. He didn't need to work but equally, he couldn't just sit around and grow old. He hadn't even done that in his curtailed retirement in France. He'd had a big garden to attend to and he'd given some local schoolchildren lessons in conversational English. He hadn't been idle.

Greg and Denis had discussed Anton's death and Birgit's. It had been difficult for both of them to really open up about how they felt. Greg still didn't really know how he felt about Birgit. He felt guilty because Anton had died, but then Anton had already been involved with Birgit and was even instrumental in getting Greg involved.

The two men spent a fair amount of time in The King's Head. Greg noticed that Denis seemed to be drinking a lot more than he used to. Time was when he would be telling Greg he shouldn't be going to the pub so often, but now it was Denis instigating the trips across the road.

Wendy and Alan had joined them regularly and, as time went on, talk of Anton and, particularly, Birgit, were confined to late-night chats between just Denis and Greg.

Gareth was on holiday, which was a relief to Greg as he knew he'd want to talk about Berlin. Greg had had enough of talking about that place. Gareth being on holiday had not been a relief to Tallie and Soozie, however, both of whom had spent all their time complaining to anyone who would listen about how unfair it was for him to go off at the busiest time of the year – just before Christmas.

Greg had done some pre-publicity for 'Once in a While' and had managed to convince the producers that any mention of his exploits in Germany would only be detrimental to the series. Besides, he told them conspiratorially, it was still all very hush-hush as far as the British and German authorities were concerned.

He'd met up with Trudie Carling again. She'd given him a big hug. 'I was so worried about you,' she'd said. 'That poor girl. You're so brave.'

Greg had detected a certain amount of whimpering which he didn't believe. 'Well, it's all over now, Trudie, but thanks for your support.'

They'd both had to endure interviews with the press regarding the upcoming series with Greg refusing to answer any questions about Berlin, stating that the Government

394

would not allow him to even mention it. The two of them adjourned to a West End club for drinks afterwards.

'I'm really looking forward to the new series, Greg.' Trudie was sipping some sort of trendy flavoured gin through a straw. 'My agent thinks it could be even bigger than the last one.'

'I bet he does,' Greg replied, pouring some lager down his throat.

'She.'

'She? Gene Waters had a sex change?'

Trudie smiled. 'I think he's doing eighteen months for fraud – amongst other things.'

It was Greg's turn to smile. 'Oh dear.' He didn't even try to sound sympathetic.

'He ripped me off!' Trudie pouted and slammed her glass down on the table. 'And most of his other clients.' She looked away. 'I think he may have arranged that nonsense that you...you know.'

Greg leaned over and put his arm round her shoulders, giving them a little squeeze. 'Don't you worry your pretty little head about it,' he said, condescendingly. 'As long as there are no photographers hiding in the shadows here.'

'It wasn't my fault, Greg. I really am sorry.' She looked up at him with her big eyes. Greg had wanted to feel angry with her but, instead he felt only elation. It was like another monkey had jumped off his back.

*

Gareth came back from his holiday in time for the Christmas rush and he sidled up to Greg one afternoon as he sat alone in the 'members' bar' at the King's Head.

'I don't want to talk about it, Gareth,' Greg said, not looking up from the book he was reading.

'You don't know what I was going to say,' replied the landlord.

Greg looked up at him.

'I was just going to mention that we had a visit from your friend while you were away.'

'What friend?'

Gareth looked over at the wall by the window. There was a rectangle that was a different shade to the rest of the wall, where the picture of old Maldon had previously hung.

'Do you mean Kate?' asked Greg.

'If that's the name of the one that threw her glass at my picture, yes.'

'I'm sorry about that, Gareth. I'll pay you for it.'

'No need, Greg, I never liked it anyway.' Gareth sipped his coffee. 'She's been kicked out of Philip Morris House it would seem. I thought I should warn you in case she comes a-stalking again.'

'How can they kick her out? Where's she supposed to go?'

Gareth shrugged his shoulders. 'As long as she doesn't come in here again, I don't care.'

'What did she say?'

'She wanted you. Said she couldn't get into your house and she had nowhere else to go.'

'And you just turned her away?' Greg frowned at Gareth, who folded his arms defensively.

'What did you expect me to do? I couldn't put her up here, even if I'd wanted to.'

Greg sighed. 'I know. It's just that she's a very sick girl. I'm amazed they've just kicked her out.'

Gareth stood up. 'She said something about going to London.'

'London?'

'That's what she said.'

*

Kate Freeman's idea of London was very different to the reality. She'd left Philip Morris House with fifty pounds in cash that she'd been stashing away from her allowance. After leaving The King's Head she'd caught a bus to Chelmsford and then a train to Liverpool Street station in London. On arrival she'd found herself wandering around the vast concourse feeling very lost. Someone had told her about a place called Centrepoint in London where they would find her somewhere to live. Well, she was in London but couldn't see anything called Centre Point.

A young policewoman came over to her. 'You look lost, love. Are you alright?'

'Of course I'm alright,' replied Kate curtly. 'Where's Centre Point?'

'What, the building or the charity?'

Kate thought for a moment. It must be a building, surely. 'The building,' she answered confidently.

The policewoman looked at Kate. She seemed reasonably well-dressed and was certainly assured, if a bit lost. She didn't look in need of a homeless charity. Maybe she had a meeting at the Centre Point office block – she couldn't think why anyone else would want to go and visit the awful concrete monstrosity. It was hardly on the tourist trail. 'It's opposite Tottenham Court Road tube station,' she told Kate. 'Get on the Central line over there,' she pointed to the Underground station entrance. 'It's about five stops and there's an exit that takes you straight up to Centre Point.'

'Thank you very much for your help.' Kate wheeled her suitcase towards the tube.

The policewoman smiled. It made her feel good when she could help someone and they appreciated it. She was more used to fielding abuse these days. This young woman had brought a ray of sunlight into her otherwise drab day.

Kate Freeman was fascinated by the tube station. It had moving staircases that went on forever. She plucked up her courage and jumped on, dragging her suitcase behind her. There were pictures all the way down. Adverts for all sorts of things. Pictures of beautiful people in lovely clothes: adverts for shows in real theatres. They trouble was, they went by so fast she couldn't read them, so she went straight over to the up escalator and retraced her journey. Up and up and up she went, ignoring the people who tutted and grumbled as she stopped and tried to walk down the steps by one of the theatre posters. Someone pushed her and she found herself being swept upwards with the crowd. She'd never seen so many people! But Kate loved it. This is what she'd longed for all her life. She'd never been allowed to come to London before – her Pops had told her it was an evil, dangerous place – but he was dead now; he couldn't stop her. She was nearly thirty years old and she could look after herself; no more curfews from that horrible Philip Morris place. She was glad she'd run away from there. Why hadn't she done it sooner? It had been so easy. She'd packed her case and just walked out of the door. No-one had tried to stop her. 'I bet they're looking for me now,' she thought. 'But they'll never find me. I'm never going back there again.' She was happier than she'd been for as long as she could remember. She laughed out loud and stood, stationary, in the middle of the throng of people at Tottenham Court Road, hurrying to their work or wherever they were going in such a rush. A man in a suit gave her a shove and told her to get out of the way. She did. It didn't upset her. 'He must have some problems he's dealing with.' she said to herself, nodding her head. A woman snorted and looked down her nose at her. Kate smiled back at her. No-one was going to spoil this moment for her.

She spotted a sign with an arrow saying Centre Point exit, went through a barrier which a kind man in a uniform opened for her and out into the smoggy open air of Central London.

There, in front of her was the most magnificent building she'd ever seen. It was tall – as high as the sky – with windows all the way up. She looked for a way in and found a door that was made entirely of glass: It wasn't the sort of glass you could see through clearly though, it was sort of smoky but she could just make out some silhouettes of figures moving behind it. She stepped forward, put her hand on the glass and pushed.

She was in a brightly-lit open space that had a desk at one end, behind which sat a man in a smart uniform. She strode up to the desk.

'Hello. I want a house,' she said to the man.

'Don't we all,' he replied. 'But unless you're a millionaire, you won't afford one round here – or anywhere in London really.'

Kate looked puzzled. 'I don't want to buy one; I want you to give me one.'

The man smirked.

'Well?' said Kate, leaning on the desk.

A light went on in the man's brain. 'Are you homeless?' he asked.

Kate thought about this. She didn't actually have a home but she wasn't one of those hobos she'd seen begging outside the tube station. 'I need a house,' she repeated.

The man reached into a drawer and took out a folded piece of paper. 'I think you're in the wrong place, love. It's the charity you need. I wouldn't hold out any hope of them finding you a house, though,' he added.

'Why isn't it here if it's called Centrepoint,' she said. 'This place is called Centre Point. The nice policewoman told me.'

'Apparently, they named the charity after this building in the Seventies when it was just a big empty block of expensive flats, love. Something to do with showing the inequality between the rich and the poor; didn't make any difference, though, did it?'

Kate didn't understand what he was talking about. 'But I was told they'd help me!' she said.

The man handed her the paper. It was a leaflet for a homeless charity.

'Give them a ring and see what they can do for you.' He smiled at her.

'Well, thanks for nothing,' she said. She turned round and stormed out of the door.

Kate Freeman did not have a mobile phone and was surprised to discover how difficult it was to find a public phone-box – especially one that actually worked. Eventually she had found one that smelt of urine but appeared to be functional as a means of communication as well as a lavatory, and had managed to get in touch with the charity. She was to register with them at their office in East London. She happily took herself off to play on the tube again to get herself across the city to the charity's offices.

She was about to be disappointed. Not only did the charity not 'give out houses', their policy was to help 18-25 year-olds. Kate, being twenty-eight did not qualify. The people in the office were very helpful and told Kate about a couple of hostels that she could try to get a night's accommodation in, plus the phone number of Shelter, another homeless charity.

Kate felt dirty, like she was some burden on society - not wanted, not a proper person and certainly not loved. She considered the best thing to do would be to head back to Maldon – London was losing its lustre – but the thought of going back to Philip Morris House seemed worse than her present predicament and filled her with despair.

The Centrepoint people had given her a map with the hostels marked on them and she made her way back across East London until she found one of them and knocked on the door. There was no reply. She banged harder – the place looked deserted.

'Don't open till night-time.' A man with grey stubble was sitting on the floor a few yards from where Kate was standing.

'I have an appointment,' she said.

'Still don't open till night-time,' came the reply. 'Can you spare something for a cup of tea?'

Kate opened the front of her suitcase and took out her purse. The man heaved himself up from the ground and held out his hand.

'How much is a cup of tea?' she asked.

'Few quid,' answered the man.

Kate took out two pound coins and gave them to him, putting her purse carefully back in the front of her suitcase and zipping it up. 'What time do they open here at night-time?' she asked him.

The man looked at her. He was in his early thirties but looked twice his age. His hands were coated with grime, his nails black. He was wearing a hoodie, through which his face peered out. Kate noticed that the few teeth he had were as black as his nails. He grinned at her. It was not a pleasant grin, more of a grimace, Kate thought. She took a step back, suddenly afraid.

With a speed that defied his appearance, the man grabbed Kate's suitcase and ran.

Kate screamed and ran after him but he was too quick. She followed him round a corner but he'd vanished. She looked up and down the street but he was nowhere in sight. Nor was her suitcase, which contained all her clothes and, more importantly, her purse with all her money. She slumped to the floor and cried. Several people passed by, looking the other way, before a woman stopped and bent down to her.

'Are you alright, darling?' she said.

Kate glared at her. 'No, I'm not!' said Kate. 'Some man just took my suitcase.'

The woman looked up and down the street. 'What did he look like?' she asked quietly.

'Dirty,' replied Kate through her tears.

The woman sat down next to her and put her hand on Kate's knee. 'Men are bastards, aren't they?'

Kate thought about this. She thought about her Pops, about the men at Philip Morris House, about Greg Driscoll. She blamed Greg for the situation she now found herself in. Why hadn't he been at home when she called? Why had he sent her back to Philip Morris House? Why had that nasty man at the pub sent her away? Why was Greg Driscoll not here looking after her? She looked back at the woman. 'Yes they are,' she agreed.

The woman took hold of her hand. 'Where do you live, love?'

Kate shrugged her shoulders

'Is there someone I could call?'

Kate frowned. 'What for?'

'To let them know what's happened.'

Kate sobbed again. 'No! No-one at all!'

The woman put her arm round Kate. 'My name's Petra, what's yours?'

'Kate.'

'That's a nice name.'

Kate looked at her in astonishment. 'No it's not! It's a horrible name. I hate it!'

Petra laughed. 'I know what you mean. My name used to be Edith. Now that is a horrible name. So I changed it to Petra.'

'Petra's a nice name.' Kate looked at her and smiled.

Petra leaned over and wiped the tears from Kate's face. She moved her hand to Kate's breast and her lips towards Kate's.

'What are you doing?' yelled Kate.

'Would you like to come home with me?'

Petra's hand was caressing Kate's breast. She screamed again. Petra stood up quickly, spat at her and hurried off down the road. Kate rolled onto the floor, her head in her arms, her body jerking with the force of her bawling.

'Are you alright, love?'

'Go away,' screamed Kate. 'Get off me! Get off me!'

A hand reached tentatively for her shoulder and lifted her face. Kate looked into the eyes of a police constable. She reached up and grabbed him round the shoulders.

***

CHAPTER TWENTY-SIX

Denis threw a party for all their friends in the 'members' bar' at The King's Head to celebrate the Festive season. Neither Denis nor Greg felt particularly festive but they put on a good show for the sake of the others. Gareth kept the 'member's bar' open late for Denis. The party-goers were all local – Denis didn't want Helen or any of her crowd there and Greg certainly didn't want any of the cast of 'Once in a While' there – especially not Trudie Carling!

The two of them spent Christmas Day alone in Greg's house. They didn't even go over the road for a lunchtime celebration – much to Wendy's annoyance. She had already dubbed them the odd couple – Denis being the neat and tidy one, Greg being the slob. Denis was getting a bit fed-up with well-meaning jokes at their expense and was happy that his new flat in London would be ready for him to move into in the New Year.

Denis left for his new flat the day before Greg was due to start rehearsals. They'd spent the previous night in The King's Head. There had been drunken tears back at Greg's and promises of invites for everyone once Denis had properly settled into his new place.

The King's Head had started doing breakfasts and Greg and Denis treated themselves to a fry-up before Denis' taxi arrived. Greg's rehearsal didn't start until the afternoon. It was a read-through of the first episode, followed by drinks to get to know the new cast members.

The taxi duly arrived as they were finishing their coffees – the fry-up having assuaged most of their hangovers. Greg gave his old agent a hug and started for the door with him.

'You stay here, Greg. I don't want to cry getting into a taxi!'

Greg gave him a friendly punch. 'I'll see you soon.'

Denis blinked tears away and went out to get his lift to London.

Gareth was behind the bar and he waved as the taxi set off before turning to Greg. 'Another coffee?' he said.

Greg had intended to go home and get ready for his own cab but that wouldn't be here for another hour or so.

'Don't want get a caffeine overdose,' he replied. 'Is it too early for a pint?'

Gareth smiled and went behind the bar.

*

'Are you alright, Greg?' Trudie Carling was sitting with him in a corner of the Studio bar. The cast were no longer allowed to use any outside bar near the studio and, anyway, the producers had arranged this drinks session here following the read-through. Janet Milner had given a speech saying how proud she was to be producing such a popular masterpiece and how much she was looking forward to the new series, proven by the producers providing a few bottles of bubbly for the cast – Prosecco, Greg noted rather than Champagne. She obviously saw the programme as more popular rather than a masterpiece! Greg had declined the Prosecco and bought a pint whilst Trudie happily sipped the free sparkling wine.

The cast had split into cliques, the few new members getting to know each other while the oldies sat and reminisced about the first series.

Trudie had taken Greg to one side to talk to him. 'You seemed really out of it today. Is something wrong?'

'Sorry,' he apologised. 'I've got something on my mind. Shouldn't let it interfere with my work, should I?'

'Berlin?' Trudie took hold of his hand. He took it away.

'No, not Berlin.'

Trudie stared at him her eyebrows raised in question.

Greg sighed. 'There's this girl...' he started. Trudie raised her hands as if to say she didn't want to interfere with his love-life. 'No,' he continued. 'Not a girlfriend. She's...um...a girl I used to know. She's had some problems in her life and was living in a sort of halfway house and now she's gone AWOL. She's somewhere in London, apparently. I thought I ought to try and find her.'

'In London? Do you know whereabouts in London?'

Greg felt stupid. 'No,' he said, shrugging his shoulders.

'Well you're not going to find her, then, are you? Do you want another pint?'

Greg resigned himself to the fact that he was not going to be able to help Kate and, reminding himself she was not his responsibility, accepted Trudie's offer.

*

Kate Freeman had been in London for over a month. The policeman in east London had taken down the details of the robbery of her suitcase but said he didn't hold out much hope of catching the man. He hadn't seemed interested in Petra's attempted assault on her. She'd wandered around in a daze until it was dark, when she'd joined a queue of dishevelled down-and-outs waiting by the door of the hostel. She'd filled in a form and been given a sleeping bag, shown to a dormitory with some mattresses on the floor and told she could sleep there for the night. She would get a breakfast in the morning but would have to leave for the day and see if there was a space for her the next night. She'd been told emphatically that this was only a temporary place

410

for her to stay and that they could not provide her with a house.

She didn't sleep all night. People were shouting; men had kept trying to get into the women's dormitory – often encouraged by the hags she was sharing with. She'd tried to complain but everybody seemed too busy to be bothered with her. She never went back to the hostel.

She'd found a place under a bridge where several other homeless people had made some sort of shelter. She'd been befriended by a young man, Steve, he'd called himself and he'd said he would look after her and he had. He'd welcomed her into the circle of people who lived under the bridge. He'd tried to sleep with her, of course, and, at first, she'd resisted. In the end, hungry and cold, she'd allowed him to lie next to her. She'd felt very self-conscious as he'd lain on top of her that first time. There had been other people there but they'd taken no notice and, after that she hadn't cared. She'd started to feel like she had a family again – something she'd been denied for many years. The family had evolved around her; not just Steve but the others too. They'd shared what little food they'd procured and shown her the best places to go to get people to give her money. It wasn't begging, they'd told her, it was the community sharing its spoils. She hadn't liked the drinking though. She'd had no idea what was in the bottles inside the brown paper bags and never took more than a sip or two.

On Christmas day they had all been invited to a big empty hall – some sort of sports centre, it looked like – by a group of young people wearing fluorescent jackets, with the name of some charity on the back, and reindeer antlers on their heads. Kate had laughed, they looked so silly. They fed them a proper Christmas dinner and handed out some clean clothes that they could keep. There were also little presents wrapped up in sparkly paper. Kate's parcel held a necklace made of shiny buttons. Steve had said it made her look like a princess. It was the best day Kate remembered having since before her mother had died.

The best places to get money were the places that the tourists hung about. Kate was quite good at accumulating a good hatful as she was still relatively attractive; she had all her teeth for a start. She'd spent the last week outside several of the many West End theatres that she'd once dreamed of performing in. Steve had told her she was probably earning more than some of the performers on the stage. She'd laughed. She didn't want to perform just for money and she'd tried to prove it by regularly singing and dancing for her family under the bridge.

After the theatres had poured out their punters, Kate used to move to the tube stations. She still loved the tubes and she'd buy a ticket and just sit on the floor watching the trains come and go. If there was no-one official-looking, she'd take off her hat and lay it in front of her, ready for the tourists, elated from their night out in the capital, to throw her their loose change.

*

Greg and Trudie left the studio party early and caught a taxi into the West End. They went to a pub just off Oxford Street. For a West End pub it was quiet. Greg had discovered it one day following a radio recording he'd done at the BBC years ago and he had visited it every time he'd been in Central London.

It was an old-fashioned pub – not one of those modern trendy place made to look Victorian for the tourists. This was a place that had hardly changed in a hundred years. There were booths with engraved glass partitions, where one could sit and have a private conversation and, best of all, no television or background music.

He used to come here often with Denis when his office was just a few hundred yards away and it felt strange to be sitting here with this young girl voted 'most glamourous woman in Britain' by a well-known magazine, instead of a rather camp older man. He noticed he was still getting funny looks from the few customers scattered about the premises. He smiled to himself.

'Penny for them?' Trudie nudged his elbow.

'I was thinking about my old agent, actually,' said Greg.

'Don't talk to me about agents!' Trudie swigged back her gin.

'Sorry, I forgot.'

Trudie laughed. 'Don't apologise.' She put her hand on Greg's leg and he let her.

'Do you want to come to my wedding, Greg?'

Greg nearly choked on his beer. 'What?'

'I'm getting married,' Trudie was whispering. 'Don't tell anyone.'

'Who's the lucky man?'

'You don't know him. He's just an ordinary bloke. Not in the business or anything.'

Greg raised an eyebrow.

'He's called Charles and runs a bank in the Channel Islands.'

Greg raised his other eyebrow.

'It'll just be a small affair – registry office.'

'You are joking? The 'most glamourous woman in Britain' getting married in secret? That's not going to happen, is it?'

'Well, we're hoping so. My agent doesn't want me to do it at all.'

'Really? I'd have thought it was an ideal situation for a bucket load of publicity.'

'She's not like Gene Waters. She doesn't want publicity. She believes in my work and considers all the rest of the crap detrimental.'

'Most glamourous woman in Britain?' Greg smirked.

'Believe it or not that was the genuine choice of the readers.' She smirked. 'Well that's what Gene Waters said but I'm not with him anymore, am I?'

Greg looked over the top of his glass. This girl was very naive. 'Well, congratulations. I suppose this means you're not going to invite me home with you this time?'

'Depends how drunk you get me, I suppose.' Trudie grinned but removed her hand from Greg's leg.

'Better buy you a celebratory drink, then,' he said, standing up.

'I'll have another gin,' she replied.

Greg started for the bar and Trudie grabbed his arm. 'I was only joking about getting me drunk, by the way.'

Greg pulled a sad face. 'You've disappointed an old man,' he said. 'I'll just get you a single, then.'

Trudie grinned and Greg went to the bar to order her a double gin and a pint for himself.

They left the pub at closing time. Greg had foregone his right to the studio providing a cab to get him home by leaving the studio premises, so he decided to slum it and get the train back to Chelmsford and then a cab from there to Maldon. Trudie hadn't asked him back to her place and, even though he had drunk a lot, he wasn't too disappointed. Maybe he was growing up after all.

They kissed each other's cheeks and she went off to hail a cab while Greg went down into the tube station at Oxford Circus.

He stumbled as he came down the stairs to the tube station platform. He giggled to himself. He'd had too much to drink. It took him back to his days at Drama School, travelling home on the tube, after a night in the pub. He was starting to wish he'd taken a cab all the way back to Maldon. He could afford luxuries like that now. Helen Clarke had achieved a greatly improved contract for this new series but, somehow, forking out over a hundred quid for a ride home didn't seem right to him.

The platform was busy and it cheered him to see several people who had had even more to drink than he had. A group of young men were singing loudly and out of tune whilst jumping up and down, their arms round each other, presumably for support as much as fraternity. Greg squeezed his way through the throng and leant himself against the wall.

He could feel the wind blow through the tunnel as a train approached. The crowd surged forwards, keen to push their way onto it. Greg stayed where he was. He knew there'd be another one along in a few minutes. That was the wonderful thing about the London transport system. Although he used to complain about waiting sometimes up to ten minutes for the next tube, it was only after he'd moved to Maldon that he'd appreciated how good the public transport was in the capital city. In Maldon it seemed as if there was a bus every three weeks, if you were lucky. There were no trains in Maldon, of course. Dr Beeching had seen to that in the 1960's when he closed the line. The station was still there, though, he knew that. His mind wandered back twenty years to the last time he'd been inside the dilapidated building, holding Jenny Gulliver in his arms.

The train moved off and the platform was slightly less crowded now. The singing group had taken their discordant performance into a carriage and were, no doubt, currently entertaining an ungrateful crowd of people all squashed together and unable to get away.

A commotion at the far end of the platform attracted his attention. Three young men with shaved heads, wearing combat trousers, green vests and sporting tattoos were skirmishing around someone who was sitting on the floor. Greg's mind flashed back to Berlin. It was the same, only these boys were English. They were shouting abuse and pointing at the dishevelled person who was cowering at their feet. They poured a can of beer onto the platform in front of the figure.

Without thinking of the consequences, he moved through the confluence of people moving away from the pandemonium and went towards the young men. He noticed one of the youths had a swastika tattoo on his neck in the same position as Birgit. It made his alcohol-fuelled blood boil. He wanted to lash out – to show the idiot how utterly stupid he was. He yelled out to them to stop harassing the cringing figure who was trying to disappear into the wall.

'Here's your knight in shining armour,' boomed the youth with the swastika. His friends laughed and stood ready for a fight. Greg stormed towards them. He wasn't normally a fighting man but with Birgit's dead body filling his mind, his rational thought had gone walkabout. He threw a punch, aiming at the swastika and caught the youth on the chin knocking him down. The other two looked at him, shouting something Greg couldn't comprehend and then, surprisingly, ran up the stairs out of the station, the swastika scrambling up and following. The crowd behind applauded briefly before getting themselves into a position to be first onto the next train. There was already a wind blowing through the tunnel and it momentarily blew the hood from the face of the body on the floor.

The recognition wasn't instant. Greg squatted and looked into the face, trying to focus.

'Katy?' he said.

The woman looked up at him, her face contorted. 'Get away from me,' she screamed.

'Katy, it's me, Greg.' He could hear the tube train getting nearer. It didn't matter; he could wait for the next one. What was Kate Freeman doing here, looking like some tramp? Is this what they meant by 'care in the community'? 'What are you doing here, Katy?'

Kate Freeman raised both her feet and lashed out at Greg, catching him on his left shoulder. The force sent him sprawling across the platform, skidding through the spilt beer. He stood up dazed and disoriented. He staggered backwards towards the platform edge just as the train exited the tunnel. He was aware of people screaming and rushing towards him as the front of the train smashed into the side of his head throwing him into the path of his would-be saviours.

Kate Freeman grabbed her few possessions and ran up the stairs.

A crowd gathered round Greg Driscoll's body as it lay prostrate on the platform, a pool of blood starting to engulf it.

'It's that actor from that series,' yelled someone and flashlights from people's camera phones sent eerie shadows across the concourse. A couple of men in Transport for London uniforms tried to disperse the onlooking multitude and provide first aid to the casualty.

The train had stopped and was not going any further that night. Several people complained that because of the selfish 'jumper' they would miss their connections at the main-line stations they were heading for. People still on the stationary train were pointing at Greg. Some were crying, some were just sitting waiting, resigned to yet another delay to their journey.

The platform was cleared. Passengers from the train were herded out of the station and told to find alternative means of reaching their destinations. The police and paramedics arrived and took over from the TFL employees, who went to help their stricken customers who still thought they could carry on travelling by the tube.

It was nearly one o'clock in the morning when Greg Driscoll left the tube station zipped up tight in a black body bag.

***

EPILOGUE

Greg Driscoll's funeral was held in St Mary's church in Maldon – just a stone's throw from The King's Head on the quay. It was the first and last time Greg had ever been in the ancient building. It seemed like hundreds were crammed inside, which would be by far the biggest congregation they'd had for years.

Wendy Jenkins thought she had organised everything but, on arriving at the church she was handed a flashy programme that had, supposedly, been printed on her behalf by the production company of 'Once in a While'. On reading it she discovered that the whole service had been altered. Wendy had known that Greg wouldn't have wanted hymns but now there were four of them scheduled to be sung by the choir, who were, even now, processing into the nave, behind a man in a cassock carrying a large crucifix. She had arranged for a CD of Greg's favourite songs from the 1980's to be played as the coffin left the church so, at least, there'd be something he would have liked.

She expertly evicted several tabloid journalists who were there to get a story, no matter how sad the occasion was. Gareth had made sure that anyone he didn't know to be a legitimate mourner was not allowed into the King's Head. It was closed to the public. A wake was to be held in the 'members' bar' and the overspill would have to encroach on the rest of the pub.

The only will Greg had left was a message he'd written on a napkin during a drunken night with Denis where he'd promised all his worldly goods to his old friend and agent. Denis didn't think it would stand up in court but, as there were no living relatives that anyone knew about to contest it, he produced it to the coroner who said he'd look into it.

Denis sat on the front pew. He'd agreed to say a few words. He hoped he'd be up to it. There were all sorts of thought and images shooting through his muddled mind: Anton, Jenny Gulliver, the girl he'd known as Virginia, and most of all – even more than Anton, he was surprised to discover – Greg Driscoll, his oldest friend; his foolish, drunken, oldest friend. A tear escaped and he wiped it away. He was sitting between Wendy, who was sobbing quietly and Helen Clarke, who appeared to be noting down the name of any famous person she could spot in order to enhance her business. Denis ignored her. He put his hand on Wendy's and squeezed it. She turned and smiled briefly before the taps turned on again and the tears flowed.

Most of the cast of Greg's community Shakespeare in the Park were there – even Scott Stevenson who'd gone on to Drama School and into the profession, inspired by Greg.

He'd travelled from Newcastle where he was appearing in a show and he told Denis that paying his respects to Greg was the least he could do. He was to leave straight afterwards to catch a train back up north. Dave, the cafe owner was there. John the previous landlord from The King's Head had journeyed from his retirement villa in Spain for the service. Gareth, Tallie and Soozie were near the back, ready to leave at the last minute to re-open the pub for the wake. Han and Ilse had come over from Cuijk and, in the back row sat two men, each contemplating the effect Greg Driscoll had had on their lives and careers. Ex-Detective Inspector Roger Milne and DI Gerald Thornton had never met before, Milne having left the force before Thornton had been seconded to Essex, but they both knew of each other - Thornton from police files and Milne because he had followed Greg's career, theatrical and felonious, since his retirement.

The vicar, the Reverend Richard Poole, had only met Greg once – at a council do that neither had wanted to attend. Greg, not being a church-goer, hadn't been of much interest to the Reverend Poole. He now stood over Greg's coffin, which was festooned with flowers – mostly supplied by the production team of 'Once in a While', who filled the middle pews of the church, secretly grateful that they hadn't started recording the second series yet.

Richard Poole looked out at the congregation and smiled. He welcomed everybody and delivered his eulogy. Denis didn't recognise his old friend from the words the vicar spouted. He wanted to ask him, every time he mentioned what a wonderful programme 'Once in a While was, whether he'd ever actually seen an episode or not. He suspected the vicar had been 'got at' by the production company – especially as he kept going on about what a supportive friend Trudie Carling had been. He was appalled to hear people applaud at the mention of her name and Wendy had to hold tight to his hand to stop him getting up and confronting the Reverend.

Denis gave his speech, correcting much of what the vicar had said. He nearly got to the end before he had to pause and swallow back his emotion. He returned to his pew and sobbed as the choir all stood to sing an elegy by some worthy Victorian composer.

Alan, Scott, Gareth and Denis came forward to carry the coffin from the church. Ian, being so much taller than the rest, stood at the back whilst the others lifted the box onto their shoulders. They stood waiting for the CD to start playing the selection of Greg's favourite songs but instead of Wendy's choice of Paul Young the speakers blared out the theme tune from 'Once in a While'.

More applause accompanied Greg's last journey from Maldon towards the crematorium. A loud wail emanated from the pews as the coffin passed Trudie Carling and cameras flashed.

A sweet aroma pervaded the stale air at the back of the church. Wendy smelt it and a strange sensation came over her. It reminded her of something but couldn't recall what it was. She looked over at Trudie Carling, who was sobbing theatrically, and sneered. The congregation's eyes were all focused on the passing coffin. A young girl with long, pre-Raphaelite, auburn hair was standing behind the last row of pews, smiling. Not a soul saw her and nor did anyone notice Greg Driscoll join her, take her hand and wander off in the opposite direction to the mourners, leaving behind nothing but a trace of orange-blossom.

***

Made in the USA
Middletown, DE
23 August 2017